T0274638

LAST
BEST
CHANCE

First published 2024 by
FREMANTLE PRESS

Fremantle Press Inc. trading as Fremantle Press
PO Box 158, North Fremantle, Western Australia, 6159
fremantlepress.com.au

Cover image Ulas&Merve, Stocksy.com
Cover design by Nada Backovic, nadabackovic.com
Printed and bound by IPG

 A catalogue record for this
book is available from the
National Library of Australia

ISBN 9781760992934 (paperback)
ISBN 9781760992941 (ebook)

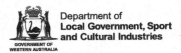 

Fremantle Press is supported by the State Government through the
Department of Local Government, Sport and Cultural Industries.

Fremantle Press respectfully acknowledges the Whadjuk people of
the Noongar nation as the traditional owners and custodians of the
land where we work in Walyalup.

LAST
BEST
CHANCE
BROOKE DUNNELL

 FREMANTLE PRESS

Brooke Dunnell has worked as a manuscript assessor and mentor, creative writing competition judge, and workshop facilitator. Her short fiction has appeared in journals and anthologies including *Best Australian Stories*, *Meanjin*, *The Big Issue* fiction edition, *New Australian Fiction 2021* and *New Australian Stories 2*, and she was one of *Westerly*'s Mid-Career Fellows in 2023. Her short story collection *Female(s and) Dogs* was shortlisted for the 2020 Carmel Bird Digital Literary Award and the 2021 Woollahra Digital Literary Award. Her unpublished manuscript *The Glass House* won the Fogarty Literary Award in 2021 and was published in 2022 by Fremantle Press. Brooke lives in Boorloo/Perth with her husband and two snoring Cavalier King Charles spaniels.

For Andrew

Rachel
Cycle day 2 (CD2)

It wasn't yet seven-thirty in the morning when Rachel Mather wriggled out of her underpants and kicked them across the exam room floor. Once they'd skidded safely beneath the chair that held her handbag, she turned so her bum brushed the edge of the gurney, then hoisted herself up. Friction made the protective square of white cotton, like a giant sanitary napkin, rumple, and she yanked the corners to straighten it beneath her buttocks.

Her legs pimpled in the cold. She slouched to look at her feet, wiggling her toes to get warmth into them. She'd brought socks but left them in her bag. Staring at socked feet was in some way worse than the artificial chill.

Someone knocked, then turned the door handle. 'Ready?' a female voice called, shoes squeaking. Rachel couldn't remember seeing her before. 'Rachel Mather?' A flat-ironed fringe hung in the nurse's eyes.

'That's me.'

The nurse pulled a clipboard from under her arm and flicked through the papers. 'You've started to bleed?'

'Yes.'

'Fresh red blood? Not brown?'

Rachel had been getting her period for thirty years; she knew what it meant to say it had started. 'Red as jam. Strawberry jam,' she elaborated. 'You know. I guess it could be—what, blackberry.'

The nurse eyed her through the curtain of her fringe.

Rachel tried to smile. 'Sorry. I guess that's a bad example.'

'Are you nervous,' the nurse said, without the upwards inflection of a question. Leaving the clipboard on a bench Rachel recognised from IKEA, she sat heavily on a wheeled stool and scooted it towards Rachel's feet. 'You can lie down now. You know the drill?'

'I do.'

Holding the hem of her skirt between her legs until the final moment, Rachel swung one calf at a time into the stirrups, then lowered herself down until her back met the rustling cover. Some nurses offered a pillow, but not this one. Rachel touched her chin to her chest so she could see.

The nurse scuttled like a crab to one end of the room and withdrew the white wand from its holder. *Excalibur*, Rachel thought, as she always did at this moment. Next, the nurse snapped a cream-coloured sheath over the end, then squeezed clear lubricant onto it. The device prepared, the nurse rolled back to Rachel and used the wrist of her free hand to swipe her hair out of the way.

'Right,' she said. 'Bit of pressure.'

That was Rachel's cue to drop her head back and close her eyes.

There was the brief sting of resistance, then the rush of warmth as the transducer entered. Rachel had been told many times—by medical professionals, not boyfriends—that her cervix was low, and she sucked in her breath as the probe butted against it.

'Is that a bit uncomfy?' the nurse asked. 'Sorry.'

'It's okay,' Rachel lied.

The nurse reached for a notebook and pen. 'Secretarial duties.' Her eyes met Rachel's and there was the faintest trace of a grin.

Emotion drove up Rachel's oesophagus and collected at the top of her throat. Just one hint of humanity and she was ready to sob.

She clicked the pen hard to drive away the feelings, letting the notebook fall open. At the top of the page was the letter E with a box next to it, and below that two columns headed L *and* R. Gritting her teeth as the probe moved, Rachel wrote her name and date in the space provided.

The nurse had turned to peer at a big screen crowded with black-and-white constellations, tracking a course through the stars. 'Okay.' She pressed buttons on a keyboard until there was a beep. 'Endometrium, three point two.'

Rachel copied the number into the box labelled E.

'Day one today?' the nurse asked. 'Or day two?'

'It started yesterday afternoon, so. Day one and a half, I guess.'

The probe swung to the left. For a moment Rachel held her breath, sure she'd just been gored through the kidney, but almost as soon as it struck, the pain was gone. 'Bowel, bowel, bowel,' the nurse murmured. Rachel looked at the screen, unsure how these clouds of particulate were different from the others. 'Lots of bowel this morning.'

'I had my All-Bran.'

'Here we go.' The keyboard emitted another beep. 'One, two …' Rachel's hopes rose. 'No, that's not—three. Okay. Left, three small.'

Rachel wrote this in the L column.

The nurse found the right ovary and scanned its surface. 'Three as well.' Rachel put the numeral under R, fingers slipping around the thin pen. 'You're forty-one?'

'Forty-two.'

The nurse frowned as if she knew better. Counting follicles wasn't like reading tea-leaves, Rachel thought, then corrected herself: it was. It was predicting the future.

'All done.' The nurse pulled the wand from between Rachel's legs and held it up, showing the rust-coloured stain at the end. After a long, silent second of contemplation, she pulled the sheath inside-out.

Cheeks flushing, Rachel shut the notebook and held it out. 'My birthday was a few weeks ago,' she said. 'It's March.'

'Jeez.' The nurse looked grim, and for a moment Rachel felt the sharp pain of another person's doubt. 'March already? Wasn't it just Christmas?'

'Tell me about it.'

The nurse took the notebook. 'Six follicles isn't terrible for forty-two. Are you for IVF or embryo transfer?'

'Transfer.'

She smiled. 'Oh well, it doesn't matter then. Just the lining. They put you on HRT?'

All this information was in the clipboard. Freeing her legs from the stirrups, Rachel sat up. 'I'm doing the ovulation induction injections.'

'Really?' The nurse shrugged. 'I would've thought…' She rolled her stool over to the wall calendar. 'Well, if all goes to plan, let's see.' Her chin bounced as she counted the dates. 'Two weeks, then three, four, five days—the first likely date for your transfer is the nineteenth, if you want to pencil that into your diary.'

Feeling fluid seep from the tunnel the wand had pressed through her, Rachel reached for the box of scratchy tissues and held a handful between her legs. The screen was frozen on an image of her ovary, mostly white with three black seeds scattered across it.

Three was not her worst number, but it was close.

But, as the nurse had said, the follicles didn't matter. They were the means to an end.

The nurse squinted at the coloured dots that coded each date on the calendar. 'I'm on transfers that week!' she said, and Rachel's heart sank at how genuine she sounded. 'I'll probably see you.'

'I'm not—I won't—' Rachel inhaled to collect her thoughts. 'I'm not doing the transfer here.'

The nurse's face tightened in suspicion. 'What? Where are you having it?'

'Overseas.'

'Oh.' For a beat, they were both silent. 'Right. You're that patient.'

Rachel wanted to tell her that this betrayal was also contained in the file, but instead she just nodded. 'That's me.'

***

Rachel had first visited this fertility clinic years earlier. Her marriage to Ben had been over for six months, and the devastation left in its wake found a focus: she didn't want to get old without at least trying to have a baby. This was the biggest clinic in Perth, advertised on FM radio and fertility podcasts, and she figured it was worth a consultation. She was thirty-eight then, rosebud young compared to now, with rich ripe eggs going to waste every month.

The doctor who saw her suggested she go straight to IVF instead of insemination. She was older, in her late fifties, with waves of elegant grey hair. As she spoke, the doctor drew perpendicular lines on the back of a prescription pad: the rough axes of a graph. 'The reality is that, at your age, fertility has already begun to decline.' The next line she drew travelled parallel to the horizontal one for a moment, then sank like Rachel's expectations. At the point where it dropped away, the doctor wrote *35*. 'You could try sperm donation with ovulation stimulation, but it might be a waste of your time.'

As Rachel's head buzzed from the terminology, the doctor found a different slip of paper in her drawer. 'I know I'm blunt,' she said, 'but I don't like to get anyone's hopes up. The truth is, if you want this, you need to give yourself the best chance.' She marked the paper, then looked up. 'Do you want a baby now?'

Rachel couldn't have said no, even if that had been the answer.

'I want to try.'

The doctor pushed the paper across the desk.

It was a list of fees for treatment, with a sharp tick beside one of the highest amounts. Donor sperm insemination, the procedure Rachel had inquired about, was a few rows above. The price alongside it was much, much lower.

She told the doctor she'd think about it, but never went back. The difference in price was egregious, wasn't it? The situation couldn't be *that* dire. Rachel had regular periods, minimal cramping, if that meant anything. Her cervical screens were always clear. Why did the clinic offer low-intervention treatments if they didn't want to perform them? To get patients in the door, probably.

The boutique clinic where she'd ended up had the more charismatic Dr Leonard, who had agreed with her position: she was only thirty-eight, with reasonable test results; no reason to think a couple of rounds of insemination wouldn't have the intended outcome. When they hadn't, and subsequent cycles involved more and more interventions—induced ovulation through pills and injectables, then basic IVF, then hormone replacement therapy and genetic testing and even fertilisation by way of a microscopic needle depositing a single spermatozoon into each egg, a procedure Rachel hadn't even know was possible until they recommended it—she was embarrassed to remember the doctor at the big clinic and how her prediction was turning out to be right. Rachel had already spent double the amount that had driven her away, and she felt herself chasing this dream until there was no money left.

She was only back because no other clinic would work with the overseas doctors. They considered it too risky, not knowing exactly how things would proceed. Dr Leonard himself had been grave, like a father warning his daughter off a bad-news boyfriend.

'These foreign places can be cowboys. It's never quite clear what you're getting into.' He folded his hands together sadly and Rachel despised him, this man who now spoke like she should have known better. 'If we'd started with IVF earlier, perhaps …' He'd given her a weighted look.

Trying to keep her voice from trembling, she said, 'You thought my chances were good when we started.'

'Hindsight is difficult,' he said, as if he hadn't just indulged in some revisions of his own. 'There's a lesson here for everyone.'

Rachel's was in humility. She went back to the big clinic and the female doctor gave her the grace of pretending they'd never met. Her hair was white now, like a queen in a fantasy novel. They'd do bloods and scans for the first few days of her cycle, before she left the country. At the end of the appointment, the doctor handed over a different slip of paper.

It was a statement indemnifying the clinic if there were any issues overseas. Rachel signed eagerly this time.

***

The waiting room was full when Rachel emerged, sanitised and dressed, to register for her next scan. You could only book in for a particular date, not a precise time, so a queue of women formed even before the clinic opened. The patients came in waves: shift workers first, either on their way from work or in a hurry to get there, clutching thermoses and looking bleary; then office workers in slacks and shell tops, thumbing emails as they waited; and last, patients whose jobs were mysterious or non-existent, catching the end of the monitoring window after sleeping late or dropping children at school, dressed in gym gear or loungewear or jeans. Once she'd seen a woman in a cocktail dress sticking on fake eyelashes as she waited.

The transition to the last group had begun during Rachel's ultrasound, and she saw shorts and thongs on lower limbs as she made her way to the desk. In the public parts of the clinic she kept her eyes lowered, trying to maintain a sense of privacy and avoid the wistful, knowing looks that could sometimes be exchanged here, the other patients acting as if they'd seen to the very depths of her soul and been startled by their own reflection.

There were a couple of women ahead of her, so Rachel snagged a copy of the day's newspaper to flick through. A few pages in, below the headline CASPIE APPEARANCE ALMOST CONFIRMED, was a large image of a woman hurrying towards an SUV. The shot had been taken on the sly, from beyond the vehicle Cassandra Caspie was approaching. The tech entrepreneur had an irritated expression, which was unflattering. Rachel guessed there were at least a couple more photogenic versions snapped in the seconds before Caspie spotted the paparazzo and that the one with her mouth hanging open and a V creased into her forehead had been chosen deliberately. Rachel felt sorry for her until she reached the caption: *Caspie is rumoured to have delivered triplets in a home birth at her Auckland mansion.*

Sucking her teeth, she folded the paper and dropped it back on the rack. The woman was ten years younger than Rachel, a genius and a billionaire, and now apparently the mother of an instant family. She didn't need sympathy over a bad photo.

After paying for the appointment and getting a reminder card with Sunday's date, Rachel was able to leave. It was bright outside, and the heat roused every pinprick of lubricant she'd attempted to wet-wipe away. She crossed the road to her car with inner thighs tacking together, humidity releasing the sharp odour of antiseptic.

Without a proper shower, you couldn't be truly clean after a scan. It was like sex in that way, the clammy pressures leaving a latent dampness set off by warmth and movement. When Rachel got to work, she would immediately lock herself in a cubicle and perform a second cleansing, change into a clean pair of knickers, and trade the thick sanitary napkin for a tampon. But the moisture would linger; she knew that from experience. This was not her first date with the wand.

The law firm where she worked was a crawl through peak-hour traffic to the other side of the CBD. At a red light she stopped behind a four-wheel drive with three kids in the back, straw boaters knocking together. Behind the wheel, their father rested his forearm on the edge of the wound-down window and tapped along to a beat Rachel couldn't hear.

Glancing in her rear-view mirror, she tried to imagine a child in the back seat of her own car. A chunky backwards-facing bassinet; a cushioned black booster; a primary-schooler colouring in a book; a teenager with earphones, eyes fixed on a screen. But the space was too empty for the superimposition, the seat crevices too free of crumbs.

Someone beeped to let her know the lights had changed, and she yanked her foot off the brake.

A few years earlier, Rachel had asked her mother if she'd pictured herself with kids before having them. She was thinking about trying to have a baby on her own but felt thrown at never being able to imagine her future offspring. Some of her friends claimed they'd known their own kids since before conception, like they were hanging out in some other realm, waiting patiently to be born.

Usually, Jean Mather wouldn't have indulged a question like that, would've waved it away like an annoying fly, but they were looking after her brother's twins and she must have been feeling nostalgic.

'I always saw myself with older children,' she commented, rocking the boy on her lap. Rachel was feeding the other, trying to aim the bottle between the dense gums. 'Eight or nine years old. Never with a little baby.' Jean offered a dazed smile. 'But they have to be babies first, don't they?'

Unless you adopt, Rachel thought, but didn't want to interrupt when her mother was being honest. 'But you always knew you'd have kids?'

'Well, that's what you did, in my day.' Realising what she might have admitted to, Jean's neck stiffened. 'Fine with me, of course, because your father and I wanted them. We had Conny right away, didn't we?'

Her brother was a honeymoon baby, born within the first year. Jean had been twenty, their father Michael twenty-three. If she'd followed in her parents' footsteps, Rachel's own eighteen-year-old might have been with them, stacking the dishwasher or watching TV.

'Did you end up liking it best when we were eight and nine?' Rachel asked. 'Was it what you imagined?'

'I don't remember any of you being eight years old, if I'm frank.'

Rachel's father had died in a workplace accident three days before his thirty-second birthday, when Conrad was eight-and-a-half, Rachel five, and Antony three. Jean often referred to the daze of their childhood; that she'd gone into a fugue after the funeral and blinked out of it fifteen years later at Antony's high school graduation. Rachel found this unnerving, because she remembered a mother who was alert, if highly emotional. It was difficult to think that Jean had no memory of kneeling by Rachel's pillow at bedtime, pausing for a moment, then tipping forward and sobbing a salted patch into the sheet.

But then, Rachel didn't remember her father. There were things Conrad said, and Jean, about what Michael used to like and do, some of the stuff he'd say, and she was sure she'd cobbled these into false memories. Jean told her that, the day of the accident, he'd bent down to give Rachel a butterfly kiss while she ate her toast and called her 'my girl'. This scene played in her head like a film, its hyper-reality making her doubtful, along with the report she had that identified the accident as occurring at around six-thirty in the morning. Surely she wouldn't have been up and eating toast by six, giving Michael the time to get to the site, climb in the cherry picker and tip over.

Rachel intended to be a single parent, but she knew her experience would be nothing like Jean's. For Rachel, there may never be a partner, which meant no-one to share the load with, but also, nothing to lose. Nothing to make up stories about—well, apart from the origin story. She'd do the toast and butterfly kisses herself.

***

After lunch, Rachel had a meeting with her supervisor to prepare them both for her upcoming leave. She'd be away for three weeks from the following Friday, which she hoped would be enough time to get her through the embryo transfer and home again. Something did feel unnatural about getting on an international flight when she hoped to be mere days into a pregnancy, but she couldn't stay away forever. If she was going to have a baby, she'd have to rack up her working hours while she could.

Jamie suggested going out for coffee, so they crossed the road to a café that was always being sold to new owners, remodelled and renamed. Since Christmas it had been called Vibes, a name Rachel felt was doomed. The regular café tables had been replaced by high tops, with padded crates on poles in a quirky version of stools. The barista worked alone, his hair in a tight knot, staring into the middle distance as the milk frother screamed. Jamie paid for their drinks and an oversized chocolate chip cookie, breaking it in half inside a serviette so they could share.

The meeting was a formality, but Jamie was the king of formalities. Rachel had worked in half a dozen HR departments since getting her degree, and Jamie was far and away the best boss she'd ever had, as well as the most exemplary. He was like a living human resources textbook. Everything was written down, agreed to and signed off on in the easiest and yet most professional of fashions. He had deep knowledge of employee entitlements and shared them generously, as if from his own pockets. He could almost convince a jaded employee that human resources worked in the best interests of the staff rather than the business.

'So,' he said, typing the last words on the email summarising their meeting, 'looking forward to your time off?'

'I've been so busy, I haven't had time to get excited yet.'

'It's always the way.' Jamie closed his laptop. 'It isn't until you've finished work that you catch your breath and think, *I'm actually doing this!*'

Rachel knew he was fishing for information. Company guidelines said employees were entitled to do whatever they wanted while on annual leave, provided it didn't bring the business into disrepute, and he'd never come out and ask what hers was booked for. Jamie was extremely skilled at making the vague seem specific.

Taking pity, she decided to give him the version of the trip she'd share with her mother and brothers. Jamie made a good test run, because his training and personality precluded him from asking invasive questions like Jean and Conrad definitely would.

'I got a bit spontaneous,' Rachel explained. She found the website for the hotel she'd be staying at on her phone and showed it to Jamie. 'You can get spa treatments and things dirt cheap because the currency is weak. And the capital's meant to be this hidden gem, the next Prague or Budapest.' She leaned across and swiped through the photo set until the exterior shots came into view: cobbled streets, bridges, ornate public buildings, a castle on a hilltop.

'Wow.' Jamie bent close, keeping his free hand on his coffee so Rachel was the only one touching her device. 'Looks lovely. I have to admit, I've never heard of it.' He offered a self-effacing look. 'But then, I haven't been to Prague or Budapest.'

Rachel had. She shook off memories of standing with Ben at the base of the Astronomical Clock, his hand sliding up the leg of her shorts as tourists pressed eagerly around them. 'They're gorgeous but getting a bit touristy.'

Jamie looked apologetic. 'Can you show me on the map?'

Rachel opened Google Maps and zoomed in to south-central Europe until the long speech-bubble shape of the country filled the screen, with the capital roughly in the centre and a mountain range just inside the eastern border. Jamie's brow furrowed as he tried to make sense of the geography. 'It's quite small, isn't it? I had no idea.'

She scrolled around, showing him neighbouring countries: Serbia, Romania, Hungary. 'There's a lot of good daytrips. The mountain towns are meant to be beautiful.' Not that Rachel would see them: she was going for one thing, and one thing only.

'But safe, right?'

'It's no more dangerous than anywhere else.'

'Well,' he said, 'good for you. I hope it's everything you want it to be.'

Sliding her phone back into her bag, Rachel felt a flood of appreciation for Jamie. He would've made the perfect husband and father, if only these very attributes didn't make him appallingly unattractive to Rachel. Plus, he was her boss, and already married, et cetera.

If the procedure worked and she came back pregnant, her story would be that she met a local man in a bar, they'd been together only once, and she had no way of getting in touch. Jamie wouldn't want to know any of that. He'd treat it like the Immaculate Conception, a hushed thing to be revered, and protect her from any office gossip. And if the treatment didn't work, he'd just ask if she enjoyed her holiday and never mention it again.

Jess
Friday

Fifteen thousand kilometres away, at the same time Rachel was kicking off her underpants and climbing onto the exam table, the earth was beginning its roll into the new day.

Here, in the northern hemisphere, the sound of keys scratching in the lock woke Jess Neave from a light sleep. She felt warm with anticipation as the door creaked and Viktor's heavy boots met the wooden floor. She could trace his movements through the darkness of the flat: keys and wallet dropped on the tallboy in the entryway; the hiss of urine and rumble of the cistern; taps moaning as he drank water in the kitchen. Finally, he entered the bedroom, smelling of beer and the fruity aftershave he wore unselfconsciously. She rolled towards the doorway and lifted the doona, inviting him in.

His skin was cold from being outside, and on top of his own scents were ozone and pavement. He pressed the icy tip of his nose to her neck, making her squeal. 'Warm me up,' he suggested, unbuckling his belt and wriggling the waistband of his jeans towards his knees. 'I think about you all day, darling.' As proof, he took her palm and pressed it against the radiant heat of his groin.

After they were done, Viktor turned Jess so her spine was rounded into his belly, his top arm looping around to lie between her breasts.

'All day,' he repeated, breath moist and sweet against her earlobe. She reached back to find his head, rubbed his thick curls with her fingers, then let her arm slacken back against the pillow.

Like that, they slept.

***

After eight, Jess woke again. The light through the bedroom window was milky white, like watered-down paint, and the cold shimmered in the glass. Viktor slept facedown, arms and legs bent like a body fallen from a high building. Trying not to disturb him, she rolled her half of the doona into the middle of the bed and scooted to the end. The chill of the floorboards made her gasp as she hurried down the hallway to the kitchen.

When Jess had finally agreed to move here, Viktor promised they'd live somewhere nice. Before that, when she'd visit, his accommodation had ranged from remote to crowded to crumbling. Viktor could make do with a sleeping bag on a cement floor, but he understood Jess's Western middle-class tastes and stretched their budget to breaking point for a second-storey flat in the Old Town with views from the kitchen and bedroom. The bay window in the kitchen was Jess's favourite place, and the warmest because it collected the heat from the stove. Viktor found a sturdy chair so she could drink coffee and look out at the mountains. The apartment and the view helped to keep her in the country, but to pay for it they both had to work whatever hours they could find, making times like these, when she could sit still and gaze, both priceless and costly as hell.

The morning sky was pale and cloudless, the sun weak, despite the spring equinox being only a few weeks away. Jess had read somewhere that, instead of the black of night, the real colour of the universe was a kind of middling beige. The sky in the region was the same, with no ocean reflected in it. It was as if any blueness got caught in the mountaintops as the sun rose, leaving just a thin film to drift westwards.

The water boiled in the coffee maker, and she turned off the burner, then poured coffee and milk into an oversized mug. The custom here was to serve hot drinks in bowls, which were lifted by circling the thumb and second finger of each hand around the rim and tipped towards the mouth. The sensation reminded Jess of drinking the leftover milk from a bowl of cereal, and she was always afraid of spilling. She conformed in public, but in her own home, she wanted a mug.

Smelling the coffee, Viktor came out shirtless, unzipped jeans hanging from his hips. She filled a bowl for him and received his kiss, short but full, his entire body pressing against her for a moment. 'Today is busy for you?' he asked, sipping the black brew, then continued as if it were she who'd asked the question. 'I go to university, then the gym, then work at the buffet. I will see you, my love?'

'I've got my English class, then tutoring in the afternoon and an early shift at the bar.' She lowered her mug. 'When do you finish teaching? We could meet up.'

'Lunchtime,' he said, then smiled fondly as her face fell. They wouldn't see one another until Viktor returned from the restaurant, and that would be long past midnight. 'Don't worry, darling. It is Friday. The end of the working week.'

Jess rolled her eyes, as he'd wanted her to. They made their living through a patchwork of casual jobs and under-the-table shifts, and these opportunities were easiest to find on the weekends.

Viktor tipped the last of his coffee down his throat. 'Boris has a speech on Sunday in City Square,' he said. 'There are drinks after. You would like to go?'

Jess yawned. 'What's he going to talk about?'

'You have heard of the green energy expo?' When she shook her head, Viktor elaborated. 'It is now two weeks away. There are many thoughts about it, many points of view. Is this a turning point for the country, or another dead end?'

'Dead end?'

'Some of the proposals ...' He turned to rinse his bowl in the sink, then dried his hands on the tea towel. 'It is not yet clear.'

'What does Boris think?' Jess would never say, but she thought Boris was the smartest of their friends. Smarter even than Viktor, and that was saying something.

Viktor shrugged loosely. 'We find out on Sunday.'

'What time?'

'Eleven o'clock.' He ran a finger along her arm.

She tilted her chin so they could kiss, Viktor's lips tasting of coffee. 'Sounds good.'

'A date!' he shouted, stamping his foot with glee. Jess laughed. 'I look forward to it so much, darling.'

Viktor went to shower, and Jess poured herself a second coffee, making it lukewarm with the last of the milk. Returning to the window, she saw clouds gathering over the mountains, slowly ascending the peaks like a diver climbing a ladder. In the same way, the clouds would soon leap from the range and cascade down the leeward side in a minorly famous weather event that still thrilled her, seven years after she'd first seen it.

It was motion that made the cloudfall phenomenon so gorgeous; static pictures of a cloud mass against the steep edge of the range always seemed unremarkable. Even video took a while to pay off, since the viewer had to appreciate the arrival of the clouds from the east, their collection at the highest point, and then the moment of pause; the diver taking a breath before the jump. Jess had seen the northern lights once and found the slowness of the colour change to be maddeningly gorgeous; the realisation that a shimmering crosshatch of green was a completely different shape than it had been moments before. She thought the cloudfall was similar in the near imperceptibility of the shift, how it took sustained attention to truly appreciate.

When Jess showed footage to people back in England, most were bored long before that point. Their questions undermined the beauty she found there: Where was this? Were a few clouds skidding down the side of a mountain really the country's most appealing feature? Who'd leave their home behind and move more than a thousand miles just for that?

***

Jess's morning language class was held in a library in the centre of the Old Town, a brisk five-minute walk from the flat. She left the warmth of the kitchen reluctantly, dressing in layers and zipping herself into a quilted coat. Her quick stride should have kept her warm, but the air over the plain was icy and relentless from the moment she stepped onto the street.

Despite its name, the Old Town wasn't as picturesque as it might have been. The oldest of the buildings dated from around four hundred years before, but there were few of these left, with the materials being so low quality and the city's various leaders so often in a mood to raze and rebuild, raze and rebuild. The resulting mismatch of styles had its own contradictory beauty: brutalist against mid-century modern, Edwardian extensions on baroque.

There was a lack of green space too, with the squares either bricked or cobblestoned (until Viktor pointed out the 'cobbles' were large, fake tiles installed in the late nineteen-nineties to cover over a particularly bad bitumen job), with the odd spindly sapling planted in dirt at random points on footpaths. The only point of relief was down by City Square, where Boris would make his speech on Sunday. City Park was an oblong of flattened grass ringed by irregularly spaced fir trees, with a playground for the Old Town's children laid with rich-scented woodchips.

The Old Town was set out on a grid of five avenues by four streets, all pedestrianised and accessible only to emergency and delivery vehicles. The blocky right angles and straight lines diluted the charm, but their regularity came in handy when the frantic building-on-building led to a confusion in addresses. The library was on Street Three, just east of the central avenue, with no number—Jess guessed the town planners thought the four-foot-tall BIBLIOTHECA carved into the base was identity enough—and no space for one, because the hairdresser across the avenue was 86 and the tax accountants in their square brown building next to the library were 88. From there, heading east, were 90 (a union office), 92b (four townhouses), 96-1 (a deli), 96-2 (bicycle repair shop) and, again unnumbered, the main post office on the corner of Avenue Quattro.

The avenues ran north–south and were named using an almost-Italian, the language used for fancy things: Avenue Uno, Avenue Duo, Avenue Centro, Avenue Quattro, Avenue Quincy. Running east–west away from the river were the less imaginative Street One, Street Two, Street Three and Street Four. At first Jess assumed the two different naming styles were to distinguish between the road types, avoiding the confusion of finding yourself at the corner of Street Two and Second Avenue, for example, but she soon realised it wasn't a matter of thinking ahead. Nothing here was.

The library building was pretty, with wide, flat steps cutting through the words BIBLIO and THECA to reach the entrance. The grand revolving door was framed on each side by a pair of massive pillars with banners for upcoming events strung between them. But there were disappointments here too: the yellowing of the marble like smokers' teeth; the original termite-devoured wood of the doorframe replaced with cheap aluminium; the wilted-lettuce colour of the carpet tiles as you stepped inside.

Jess knew these kinds of complaints were snobby, and she'd never share them with Viktor and his friends. But that meant her feelings could build up to a point like now, when she stumbled over a fraying corner of carpet square, twinged her knee, and experienced a sudden, hot rage completely out of proportion with what had happened. She tripped over so much in this fucking country, both literally and figuratively, that sometimes it was impossible to keep the frustration at bay.

As she paused to take a breath, she was jostled by patrons entering after her and not leaving a wide enough berth, despite the excessive size of the foyer. She crossed her arms and hunched as if bracing against a hard wind. No-one said anything, whether to excuse themselves or admonish her for standing in the middle of a thoroughfare. They passed as if she wasn't there at all.

Jess took a few moments to massage her knee and catch her temper before heading for the side room where her class took place. The space was heated to the point of nausea, and she had to shed the layers she'd put on only minutes before, down to her white button-down shirt and black dress slacks. It was the same uniform she wore for all her teaching and waitressing jobs. Her temperature regulated, Jess found the day's tape in the drawer and clicked it down into the ancient cassette player.

This was her most reliable work, an English language class for older people. The eight-week courses ran several times a year, offering forty-eight hours of instruction in total. Enough to grasp the very basics, she hoped. Most of the teaching was done through the tapes, whose male and female voices featured mid-Atlantic accents straight out of a post-war newsreel. Jess was the native speaker promised in the promotional materials, available to answer questions and check answers, but chiefly the player, pauser and flipper of the tapes. Usually, the most anyone asked her was 'Break, yes?' and 'Home, yes?', but to be fair, one of the class rules was that they could only speak in English during lesson time, and they didn't know English.

Despite being offered every few months, the course was never well attended. It ran on weekday mornings—Mondays, Wednesdays and Fridays—to suit older folks, but this was the demographic who cared least about the world's dominant language. While young people could be dismissive of their native tongue, calling it parochial and pointless, only good for communicating with granny and the government, those aged over sixty were proud of their heritage and suspicious of English, an instrument both too pointed and too blunt.

Viktor's late grandfather had been one of this generation, a man who'd never lived more than twenty kilometres from the shack where he was born and considered the ninety-minute trip to the capital to be a journey on par with Arctic expeditions.

'You are a stupid boy,' he once told Viktor solemnly. Jess had been living there for a year, and they'd just celebrated a third cousin's baptism, with relatives far and wide gathered; Grandfather saved all his criticism for an audience. 'If you want to leave so badly, why do you always come back?' He pointed at Viktor's brother Feodor. 'He is the good boy. He still loves the farm.'

Viktor had shrugged, unbothered. 'I come back because I love my grandpapa, right? He is the smartest man around.'

His grandfather snuffled proudly. 'Stupid, what did I say?' He nodded at Jess, who was only barely keeping up. 'You are stupid too. Leaving your own home behind.'

Jess licked sweat from her lip. 'Stupid from love,' she said in the old man's language.

There was a pause as the family members turned to the grandfather, waiting for his reaction. After a second he smiled widely, his upper dentures square and numerous.

'Perhaps it is good you are stupid,' he assented, beckoning Jess so he could embrace her from his armchair-throne, long fingers cupping her skull. 'Stupid and stupid, a matching pair.'

The grandfather had not been impressed by English. Along with his own language and two other dialects, he spoke Romanian, Serbian, and a bit of Hungarian and Czech. Besides, only a couple of million people understood his language; the rarity made it valuable. If he could make his grandson's foreigner girlfriend speak to him in his own tongue, was English really that powerful?

When he died, he'd been buried behind the church where he was baptised, confirmed and married, in a plot beside his late wife, parents and sister. All the townspeople had come, along with family from throughout the region. Not a word of English was spoken, not even at the wake, and when they got back to the flat, Jess felt tired and thickheaded from concentration. Viktor had wanted to look at photographs, but he didn't need to talk, so she could lie against him in a comforting stupor as he ran his finger down the edge of old polaroids and wept.

Viktor had told her she'd have no trouble finding work as a native English speaker, but it hadn't turned out quite like that. The younger generations learned it at school, and most adult education venues required teaching and ESL qualifications that Jess didn't have. She'd got the library classes through a contact of Viktor's and ran conversation lessons with a few teenagers from well-off families, but if she wanted to get into better-paid stuff she'd have to take on additional training, and that would eat up too much of her scant time and money.

Besides, speaking English wasn't all Jess wanted to do with her new life. She had other ambitions. She wanted, one day, to move to the eastern mountains, the site of the cloudfall. The government didn't do much to sell the area's natural beauty, and Jess was certain there was potential there, ecotourism or bike-and-hike holidays or something. There was just never enough time or money to figure it out.

She was lucky to have the senior classes at all, because the venture was wholly unprofitable. To pay for Jess, the library needed to enrol ten people in every course, but the most she'd ever had was seven. Once, in a summer term, she'd started with just two, a married couple who went off on a cruise after the third week. Jess had emailed the head librarian, who told her to keep turning up in case the couple came back. They didn't, so Jess got paid to sit.

The low numbers meant nothing in the scheme of things, because this was a place that ran on momentum. She couldn't imagine the effort it had taken to get the class up and running—the conservatism of local council, the lethargy of the library staff, the suspicion of patrons—but once the boulder had been shoved to the top of the mountain, the tumble down was unstoppable. There could be zero enrolments, a total conflagration of the tapes, no native speaker within the country's borders, and still the course would run. Mr and Mrs Mid-Atlantic speaking without sound to an empty room.

The current course had started in the new year and was in its second-last week. There were five students, all women in cable-knit cardigans and long woollen skirts, four with their hair plaited in crowns around their heads. The nannas, Jess thought of them. They were very sweet. During the break, they poured tea for Jess first and waited until she'd taken a biscuit before selecting their own, then laboured with their unwieldy smartphones to show one another the latest pictures of their grandchildren. This was why most were doing the course—to be able to function, in some small way, when they one day visited their families in Ireland and Canada and Australia. To be able to speak to their grandchildren's friends when they were introduced: *Hello, how are you. I am Alexey's grandmother. I travel by plane. I stay two weeks. Nice to meet you, goodbye.*

The workbook had no lessons dedicated to emotions, no translations for the feelings that came with thinking of loved ones living far away. They learned *I am hungry, I am sleepy, I am cold,* but not *I am sad, I am lonely, I am confused.* They covered *I am lost* in the lesson on geography. No doubt they'd need it, in the bizarre places where their children and grandchildren lived. Perhaps they also used the phrase in their hearts.

But that was patronising the nannas; maybe they took it all in stride. Their grandchildren were stupid for leaving, in a different way than Viktor was stupid for coming back, but that was to be expected: all young people were stupid. You just had to learn enough English to fly to where they were and tell them to their faces.

The nannas arrived by ten minutes to ten, gossiping as they shed their coats. Jess flicked through a workbook and pretended not to listen. From snatches, she figured they were talking about the green energy expo Viktor had mentioned that morning.

The country had many such events; what her communications lecturers at university would have called 'robust performances of the public sphere'. Colloquiums, forums, seminars, summits, town halls, demonstrations—every weekend there was something, new posters taped over the old ones in layers that could be dug through like geologic time. They spilled out of the convention centre into squares and taverns and hotel ballrooms, the same burly, underemployed youths hired to direct traffic, provide security and run the bar. Cynically, Jess thought of it as a content-creating exercise. Local TV covered everything, and the tabloid newspaper filled the letters page with citizens praising or dismissing the past weekend's offerings, then casting their predictions on the next.

At first Jess had tried to keep up, to develop an interest, to pick a side. So many of the issues discussed were important to Viktor. But even as she learned more about the place where she'd chosen to live, she struggled to understand what was to be supported or derided or ignored. She was never able to capture the logic of what made, for example, the Seventeenth Colloquium on Fairness in Sport a sickening display of corruption, while the Biennial Convention for Discussion of Sports Fairness was a bastion of integrity that brought proud tears to Viktor's eyes.

Occasionally the news footage intrigued her, like the time a defector from one political party sprinted across a stage to pour expired yoghurt on his rival's bald head. In towelling off the foul-smelling goo, an assistant had missed a greenish bit of apricot. After the perpetrator was tackled and the victim resumed his speech, the chunk was dislodged by rivers of anxious sweat to slide down his forehead and off the ski-jump of his nose. Sensitive microphones caught the *plop* of the rotten fruit hitting the floor.

When she mentioned it to Viktor, he'd given a sad frown. 'Political theatre, darling. The two men remain secret allies, and it is good advertising for the rival dairy brand.'

The most interesting thing about the upcoming expo, to Jess, was how it was being talked about so far in advance. The events planned for the two weekends in between must be real duds.

One of the nannas, the most plaintive, told the others she wouldn't be staying in the city during the expo. Instead, she'd go to her sister's place in the mountains.

'It will rain there,' another said dismissively.

'Better rain from heaven than piss from a politician,' a third mused.

Jess swallowed her laugh so they wouldn't know she was eavesdropping.

'Rain in March?' the fourth nanna scoffed. 'You're kidding. Paula will be fine.'

'I'm going to stay with my son,' the last one announced. She had a warbling voice like drunken morning birds.

The others went quiet, as they always did when Rania mentioned her son. Jess had gathered from other conversations that the son was involved in something dangerous, maybe illegal, that his mother didn't know about. The town where he lived was impoverished, and Viktor had warned Jess not to go there.

'I may go to my brother's,' the fourth woman said. Vera was the only one without a braid, her hair instead cropped into a white cap. She was tall and slender, with deep crevices linking her nostrils to the corners of her mouth. She'd taught at the university before retiring and was the only student who didn't have grandchildren. Instead, she was learning English recreationally, to add to her French and Italian. Vera was almost glamorous.

'Where is he?' Paula asked.

'Budapest.'

The other women breathed in sharply. 'Aren't you being dramatic, Vera?' the second student said. 'Just stay off the street. Get milk and bread in, close the curtains.'

Vera's eyes flashed to Jess, who didn't have time to look away. 'I had enough of that in the lockdowns,' Vera said grimly. 'No, I prefer my brother's than isolation.'

'Aren't we late?' Rania interrupted in her wobbly voice. 'Teacher!' she called in English. 'Yes?'

Jess glanced at the clock. It was three minutes past ten. 'Yes, thank you,' she said. 'Sorry. I was lost in my thoughts.'

'Lost!' cried the third student, beaming brightly as she recalled the word from Monday. 'Lost, yes!' Putting her arms out like a scarecrow's, she mimed doddering around to the amusement of the others. They'd acted this out during class, pairs swapping the roles of lost person and helpful person. *I am lost,* the cassette tape had dictated. *Please help me.*

'I can help you,' the partner was meant to say. 'Let me show you the way.'

Fifty-five minutes later the tape's A-side clicked off and Jess went to boil the urn. As they finished their writing exercises the women joined her, nodding appreciatively as she bit into a supermarket shortbread. Jess returned to her desk to give the women privacy, but was followed by the retired lecturer, Vera.

'Can I help you?' Jess asked.

'Yes, please, teacher.' Though she was the fastest learner, using her French and Italian to reason out the meaning of words, Vera's English was thickly accented and difficult to decipher. 'I ask of … the assembly?'

'Assembly?' Jess imagined rows of schoolkids with their legs crossed.

Vera tried again: 'Meeting? Energy?'

'Meeting—the expo?'

Vera looked relieved.

Jess lowered her voice. 'Do you have a question?' she asked in the local language.

'You speak well,' Vera commented. 'My English is not so good.'

'English is a hard language to learn.'

It was something Jess said often, mostly when people apologised to her for their English. When she first moved, she'd made the mistake of praising people's near-perfect usage, unaware of the contempt they felt for the condescension of charmless native speakers, those unworthy winners of the global communication lottery.

'You know of this event?' Vera asked. 'The Russian president will go.'

Jess had heard this line before, but it was only ever representatives from smaller countries who came, places whose capitals she hadn't known before she came here: Northern Macedonia, Bulgaria, Albania, Moldova. In the last three years the biggest coup was the Polish Minister for Digital Affairs, and he hadn't even stayed overnight.

Vera smiled with one side of her mouth. 'It's true.' After a moment, she added, 'And France, and Germany. Italy. Spain. All of them.'

'What for?'

Vera's forehead creased, a long deep line. 'The expo,' she said, using English for the last word to prove she'd remembered it before returning to her native tongue. 'It's about the environment. Technologies to defeat the weather.' They'd done weather in class: *Sunny. Cloudy. Rain.* 'There will be many visitors, politicians and businesspeople and journalists. Security to protect them. Protests, of course.' She shrugged. 'This is why I will stay away. Travel will be difficult. Police everywhere.'

'I'm here legally.' Jess's hand went to her backpack, where her papers were.

'Of course.' Vera looked at the clock; the break would end soon. The other nannas were dusting crumbs from their hands and rinsing out their cups. 'But if you go away, you can rent your apartment to a foreign journalist. That's what I'm doing.'

'Really?' Jess couldn't imagine international reporters caring about anything that happened here.

'The hotels are full and there's nowhere to stay, so a journalist will pay a lot of money.' Vera smiled. 'Mine's from Canada.'

'Okay, well.' Jess switched back to English as the others moved towards their desks. 'Thank you very much, Vera. The word for that meeting is *expo*.'

'Ex-po,' the students repeated, speaking over one another, at different paces and with different intonations.

As the B-side of the tape ran through the names of farm animals, Jess thought about Vera's predictions. The Russian president? Western world leaders? She couldn't believe it. The place was insignificant, its capital city a pinprick. Jess had grown to love it here, or at least feel fond and protective, but it was a hard-scrabble life. Nothing came easy: money, progress, attention. It was a sobering realisation experienced over and over that she was a nobody, doing not much of anything. After three years, things hadn't improved—if anything, they were harder. At the end of the week, she and Viktor put any money they had left in a dish on the kitchen bench, and there hadn't been more than a handful of coins in months.

She tapped her teeth and considered Vera's advice. They could put the flat on the internet and leave for the expo weekend, stay on the farm with Viktor's brother, maybe. Jess would love a few uninterrupted days in the mountains, but she couldn't imagine anyone paying enough to make it worth giving up their lucrative weekend jobs. It wasn't like they'd get holiday pay. In fact, there'd probably be more work available, if the restaurants and hotels were expecting an influx. They should stay and wring every last crown out of the opportunity.

Jess's sigh turned into a yawn, and she fought the urge to lie with her cheek against the cool desk. She loved Viktor, and she'd made her decision to be here, but she wouldn't mind if things got a little bit easier.

Rachel
CD4

On Sunday, Rachel went for her day four check. Her lining was fine, and three follicles were still growing, while the others had forfeited the race. In the words of the old cliché, it only took one.

Afterwards, she had breakfast with her mother. The hatchback was in the car park when Rachel pulled in, and Jean had found a spot for them on the café's covered veranda. 'I didn't wait,' she announced, nodding at the table number she'd been given. 'I was gasping for a coffee.'

Rachel went inside to give her order, relieved Jean wasn't at her shoulder to scoff at the decaf latte with oat milk and half-serve of bircher muesli. She'd forgotten Jean's order number, so the server gave her a new one.

'What's this?' her mother asked when she returned to their table.

Rachel glanced down, looking for a problem with her outfit.

'*This*.' Jean flicked the table number. 'I got twenty-four. Didn't you put it on twenty-four?'

'I couldn't remember twenty-four.'

'So they'll be processing two different orders,' Jean huffed. 'They'll probably forget something.'

'We'd have two orders anyway.'

With the pad of her thumb, Jean pushed the second metal stand. 'Take it back and say they're both on twenty-four.'

'Mum. It doesn't matter.'

'*Take* it—'

A server rounded the corner with Jean's macchiato, and she sat up and beamed. 'Thank you. Ooh, nice and hot! That's wonderful.'

'Too late now,' Rachel said once he'd gone. She pulled her number across the table so Jean couldn't fiddle with it. 'Anyway. How are you?'

As Rachel had known she would, her mother immediately began talking about Conrad's kids. Rachel's older brother and his wife had three children—the boys were almost five, and they'd recently had a daughter—and ever since Carly announced her first pregnancy, Jean had been unable to consider herself as separate from her son's family. It wasn't even that she spent that much time with them, just one day a week babysitting the older two and some activities on weekends, but she absorbed every story Conrad told her and recast it for others as if she'd been there.

The boys had started kindy at the end of January and were proving to be geniuses. Far smarter than their teacher, who Jean was thinking of making a complaint about after Gideon came home crying once. Neither he nor Aidan had been able to explain why. She'd never do it—Jean only ever complained to her children and daughter-in-law, so everyone else thought she was nice as pie— but Rachel prickled anyway.

'It doesn't mean it had anything to do with the teacher,' she said, after their breakfasts and Rachel's coffee had been brought out and the two table numbers whipped away.

Jean leapt on this like a tiger on prey. 'Why wouldn't it? Why not?'

'Why *would* it, though? Gid's four. Four-year-olds cry.'

'Why were they so secretive about it, then? They were scared.'

'They probably couldn't remember.'

'No. No,' Jean decided, sawing her toast. 'I didn't like that woman from the first day. I think she has it out for Gid because he's handsome.'

'And Aidy's not?'

'Aidan can stand up for himself,' Jean breezed. 'My Gideon is a sensitive soul.'

Rachel assumed Jean was making up for apparently mothering on autopilot by being an indulgent grandmother, one who'd take the grandies' sides at all costs: undermine the teacher who made them frown, squash the bee that stung them, blow away the breeze that itched their noses. Jean as a mother would have told them to get on with it. To be fair, she'd had no time to indulge, having been widowed before she was thirty and needing to work a full-time job, run a house and try to provide basic emotional support for children she apparently only faintly recognised, like shifting shapes in the dark. And she hadn't done that badly, had she? Conrad and Rachel functioned most of the time, and Antony at least half.

Despite the hardships, as a mum Jean could even be fun: water-balloon fights in the backyard, letting them drag their mattresses into the lounge room and stay up watching movies, weekend treks through bushland on Perth's outskirts. She didn't hide her feelings and let the children release their own, encouraging them to cry, stomp, swear if they had to. Antony would be at the end of the passageway, slamming and slamming his door, and she'd be Serene Jean at the kitchen table, asking Conrad and Rachel if they wanted their brother's dinner, since he clearly didn't. She took them on caravan holidays and bought what the other kids had, even if it was from second-hand shops or out of the classifieds from mothers whose older children had moved on. They had a dog called Merry who slept on the other half of Jean's double bed, and when she died, Conrad dug a hole under their favourite tree and Jean carried the bag from the vet across the backyard, cheeks red and soaked with tears.

Then Jean revealed this wasn't the way she'd intended to mother them. When Antony finished school and she experienced the sensation of logging back on, of becoming present, things had changed. Rachel was unsettled by the thought that, if Michael hadn't died, she would've had this oversensitive, sniping parent her whole life.

'What's that you're drinking?' Jean asked now, with Rachel's latte half-finished. She lifted it to her nose. 'Smells funny. Are you on some health kick?'

There was no point answering: Jean would decide for herself. She took a sip and scowled. 'That's disgusting. What is it?'

'No, it isn't.' Rachel held out her hand until Jean passed the cup back, then swallowed a mouthful as proof. It *was* bad, of course— only someone who'd never tasted caffeine or cow's milk could say decaf and oat were good substitutes—but not as bad as her mother made out, and it was better than nothing.

'Is it the new thing? I remember when ordering a cappuccino was exotic. When I was your age, we had instant.'

You don't remember being my age, Rachel wanted to say. You were still a year away from picking yourself off the floor.

A server came to clear the table. Jean caught her by the sleeve to give feedback on the eggs Benedict, every word of which she intended to be passed on to the clearly busy and uninterested chef. Rachel wanted to smack her mother's hand away, tell her to stop grabbing at people and their belongings. *Keep your hands to yourself.* It was one of the first lessons she'd teach her own child, compassionately.

She'd also teach them not to let anyone grab. Even grandmothers.

While they were eating, Jean hadn't allowed the conversation to be steered towards Rachel. Now she turned the wheel herself.

'This thing,' she said, mouth pinched like she could still taste the decaf. 'It's this week, is it?'

'Friday night.'

'Where's this place again?'

Jean was pretending she forgot; Rachel knew she'd told Conrad and Carly everything. 'It's meant to be fascinating,' she said.

'Oh, I bet. If you like blocks of flats and deprivation.'

Jean had not been to Europe. Had barely been out of the country, other than two package tours of South-East Asia.

Rachel let her gaze drift. Her hands laced gently over her abdomen, inside which the follicles were growing.

'I don't know why you're going there of all places,' Jean whined. 'Why not Bali? Somewhere normal.'

If Rachel were going to Bali, Jean would have told her to go to New Zealand. If it was New Zealand, she would have told her to holiday at home. If at home, she would've crowed, 'Why don't you go to Europe? You're single!'

'It's cheap,' Rachel responded. 'And unique. There's something about it that appeals to me.'

'If I was going overseas, I'd go to France.' Jean stepped on the *a* sound so it burst, like a grape. 'Or Spain, or Italy.' She grimaced. 'But I suppose you've already seen those places. With Ben.'

Rachel nodded and tried to look wistful. It was fine if her mother thought the trip had something to do with Ben: that was her opinion of everything Rachel did. Jean was proving to be more hung up on Rachel and Ben's failed marriage than anyone.

'Is it supposed to be edgy or something, this place?'

'It was a cheap package,' Rachel said again. 'A four-and-a-half-star hotel for less than a hundred a night. Where else can you find that?'

'Probably Iran.'

A queue of cyclists in lycra had formed at the café's entrance. Rachel felt guilty, sitting at a cleared table while people waited.

'What did Conny say?' her mother asked. 'He must think it's a bizarre idea.'

'He doesn't care.' When Jean rolled her eyes, Rachel added, 'He's jealous I get to even have a holiday.'

'I expect he'd rather stay home than go to Chechnya.'

Rachel stood abruptly, the legs of her chair rumbling against the wooden deck. 'Come on, there's a line of people wanting tables.'

'They can wait. We had to wait.' Jean rose, then paused to smooth the fabric of her blouse over her stomach, enjoying the people who tilted in their direction, attempting to work out if the table was being vacated. Rachel nodded to the pair of men who'd been waiting the longest and took her mother by the upper arm, aware that she was the one who was grabbing now. Jean shook her off.

'This is the last time I see you before your nutty sojourn?' she asked when they got to her car.

'I'm working all week, and I'll have to pack.'

'Well.' Jean put a hand over her eyebrows to block the sun. 'Good luck. I hope no-one dismembers you.'

Rachel laughed.

For a moment her mother looked flattered, but the expression was soon chased by a scowl. 'I'm serious, though. It's a worry.'

Rachel leaned in to receive a farewell kiss, a tight scrunch of Jean's dry lips against the curve of her jaw. 'I promise I'll come back in one piece.'

She hadn't told her mother about any of it—the failed IVF

attempts or her desire to be a single parent or even her thoughts about having kids. When Jean said she'd pictured herself with an eight- or nine-year-old rather than an infant, she hadn't turned the question back on Rachel. Revealing her plans would allow Jean to either approve or disapprove—there was no middle ground, no 'whatever makes you happy' or 'you have your own life to live'— and that weight would be ruinous. To an outsider, Jean offering her support and Rachel having a baby might be seen as the best-case scenario. To Rachel, that just meant her mother was right.

Rachel doing IVF would surprise her mother, since one of Jean's explanations for the divorce was that Ben wanted a baby and Rachel didn't. (Not true; never true.) She was especially insistent on giving this version to Carly, as if she'd never met them. At a family dinner, Jean said to her daughter-in-law, 'I wanted to tell Ben at the wedding, you know, this one is very headstrong—' (Rachel was the least headstrong person in the family, in the world) '—but that boy thought he could convince her. Well, proved him wrong in the end. You can lead a horse to water, et cetera.'

'Proved him wrong about what?' Carly had asked, frazzled. Meals had to take place at their house because it was easiest with the boys, but it meant she needed to have eyes on everything while she hosted. 'What horse?'

'Ben wanted to run an equestrian centre,' Antony smirked. 'Rach wouldn't let him.'

'Really,' Jean admonished. 'No, it's the baby question. The age-old. Rachel didn't want to be a mum, but Ben thought she'd change her mind.'

'Oh.' Carly checked under the table for her own children.

'I'm sorry to say, but Rachel's never had the maternal instinct.' Jean prodded her on the shoulder. 'I remember you coming home from school one day screaming you were never going to have kids.

You'd just done that experiment with the dolls that cry all night. Social studies. It's meant to be a contraceptive, and it worked on you.'

'Rach loved dolls,' Conrad called from the barbecue, white smoke obscuring his face. Rachel wondered if her brother ever cooked when it wasn't for show.

Carly found one of the twins and hauled him up. 'I hope these two haven't scared you off,' she said, folding the squawking child under her singlet to feed. As usual, Jean stared.

'They're gorgeous,' Rachel murmured, a lump in her throat.

Eyes on her son, Carly patted Rachel's arm. 'I don't know about the maternal instinct,' she said. 'If you have a baby, you get an instinct, as far as I can tell.'

'All I'm saying,' Jean announced, 'is that no-one should be surprised when Ben shows up with some pregnant dolly bird.' She lengthened her throat to fend off criticism. 'I don't *agree* with it, but it happens. He's forty. There's such a thing as a man's biological clock.' She nodded to Conrad. 'Isn't there?'

He lifted a kebab with his tongs. 'Lunch is ready.'

Rachel hadn't believed her mother, but it was a relief when Ben's new girlfriend turned out to be about the same age as Rachel and already the mum of a teenage son. Viewed from the outside (and what did Rachel know?), Melissa didn't seem the type to want to go through it all again.

When Jean heard about Melissa, she decided it was what she'd meant all along. 'You can't tell me it's a coincidence that the new one has kids,' she insisted when Conrad showed her the social media photos.

'One kid,' Rachel corrected. 'And the biological father is very involved.' At least, according to Facebook.

Jean assumed a wise-owl face. 'Ben may not be the boy's dad, but that doesn't mean the boy isn't like a son.'

Rachel had already started looking into single parenthood by then: Jean's commentary hadn't set her off. Her mother had the situation back-to-front, anyway. It was Rachel who'd been on the fence about kids, Ben who was certain he didn't want them. Marrying him had brought an end to her indecision, and though there was some unease and grief, it had been a relief to know what her future held.

When they separated, she was back to the turmoil of should she or shouldn't she. Soon time would make the decision for her.

***

At home, Rachel took out the folder of documents from the overseas clinic. It had been sent via registered post, and there was a smell to the pages that Rachel now associated with the place she hadn't yet seen: a floral but also smoked-wood kind of smell, like the paper was stored for a long time with sachets of old potpourri. The edges were curled from where Rachel had gone through them over and over. By now she had them almost memorised.

In the envelope, along with the contract and an outline of Rachel's medication protocol and travel itinerary, were the profiles of the two donors she'd chosen. The creators of her embryo.

Before she signed on, the clinic had emailed Rachel a PDF with bios of all the egg and sperm donors on their books. When she first tried with her own eggs, there'd been similar folders of sperm donors to choose from, with photographs of the adult men as babies alongside anonymised personal and medical details. At the time her choice felt almost arbitrary, a matter of getting a 'feeling' from a particular profile, which for her had been a thirty-seven-year-old who worked in education, five foot ten, brown hair and eyes, and a love of surfing.

Looking back, she can see where her choice came from. The man was basically Ben.

The profiles hadn't used names, only codes containing two letters and four digits, but Rachel knew it couldn't really be him. This was only partly because he'd been so staunch about not having children; mostly, it was because she didn't recognise the picture of him as a kid. Her ex-mother-in-law had shown her all of them, many times over.

The overseas clinic's donor profiles were accompanied by given names, which humanised them more. Rachel wondered if they were real or pseudonyms. Was the little blond boy in a furry brown onesie squinting into the sunlight truly called David? Was the nappy-wearing toddler standing in her mother's teal leather sandals actually Katerin?

Her own ova were unusable now, the doctors had determined. The few they could extract disintegrated in the dish before a sperm cell came near them. She could try to get a donated egg from a local clinic, but the waiting lists were extensive, and it had already been over three years. She was sick of her surroundings, staring at the same walls while needles and wands and speculums went in and out of her. There was that Albert Einstein line about it being crazy to do the same thing over and over. If she wanted a different result, she had to make a change.

She'd always needed donor sperm—enter the thirty-seven-year-old surfer—but now that she was shopping for an egg too, different options opened up. She could seek out a fresh one, created by another woman undergoing treatment at the same time Rachel did, but even in a much cheaper country, that was extremely pricey. An affordable alternative was to buy a clutch of frozen eggs and have them thawed to pair with fresh sperm. Simpler and more economical still, and with a greater chance of success than a once-frozen egg, was to get an embryo that had been created with a fresh ovum and sperm and frozen at blastocyst stage, ready to be transferred the day she needed it.

Rachel liked that her embryo would come from two random donors. A more common option was to adopt one another couple had left over, but she didn't want her child to have full-blood siblings if she could avoid it. She did have to stop and consider the ethics of embryos being created based on anticipated need; if supply outpaced demand, some must end up being destroyed. But the literature said that having the highest-quality blastocysts led to more live births, and other international clinics offered the same service, only their prices matched those at home.

Making choices based on money bothered Rachel. In one sense, she'd spend anything to have a child; in another, she felt aggrieved at having to pay a single dollar to conceive. In the time she'd been trying, the amount she'd handed over to the boutique clinic had become unlinked from any idea of value. While she didn't have a baby, the amount was everything, infinite, but as soon as she saw those two pink lines the meaning of it would zip down to nothing.

Going with a pre-made blastocyst meant Rachel couldn't pick individual donors; instead, she was offered a slimmer document listing the egg-sperm pairs already combined in the lab. Trying to be methodical, first she narrowed the donor mothers down to whose baby pictures bore some resemblance to her own: Nadya, Irina and Johanna. From there, she scrutinised the potential fathers for traits she might like in a child of her own, trying not to compare them to Ben.

It was harder than she'd imagined. Did she want an outgoing child, or one who was reserved? One who liked the arts, or preferred the sciences? Was it better if a male parent had played football as a child, or basketball or athletics? Was there some code she was missing—was this why she was single?

Eventually she'd changed tack, deciding to rule out the men who put her off instead of being choosy about who turned her on. It was like looking for company as the pub closed. Then she was left with two, Georgi and Pyotr, and three combinations to choose from: Pyotr and Irina, Pyotr and Johanna, or Georgi and Nadya. Each pair had bundles of three genetically normal embryos for sale. Three was the number required for the statistical likelihood of a live birth.

If she chose a Pyotr embryo, the half-sibling set would remain available. The idea made her uncomfortable, though she knew any of the donors might already have kids of their own, and the clinic said they stopped contracting donors once their genetic material had produced babies for three different families.

In the end, Rachel chose the Georgi and Nadya embryos for reasons that in one sense felt well-considered, and in another were as arbitrary as any of the decisions made when choosing a partner or having a kid. Nadya was in human resources, like Rachel. Georgi liked coffee and books, like Rachel. And he looked nothing like Ben. In the baby photo, Georgi was bald as an egg, though the dossier said he was now blond, six feet tall, twenty-nine years old, and working as a software developer. The kind of information she could have got from a one-night stand.

It was ironic that no-one would ever know of Nadya's background or even her existence, because she was Rachel's main focus. In the picture of her as a one-year-old, Nadya's dress resembled one Rachel had at a similar age, a scarlet corduroy pinafore with big brown buttons down the front. Rachel wondered if, after cycling through second-hand shops for a decade and a half, it had ended up overseas, purchased by Nadya's mother in the years after the dictatorship collapsed. Or perhaps the fashions had taken that long to make it halfway across the world.

The donors were both listed as living in the capital. It was a relatively small city of half a million people, around a third of the country's population. Rachel wondered if she might pass either of them on the street. If she ran into Nadya, would they still look similar? Would there be something in the egg donor's eye that caught Rachel's attention, made her feel … what?

In the final stages of signing up, Rachel had a video call with a clinic representative. She chose the neutral background of her dining room wall and lit a lamp just out of sight to give herself a glow. When she logged in at the appointed time, late evening in Western Australia, the clinic manager was already staring into the camera.

'Hello?' Rachel asked after a few seconds of the woman's cool gaze. 'Can—can you hear me?'

'Mrs Mather,' the clinic manager said. She wore a silk blouse buttoned to the throat and had the fine-angled beauty of an ageing supermodel. 'My name is Olga. I have spoken to you via email.'

'Hi, hello.' Rachel cleared her throat, which sounded too noisy in her quiet townhouse. 'Sorry, it's Ms. Ms Mather.' She'd never taken Ben's name, which simplified the divorce paperwork. Jean had once mused that it was easy to end a marriage if you'd never jumped in all the way.

'Mrs Mather,' Olga said again. Rachel rotated her earphone jack in case it was an audio problem, or maybe Olga's knowledge of English didn't allow for the distinction. 'Let us confirm your details and reach an understanding before we go ahead with your treatment.'

'Yes.' What to say? 'Thank you.'

'Mrs Mather.' The repetition was putting Rachel on edge. She tried to exhale without sending a whistle down the microphone. 'You are currently childless but wish to become a parent. Due to age, your own eggs are unusable. You propose therefore to attend our clinic for a donor embryo transfer in the hope of achieving a pregnancy.'

Olga stopped. It took Rachel a moment to gather herself after hearing the facts stated so plainly. 'Yes.'

'You seek a donor embryo because you also require donor sperm.'

Rachel nodded. It felt as if she was giving evidence. 'Yes,' she said, thinking of how witnesses were told to speak aloud for the record. 'That's right.'

Olga's steely eye contact finally broke, and she looked down, as if reading from a form. 'As you know, Mrs Mather, this clinic is equipped to provide fertility treatment only for married couples of the opposite sex. We are not permitted by federal law to service same-sex pairs or singles. This is because the welfare of the child is paramount.'

Rachel's sternum went cold. She'd read, in her scant research, that it was a fairly conservative country: same-sex couples couldn't legally wed, but they could register for a domestic partnership that the government claimed was just as good. Single motherhood carried a stigma, so couples tended to marry if there was an accidental pregnancy. Later they'd split, increasing the divorce rate.

In online forums, posters said the clinic paid lip-service to the rules; that it had a don't ask – don't tell approach. But here was Olga, stating the laws directly. The welfare of the child is paramount. Beneath her fear, Rachel was offended.

'However,' Olga's gaze shifted to the left of her screen, 'we are aware of your case, which is that you are married, but your husband is also beset by fertility concerns, leading to the need for donor sperm.'

That was completely wrong. 'I'm not—' Rachel began, her heart pounding. When they realised that they'd mixed her up with someone else, her treatment would be cancelled, wouldn't it, if it was illegal? She didn't know if she had it in her to start all this shit over again.

Olga glanced up, eyes sharp with warning. 'May I continue, Mrs Mather?'

Chastised, Rachel pressed her lips together. She hoped her trembling was subtle enough not to be detected.

'Moreover, your husband is unable to attend the treatment, so you will travel alone.' Olga waited for a beat, but Rachel was dumbstruck. 'This is correct, Mrs Mather?'

'But—'

'All we require is confirmation that your husband cannot be with you, and you will travel alone.' Olga's expression softened. 'If you can confirm this now, we will go ahead.'

'I'm travelling alone,' Rachel repeated. She was bolstered by Olga's tiny nod. 'I won't have my husband with me.'

'Very good, Mrs Mather.' Olga scrawled something out of shot, then looked back and smiled. 'We look forward to welcoming you in March.'

Jess
Sunday

Viktor had a shift at the Castle Hill Café's breakfast buffet before Boris's speech, so Jess walked to City Square alone. The temperature was below freezing again, the sky bricked over in white. At the end of her third full winter in the city, it was no longer a novelty to wear a coat that looked like a sleeping bag or to wind scarves so high she could barely see. She couldn't wait for the true spring to dawn.

The capital lay inland, on a plain, beside a river so insubstantial locals called it 'the canal'. The summers were broiling, the winters as hard as a metal flagpole coated in ice. Jess relished the cloudfall, and the shoulder seasons could be glorious—there was a particular variety of tree planted outside the parliament in Street Two that flared bright red in late spring and shed prettily come autumn—but it was difficult to see the upside when the temperature had been below zero for two months. They hadn't even had the pretty distraction of snow.

It was why she longed to move to the eastern region, with its wider variety of weather and colours, greens and blues and yellows instead of the greyscale of the capital. The area around Viktor's family farm was sentimentally beautiful, like a painting on a box of Swiss chocolates. But the only work out there was farming, and even that couldn't support more than one brother. Viktor hadn't moved down to the city for the view.

There was a while to go until Boris's speech, so Jess detoured through City Park to buy coffee and a pretzel. The woman who ran her favourite cart was a foreigner too, though Sandy had been around since before the Berlin Wall fell. She was young and exploring communism, she'd told Jess, when she met a sexy countryman called Novak while smoking hashish in Afghanistan. Jess had never seen Novak, but she had the bleak feeling that the tightly muscled, rug-chested man Sandy described was now like any other balding sixty-year-old. He operated their second cart, which they stationed in the forecourt of an industrial development on the other side of Castle Hill.

Sandy scowled in greeting. 'Bloody cold,' she commented, turning the knob on the coffee machine. 'They call this spring?'

Jess rocked on her toes to keep warm. 'Fingers crossed it rains soon.'

'It won't.' Sandy selected a pretzel from the warmer and used a sleeve of paper to pass it over. 'You've heard of this thing they're doing?'

That could mean anything.

'The technology show or whatever it is.'

'The expo?' Jess asked.

'You heard they're going to suspend our permits that weekend.'

'What?'

Sandy nodded angrily over the frothing milk. 'No food sales other than at static sites. Five whole bloody days!'

'Wow.' Jess thought of all the stalls and carts and vans that operated in the city. Half of the food offerings would disappear. 'Why?'

'Who bloody knows.' Sandy snapped the lid onto Jess's coffee cup for emphasis. 'Don't mind us,' she told the sky. 'Just regular people trying to make a living.'

'I'm sorry.'

'Not your fault,' Sandy sneered, in a way that suggested it somehow was. 'It's why I'm here on a Sunday. Got to bring in some cash before they shut me down.'

Jess took the hint and bought a second pretzel for Viktor.

There were two events being held in City Square that morning, with folding chairs set out on either side of the main fountain. One was already underway, three grocery pallets forming a makeshift stage to distinguish the speakers from the small crowd. Boris wasn't among them, so Jess crossed the square and saw his girlfriend, Lena, waving a mittened hand.

'Good morning!' Lena said, pressing icy lips to her cheek in greeting. 'I heard from Vika and Radu, they are almost here.'

'Is Carolyn coming?'

'She is working,' Lena said. 'We see her soon.'

Though she had no idea what he was going to say, Jess was pleased for Boris that his audience was already bigger than the one on the other side of the fountain. Lena found four chairs in the third row, and they sat at each end, claiming the ones in between with their bags.

Even so, an older man wandered up and turned as if to sit next to Lena, his once-red sweatpants thinning and grey at the seat. 'Fool, what do you think, I saved it for you?' she snapped, and the man gave them both a blank look before shuffling away.

Viktor and Radu arrived, Viktor folding his big, warm hand around Jess's and leaning to kiss her neck. He smelled of the eggs and salted fish served at the buffet. 'Thank you for coming,' he said. She handed over the second pretzel and his eyes widened.

'My darling, what do I do to deserve this?'

Without introduction or preamble, Boris stepped in front of the crowd. There was no stage, just a microphone on a thin stand that he reached on tiptoe. 'I wish to outline some of the issues presented by the expo.' His voice was calm and thoughtful, his English words melodious. 'This is to come to our own conclusions as to the fate of our nation.'

It sounded important, but most things seemed to be here. Everything hung in the balance all the time. Jess tried to concentrate.

'The proposal may sound enticing,' Boris continued. 'Why not? A chance for a new industry, a way to be part of the future. And Miss Caspie, our honoured guest, promises further investment to come.'

The name was familiar to Jess but didn't land. She was more surprised that the feted guest was female. No woman had ever risen above the rank of deputy mayor here.

'Unfortunately, this is no foolproof solution. For nothing truly is.'

Boris's tone was grave. He was a good speaker. Jess had once asked Viktor why Boris never ran for public office and her boy-friend laughed. 'Because he hopes to make change in the world.'

Jess had first met Boris and Viktor on the same day. They were a package deal, along with Radu, and now the three girls—Jess, Lena and Radu's girlfriend Carolyn—were too. The boys had been friends since childhood together in the east: Viktor and Boris's families worked farms, and Radu's father was a nurse at the town health clinic. They all moved to the city for college, leaving more amiable siblings behind. Later, studying for their postgraduate degrees, the trio were offered an exchange semester at the English university where Jess was doing her Bachelor of Arts. Each had to deliver an academic talk as part of the scholarship, and they'd handed out advertising leaflets during one of the mass communications lectures Jess attended. It was a good place for them to find an audience, because the students were mostly female, and happy to stare at three good-looking men for an hour before tucking into the free pizza put on by the student union.

In the lead-up, Jess saw them in the refectory a few times. Their pants and jackets were faded in a way that was less artful and more sincere than the self-conscious boys her age; their facial hair was thick and serious. When they drank espresso their Adam's apples cut the air, sharp as arrowheads.

Radu had given the first talk, then Boris, then Viktor. Even when he wasn't speaking, Jess's attention went to Viktor, his dark eyes and thick lips and long, puppety limbs. By the end of Boris's presentation, Viktor was gazing back at her with an energy that made her shivery. He delivered his own speech, on press freedoms in formerly communist territories, and Jess barely heard a word. At the end, when he invited questions, the tutor of the mass comm unit asked something about press councils and state newspapers. 'Who is the watcher of the watchdog?' was part of Viktor's answer. Jess remembered because as he said it, he looked right at her and grinned.

After the lecture she downed a plastic cup of wine for courage, then walked to where Viktor was standing with the tutor. His cologne swept over her: something clean and sharp, distilled alcohol and passionfruit. She nodded along to their conversation until there was a lull, then said, 'I think you made a great point about the power of communication.'

The tutor raised his eyebrows. Jess was getting straight sixties on her essays.

'You think so,' Viktor mused. He made breathtaking eye contact.

'Writing helps us to engage with community,' Jess continued. 'Tell stories. Our own, and others'.'

'You are a writer?'

Jess wished the tutor would leave, but he stood stubbornly, hand tight around his own cup of wine. 'I dabble,' she said. She'd done a couple of film reviews for the student paper. 'Do you know what dabble means?'

'I know this word.' Viktor grinned again, and it was a brilliant grin; it made her stomach quiver. 'Do you let people read what you dabble?'

'Of course.' The student paper was free. 'How else can you build community?'

'Well. And as I was saying,' the tutor coughed.

'Yes, thank you,' Viktor told Jess, and she'd felt disappointed at the rejection until he reached out for a handshake. 'We may have coffee and dabble together, do you think?'

The feeling she'd got when his hand closed around hers—the warmth, the understanding, the longing—had lasted ever since. It had brought her all the way here, to this iced city, the grey earth flat like a floor and white sky a ceiling. Subtle in Viktor's speech was everything she needed to know: if she wanted to be with him, then his homeland would have to become hers as well. He would not stay in Britain or anywhere else.

Boris's presentation on the expo was short, but there were lots of questions. Jess had zoned out, so what the audience put to him made little sense: 'What are you saying, that we must delay even longer? Are we not a laughing-stock already?' 'My father has had no work for seven years. Could this not be his chance?' 'If we do not take this opportunity, it will not disappear. It will be offered to our competitors.'

Jess still didn't know why the women in her English class were planning to leave the city for the weekend or why the government would suspend food cart permits. Boris and his audience seemed focused on the expo's possible outcomes, not the event itself. No-one asked about traffic or overcrowding or any of the other things the nannas had fretted over.

In general, the crowd disagreed with Boris's warnings, but in a friendly way. When the questioning finished, many lined up to shake his hand and clap his shoulder. Viktor and Radu went to join them, and while Lena was talking to someone else, the man in the old red sweatpants returned to Jess.

'I agree with your friend,' he grumbled, 'but it is too late to save the world this way. Might as well squeeze out coins while it remains possible.'

'Hmmm,' she said, not knowing what he was talking about. 'Maybe.'

When the audience dispersed, the five of them went for warm cider at the tavern where Carolyn was working. The beer garden's bar heaters blared down on their insulated coats. Still full from her pretzel, Jess tried to resist the crumbed cheese squares Lena ordered, but the salty softness was too good. Viktor called for olives and pickled carrots, and she ate those as well. They'd keep her from getting tipsy, she reasoned. She had work later.

The conversation went straight to Boris's speech. The others congratulated him for being articulate, concise. Radu was irritated at the audience's dismissiveness. 'All we care about is work,' he grumbled in English. He had no scarf, and his cheeks and neck were slap-red. 'There is no work if there is no future.'

'But Bory also poses a type of work,' Viktor pointed out.

'Mine is a longer-term prospect,' Boris countered. 'No-one is prepared to invest.'

'Because today we must buy bread.'

Jess couldn't tell if Viktor was playing devil's advocate, or if he really disagreed with his friends. His eyes roamed the beer garden.

'There is always work,' Lena said, rubbing Boris's hand. 'It comes along like a tram.'

Viktor shook his head good-naturedly. 'And so, this is what is coming next. Why not jump aboard?'

'You want to be Caspie's lackey,' Radu said without malice. 'Her man on the ground.'

Viktor's smile was faint. 'This is bad?'

Boris shook his head. 'I predict the pay is crap. Like everywhere else.'

The discussion shifted in a familiar direction, to how bosses ripped them off. Viktor, Boris and Radu all had master's degrees from the country's most prestigious university, but the only work they could find was piecemeal: hospitality, labouring, house-painting. Radu, Boris, Lena and Carolyn lived together, the men sharing an old scooter so they could log on to delivery apps and take jobs when demand was high. Lena and Carolyn were both in PhD programs, yet Lena worked as a hotel cleaner and Carolyn at the tavern. Jess, the least educated of any of them, was rewarded for being a native English speaker with the low-paid but regular seniors' class, steady high school tutoring, and the odd assignment for a street newspaper that published in English. Boris had an advanced degree in public policy, but no wealthy parents wanted a fellow countryman to teach their kid social studies.

While the others spoke, Jess excused herself so she could google the name 'Caspie' from the toilet. She exhaled in awe when the picture popped up, recognising the woman's tangerine-coloured plait and company logo. Cassandra Caspie was the founder and CEO of Elpis, a bleeding-edge tech firm whose hybrid solar panel batteries were alleged to be climate neutral to produce. Believers were sure Elpis and businesses like it would save the world from the coming, and present, environmental catastrophe.

To Jess's surprise, there was a *Guardian* story about the upcoming expo under the News tab. It gave her a little buzz to see her adopted country acknowledged in the world's press. Apparently, Elpis was developing battery factories all over the world, and Caspie was coming to the expo to pitch her plan to build the largest one yet on the city's outskirts. Her grandfather was from the area originally and she wanted to give back, a spokesperson claimed.

The fact that she planned to attend the expo was more news-worthy than what she was doing it for. According to the article, she hadn't left New Zealand in almost two years or even been seen in person for months. Her camera was switched off during Zoom meetings. A rumour that she'd given birth to triplets had been debunked, but the real reason for her absence was a mystery.

Intrigued, Jess clicked around the conspiracy theories: Caspie had been horribly disfigured (she was known to visit thermal springs for therapeutic reasons, and some said she'd got too close to a geyser and scalded her face off); she was undergoing epic plastic surgery; she was incapacitated or dead and the voice beyond the black screen was fake. Elpis staff denied all of it, but the internet didn't care. Major international pop stars had been replaced by imposters and cyberspace was crawling with deepfakes. Why should Cassandra Caspie, a public figure who wasn't even that public, exist? She wasn't even on social media.

Jess washed her hands and returned to the table. Carolyn was there on her break, and she stood to kiss Jess. Another round of hot ciders had arrived, and the conversation had switched from English and was no longer about the expo and Elpis, so Jess couldn't chime in with what she'd learned. Now Lena was talking avidly, her hand entwined with Boris's, both looking a little dopey from the alcohol and heat. As she slid back into her seat and lifted a cider, Jess heard Lena say something about growing babies.

'You want a baby?' Jess asked.

Lena nodded enthusiastically. 'I hope for many.'

'The more the better!' Radu said, raising his glass.

Jess assumed they were teasing her. Lena was thirty-two and halfway through a doctorate in virology, living in a share house one step up from a squat. People had babies in worse conditions, but surely Lena wouldn't do so by choice.

Carolyn noticed Jess's expression. 'What do you think, Jessie?'

'It's Lena's choice,' Jess said carefully. 'And Boris's.'

Boris beamed, his cheeks a tight magenta. 'Why not?'

Radu nudged his friend, cider spilling over the lip of his glass and onto the table, where it soaked into the porous wood. 'Our friend Bory loves money as much as the next person. It gives him the freedom to make speeches.'

The others chuckled, but Jess was confused. He must mean Boris loved money more than children, because she didn't see how they could have both. It was expensive, even here, to raise a child.

Carolyn spat an olive seed into a cup, then asked Jess, 'Would you do it yourself?'

'Viktor and I don't want kids,' Jess said. The decision wasn't private; she was sure they'd told the group before.

'No, of course,' Carolyn said dismissively. 'In fact, this makes it better. You won't need to keep the babies for yourself, so you can sell them all.'

'Sell them?' Jess asked, flummoxed.

'You think I would do it for free?' Lena shrieked. 'It takes time. It hurts.'

Jess sucked her lip, not wanting to speak when it wasn't her place.

'I've done it before, you know. I made good money.'

Jess didn't know what to say. No-one else seemed surprised; Viktor rubbed her back distractedly as he drank his cider.

Carolyn peeled the last cold cheese square from the baking paper. 'Do they not do this in England?'

'I don't know.'

'Of course not,' Radu said. His tone was sardonic. 'Too expensive. The English pay the women here for their babies. A lot of money to us, but cheap to them.'

'I would do it if it was possible,' Carolyn announced, dusting her hands together and standing up. Her break was over. 'I went with Leni before, but they didn't like my results. All that effort for one baby, maybe two? Not worth it.'

Viktor and Boris looked bored and were talking about something else. Lena grinned at Jess. 'You could come with me this time,' she offered. A slick layer of cider clung to her lower lip, like vomit. 'You are a permanent resident, that is enough. And how old?'

'Twenty-six.'

'Oh, they love this. Brilliant age. And you are from overseas.' Her nose wrinkled. 'Your young Western babies could make a lot of money.'

***

The cider and greasy food sat in Jess's belly through her shift, making her slow and clumsy, spilling spirits down the edge of glasses. No-one cared. The hotel bar was crowded with businessmen who had meetings the next day, and they were tired and docile from travelling, stripped to their polo shirts, heavy watches glinting. Later, when most had gone up to their rooms or into the restaurant for a late dinner, Jess had the chance to listen out while she collected dirty glassware from the tables, but nobody was talking about Cassandra Caspie or the expo. Perhaps it wasn't as big a deal as Boris and Vera made out. Even more of a relief was that no-one was discussing having babies and selling them to the highest bidder.

Back at their flat, Jess couldn't sleep. Viktor had gone straight from the tavern to some meeting, where he seemed to be stuck, and in his absence the bed felt cold, the sheets plasticky. The conversation with Lena and Carolyn kept scrolling through her mind. When Viktor came back in the early hours and realised that she was still awake, he turned on the lamp and stroked her forehead. 'What is it, my love?'

'I keep thinking about Lena.'

He looked puzzled. 'What about her?'

Jess couldn't believe he'd forgotten already. 'Having kids and selling them.'

Viktor frowned. 'Leni has no kids.'

'She said she'd done it before, had some and sold them.'

Realisation broke over Viktor's face. 'Not kids, my love. *Babies*.' He said this final word in their language, eyebrows raised. When her horror didn't abate, he returned to English: 'Egg. Egg. Not kids.'

'Eggs? Like from her uterus?'

He nodded. 'I'm sorry, my love. The word is the same in our language.'

It made some sense: Jess knew the translation for the eggs bought in a market was 'chicken babies', a term that had put her off for some time because it was so literal. 'Oh, thank God,' she murmured, then overcame the urge to cry by laughing.

'You thought she was selling babies, children?'

'I couldn't tell. It sounded so strange.'

'Even for lots of money, Leni does not do this,' he joked. Noticing how unsettled Jess was, he touched her cheek. 'My love. How about some tea?'

She wrapped herself in bedclothes and followed him into the cold kitchen, which warmed quickly when the stovetop was lit. Humming, Viktor directed her into the window nook, then moved around collecting the small saucepan, fragrant sachet, dried berry powder and condensed milk. He made it spicy-sweet, the way she liked it, and she took the mug gratefully. It was one of the least complicated things about living here, the availability and pleasure of tea.

Jess was frustrated by her slippage in understanding the language, something she thought she was overcoming. Precise, technical terms often escaped her—if there was an electrical or gas problem in the flat, Viktor had to be there to guide the repairman, because all Jess could say was 'power' and 'tubes' and 'smoke'— but it was months since she'd had such a big misunderstanding. She was embarrassed, wondering if the others had figured it out, or if they just thought she was a secret conservative, prudish about women donating their eggs.

She was lucky to understand as much as she did. It was a Romance language that, like the neighbouring Romania, often drew on Italian, which was one of Jess's minor studies at university. When she used to visit Viktor, she got by with a basic understanding cobbled from English, Italian and a weirdly expensive phrasebook bought on eBay, but it was immersion that had unlocked most of it. Still, there'd be these less common words that evaded her. She remembered visiting a doctor for contraceptives and explaining to him that she didn't want a baby. 'This will stop them,' he'd said as he scrawled out a prescription. At the time, she'd thought he was being typically blunt.

'Just so I've got it right,' she said to Viktor as he wiped out the saucepan, 'Lena's going to give away her eggs from her ovaries for money?'

'That's right.'

'Who to?'

'She is not told. A foreigner who does not make her own, that's all.'

'And she's done it before?'

'Twice, I think. This is not unusual. Carolyn tried, as she said.'

Jess rubbed her lips together, tasting the berries. 'And men donate sperm?'

He smiled softly. 'Yes, but not me. I promise.'

'If you did it before we met, that would be fine,' Jess said, relieved.

'I did not.' Seeing her relax, Viktor ran a hand through his curls. 'But perhaps I should. We are running low on cash.'

Jess grunted her agreement; she'd noticed that, too.

'It is to get worse, I'm afraid.' Viktor's eyelids were heavy. 'I am in meetings about the expo for two weeks, and they will take up so much time. I cannot work at the buffet.'

'That's alright,' Jess said automatically, feeling emptiness in the pit of her stomach despite the warm tea. 'We'll manage.'

'It is a setback, but I hope for a reward at the end.'

'You're going to get a job with Elpis?' she joked.

Viktor nodded seriously. 'This is my plan. Then all our problems are solved.'

Jess smiled, trying to do the sums in her head. Thank goodness they'd paid the rent on the first of the month.

Viktor touched her hand. 'Is this okay now, darling? I must sleep.'

She let him go to bed but stayed up a while longer herself, sitting in the window and looking at the blackness in the east. Tonight, the wide sky was starless.

Jess knew about the country's assisted reproductive technology industry. Like with plastic surgery in Türkiye or Thailand, the treatments were as advanced as anywhere else, but cheaper than more developed countries even when you included the cost of travel. Here, patients would stay at a nice hotel for a few weeks, do some sightseeing in their downtime, and return home with their results. The hotel where Jess bartended put up the patients for one of the IVF clinics, and they'd sometimes order mint tea or hot water with lemon, their partners requesting low-alcohol beer or sugar-free soft drinks. Until her colleagues set her straight, she'd thought they must all be in-treatment alcoholics.

Jess knew IVF involved sperm and egg fertilising in a test tube, but that was about it. Pregnancy and babies weren't part of her world. Her sister, who had three kids, sometimes made the old joke about Ryan only needing to breathe to get her pregnant, which made Jess twitch. None of her mates back home wanted kids yet, if at all, and none of Viktor's friends had them either. The low birthrate was often discussed on the news and at public debates: they rivalled Japan or South Korea for how poorly the country's population was being replaced. Because of the IVF clinics, a lot of the women who did get pregnant were tourists who had the babies elsewhere.

Jess had heard somewhere that young women should freeze their eggs if they were going to delay having kids, and she was aware of egg donation, but she knew nothing about how they did it. Donating sperm was straightforward, because it was designed to exit the body, but she was pretty sure that a woman's eggs were the opposite. Maybe they made little surgical cuts at each hip and spooned the eggs out that way? Or was a catheter threaded along each fallopian tube to the ovary, with an 'on' switch like a vacuum cleaner?

If Jess was honest, she could be judgemental of the fertility women when they came down to the bar. It was partly because the drinks they bought were cheap, so their tips were low, even when they clearly had money. They may have been travelling to reduce their costs, but the IVF patients were far wealthier than the average local, and that money was being used to produce a child out of nothing. Weren't there millions of already-born babies who needed parents? And the planet was in massive decline anyway. These people were going to the other side of the world to create new life, wasting finite resources while the earth died around them.

Back in bed, Jess pressed her palms to the bowls inside her hipbones, where she guessed her ovaries were. *Your young Western eggs could get a lot of money,* Lena had said. Jess wondered exactly how much money that might be.

Rachel
CD10

Her first flight, to Dubai, landed in the middle of the night, and after a few bleary hours in the terminal, the second took off into an early morning haze. Looking down from her window seat, Rachel saw the irregular blocks of tall buildings becoming sparser as the aircraft headed over the gulf, the coastline curling into fractal-like sandbars. On some of these she could make out isolated white structures connected by silver filaments of road. As they flew north-west over the bright green sea, the pale shapes stuck in her peripheral vision, oblongs wiggling against the brilliance like amoebae in a Petri dish. Eventually, the brightness became too much, and she drew her shade to sleep.

There was another long connection in Vienna, and Rachel, dozing in a stiff chair in the terminal, almost missed the final call to the plane stationed in a far-off gate. She was the last to board. As she slid down the narrow aisle to the furthest row she mouthed apologies at the passengers whose blank faces followed her, like the slowly rotating clown heads in fair games. The aircraft was old, and the recirculated air smelled like the inside of anti-desiccant packets, and when she fell into her seat, the thickly padded vinyl seemed to fasten tightly around her. It was lucky the flight was short, because she was both afraid to get up again and worried she'd be suffocated by the cushioning.

Once the aircraft had levelled out, the flight attendants handed out miniature water bottles and paper plates covered in sweating plastic wrap. Underneath were two slices of pink meat, a block of hard cheese the size and colour of a stack of Post-it notes, a bread roll and half a dozen dried red berries dusted in icing sugar. Lifting one to taste it, the vibration of the plane shed the loose powder onto Rachel's black slacks. She tried to rub it off with a serviette but only succeeded in grinding the sugar into the fabric, leaving a dingy grey swipe along each thigh.

Everything changed once they landed. She'd been told someone from the clinic would collect her from the airport, but she hadn't expected to be met as soon as she stepped off the airbridge. The chaperone was petite and milk-skinned, with slender wrists and a gentle smile. She must have been in her early twenties, the same age as the junior lawyers where Rachel worked.

The woman's palm was cool as she touched Rachel's shoulder, directing her out of the flow of disembarking passengers. 'Mrs Mather, hello. I am Ana. I am here to assist you.'

Ana led her away from the signs for customs and baggage and towards an unmarked door, which she held open. As Rachel passed through, she realised Ana had taken her carry-on bag and hung it from the slim hook of her elbow.

The corridor they entered was plain and smelled of disinfectant. Around a corner they came to another door with a small black panel set into the adjoining wall. Ana touched a card to the surface and the door slid open. 'Please,' she said, gesturing.

The next room was cream-coloured, featureless except for a single desk protected by a glass screen. A dark-haired man waited behind it.

'Your passport,' Ana prompted, and Rachel realised this was a private border control. The man wore a dark grey uniform with insignias on each sleeve, and he gazed over her head as she passed her travel documents through a slot. 'This is easier,' Ana explained as the officer flicked through the pages, held Rachel's photograph up to the light, then dropped the passport and crunched a heavy stamp onto it.

'Come,' Ana invited, and Rachel followed her down another corridor. 'We will get your bags. You are tired? It is a long flight.'

'It was,' Rachel agreed. 'Three flights, actually.'

Ana clucked with awe. 'Such dedication.'

At the end of the hallway was a longer room with a luggage belt along one side, Rachel's suitcase the only one on it. Ana slipped her fingers beneath the handle and pulled it fluidly to the floor. 'There we are,' she said. Her English seemed flawless to Rachel, the slightest accent giving it a sweet, glamorous twist. 'Would you like to use the lavatory? The drive to the clinic takes around twenty minutes.'

On the back of the stall door was an ad for the fertility clinic. In it, an elegant young woman touched the upper arm of another, middle-aged one, whose lips were pursed. *There for every step of your journey*, the slogan read. Rachel squinted: was that Ana in the picture? The Facetuning of the figures made it difficult to determine, but the hair and facial expressions were the same, as was the lavender-coloured blouse and pencil skirt. If they'd chosen a real worker instead of a model to play the younger woman, then was the older one really a patient too?

The terminal's revolving door swept them into the steady roar outside. Above the drop-off lane was a highway flyover, slivers of car roofs flashing above the cement slab. The air was cold and the light soft despite it being early afternoon. Rachel wondered if she should put on her coat, and Ana read her mind.

'The car is there,' she said, pointing to a low black sedan idling at the verge. 'It will be warm inside.' She set off across the pavement, the wheels of Rachel's suitcase clicking after her.

The interior of the car had a faint lilac smell, and the driver, another young woman, nodded at Rachel in the rear-view mirror. When Ana slid in beside Rachel, she spoke quickly to the driver in their language, then pulled a bottle of water from the seat pocket and held it out. 'Try to stay awake,' she said, back to fluent English. 'Please, drink.'

The water was chilled and tasted crisp. Feeling suddenly parched, Rachel downed the whole thing in one go.

The car curled up an on-ramp and joined the highway. They merged easily, the traffic heavy but not congested, hatchbacks and coupés manoeuvring efficiently between utility vehicles and trucks. Road signs swelled and shrank as they passed, the distance from upcoming hamlets given in various forms: miles and kilometres, decimals and fractions. Some listed locations in order of those furthest away, while others did the opposite. As far as Rachel could tell, they stayed on the same highway the whole time.

After fifteen minutes, Ana pointed past Rachel and out the left side of the vehicle. 'You can see the city. There is Castle Hill, and in the centre is the spire of the cathedral.'

The hill was easy to spot, a smooth grassy dome topped with an oyster-coloured fortress. There was a puddle of three- and four-storey buildings on its eastern side, among them two or three steeples; Rachel couldn't tell which one Ana meant. A few streets north, the structures grew larger, fifteen or twenty floors high and the length of an average block. Most looked to be flats painted in pastel yellow or green, their balconies barred with thick, plain steel. Of the glass offices dotted around, Rachel recognised none of the signage: no tech companies, no international banks, no Deloitte or Ernst & Young.

'The Old Town is south-east of the hill,' Ana explained. 'North of it is the New Town. The river is between, though you can't see it from here.'

They were slowing for an off-ramp. 'Is the clinic in the Old Town?' Rachel asked.

'It is nearby. We will arrive soon.'

The exit lane twisted, descending from the highway until it met the next road. At the corner, a traffic light alternated between red and orange, a car releasing itself from the ramp each time, turning into the emergency lane and speeding up to join the flow of traffic. When it was their turn, Rachel was pushed back in her seat as the driver stood on the accelerator, the engine roaring.

'There is some brilliant art coming up,' Ana said, unaffected by the g-forces. She tapped her own window. 'Here.'

On the side of an overpass was a mural in swirls of green and blue, zipping away as the car reached top speed. Rachel could make out a globe with pointed blue waves beneath it, and perhaps a face. It seemed amateurish to her, a step above graffiti, but what did she know? 'I like the colours.'

Ana nodded. 'There is so much grey here. The artist petitioned the mayor, and finally.'

The driver said something, and Ana grimaced. 'Yes. Never fast, of course.'

They were on a ring-road, travelling anticlockwise. The buildings on the inside faced the centre, their backs to the passing traffic. Rachel saw thin pipes and metal stairs running down from roofs, towels flapping on wire, skip bins and fruit boxes waiting by roller doors. The kerb was graffitied with black and white tags and scrawls, and Rachel realised why Ana appreciated the globe painted on the overpass.

In another few minutes the car turned off the ring-road and rounded a couple of corners before rolling into a basement car park.

Ana beamed. 'Here we are!'

They glided past parked vehicles towards an area marked in yellow. Directly opposite, the silver doors of a lift pressed into the cement wall of the building. As soon as the handbrake was on Ana nipped out to open Rachel's door. The air was frigid, the space smelling of moisture and paint. 'Leave your bags,' Ana instructed, taking a fob from her pocket and touching it to the lift's call button. 'The car will wait.'

The lift opened onto a lobby with pale purple walls and a marble-tiled floor. They crossed towards a floor-to-ceiling door of frosted glass, which rolled aside to reveal a waiting area that was colourful and warm, a burbling fish tank filling one wall. The rows of oak-backed chairs were empty of patients, but three women around the same age as Ana and wearing matching blouses sat behind a blond-wood desk, smiling as Rachel was led over.

'This is Mrs Mather,' Ana announced. Nodding, the women split into separate tasks: one went to a filing cabinet, another left through a swinging door and the third handed over a clipboard. Rachel thought it was for her, but Ana took it and sat down.

'May I offer you something to drink?' the third receptionist asked. 'Tea, water?'

Rachel was dying for coffee, even a decaf with crap milk, but she said, 'Water, please.'

As the third worker went to the purifier, the second came back and took a suspension file from the first. 'Everything is ready,' she told Rachel. 'Please, come this way.'

Rachel turned to Ana, who stood, still writing on the clipboard. They followed the second receptionist down a hallway lined with abstract art in splashes of blue and pink, each bottom-lit, as if in a gallery. When they'd passed half a dozen canvases, the receptionist stopped by yet another door and tapped it cleanly with her knuckles, then pulled the handle. 'The doctor, thank you.'

The office could have been any Rachel had visited in her years of treatment: the big mahogany desk with its black padded centre, the shelves containing plastic models of the female reproductive system, the posters depicting the fertilisation process. An exam table draped in a disposable cotton sheet ran along one wall, a handbasin beside it. The privacy curtain, pinned back for now, was in the same lilac colour scheme as everything else.

The two Australian specialists Rachel had consulted with were older, in their fifties or sixties. The doctor at the desk couldn't be a day over forty, with thick dark hair smoothed into an elegant wave over his forehead and blue eyes behind metal-rimmed glasses. He looked like a male model from a shaving cream ad. Standing from his chair, he held out a tanned hand, the wrist reassuringly hairy.

'Mrs Mather,' he greeted. His accent was thicker than Ana's and the receptionists', his tone caramelised, and Rachel's abdomen warmed. 'It is nice to meet you finally at last.'

Ana waited in the doorway. 'The doctor has fair English,' she said, 'but he is not quite fluent. If you are comfortable, I can stay to interpret.'

The doctor smiled. His teeth were regular and white, but there was a thinness to them, a transparency that indicated they weren't capped. His lips were a very fleshy red.

'Yes, fine, thanks.' Rachel took a seat and Ana sat beside her. There was no third chair, and Rachel wondered what happened if two patients attended the appointment. Would their chaperone stand? Lie on the exam table? Perch on the beautiful doctor's lap?

The doctor summarised Rachel's situation. He used English medical terms easily; it was with ordinary language that he required help. He had a melodious, entrancing voice and Rachel felt herself struggling to concentrate. She wondered if the clinic preferred their patients to have their first appointments straight off the plane, sleep-deprived and dirty, or if it was an oversight.

But she shouldn't be suspicious: they were trying to give her a baby. The doctor reiterated this many times, making strong eye contact, even reaching his large hands across the desk to hold hers. 'We want you to have a child, Mrs Mather. This is what we want the most. This is …' He glanced at Ana and said something.

'Our greatest goal,' Ana translated.

'A great goal,' the doctor repeated gruffly, squeezing Rachel's fingers. When he released her, Rachel had to quell the urge to press her now-warm hand to her cheek.

He went through the test results the Perth clinic had sent through, commenting favourably on her progress. 'It goes like a clock so far,' he smiled, and Rachel blushed. 'Now we do our own check, okay?' He rose from his chair again.

Ana also stood. 'Through here,' she said, indicating the nearby wall. A door had been cut into it, painted to blend in, like in the Oval Office. On the other side was a low-lit ultrasound suite with three nurses in violet scrubs and matching surgical masks, their eyes identically warm and compassionate. 'Please,' Ana continued. 'I will wait outside.'

It felt wrong, somehow, to be without Ana. Rachel hesitated.

Ana smiled. 'Please. It is fine.'

Entering the space, Rachel was soothed by the hint of floral in the antiseptic scent and the quiet piano music tinkling from a speaker. One nurse stepped forward to take Rachel's hand, leading her to a corner where there was a partitioned changing cubicle, not just a thin curtain like at home. 'Please remove pants and undergarments and put on the gown.'

She took a second to scan the space before undressing. There was a padded basket for her clothes and a small console table with a vase of primroses. Rachel bent to inhale: they were real.

When she emerged, the same nurse directed her to the exam table. 'Please put one leg here, and other here.' The stirrups had little pillows for comfort. 'Please lie back,' the nurse continued, palm hovering a few inches from Rachel's shoulder as she reclined.

Once she was horizontal, the nurses swept into action. The one who'd guided her into the stirrups stood at Rachel's right shoulder. Another was by her waist, holding a notebook and pen. The third, and apparently most senior, nurse retrieved the ultrasound wand and wheeled her stool between Rachel's flopping feet.

'We are ready to begin,' the nurse at her head said. Her accent was even fainter than Ana's, with only the gentlest curl of geography at the end of some words. 'You may take a deep breath. Do you feel okay?'

Rachel thought of how sweaty and unwashed she was, how there must be an odour down there. She hadn't been able to shower in this hemisphere yet. Taking the deep breath that the nurse had advised, she said, 'Okay.'

The nurse with the wand counted to three in the local language— Rachel had looked up some basic translations at the airport in Dubai—and slid it inside. Once again, a map of her anatomy sprang to life on the technician's screen.

'You are doing very well, Mrs Mather. This will not be long.'

The nurse with the wand dictated to the one with the clipboard while the third interpreted. 'The follicle on your left ovary is measuring eight millimetres at present. This is very good. The lining is developing the three layers, though this is slow. The scanner will be removed now, okay?' Rachel exhaled as it slipped out. 'You have done very well, Mrs Mather. Any questions?'

'You said the lining's slow?' Rachel held the hem of the gown. 'Is that a problem?'

'It is perhaps a couple of millimetres less than we expect, but this is not to worry.' The nurse brushed Rachel's sleeve. 'You are day ten, yes? Plenty of time to catch up.'

She pressed a button, so the top half of the table lifted Rachel to a sitting position. The nurse who'd made the notes brought over a needle and collection tubes and performed the smoothest blood draw Rachel had experienced in three years of treatment; she looked across after a few seconds of silence to see what the delay was to find her blood filling up the chamber. Afterwards, the nurse pressed a plaster to the crook of Rachel's elbow, smiled and gestured wordlessly towards the cubicle. They were done.

As Rachel dressed, she reflected on how the nurse who'd translated, at least, remembered her progress without having to double-check the file. Her eyes blurred at the degree of care this suggested, and she shook her head as she stepped into her underpants. She was too tired.

When she emerged, Ana was there and the nurses had gone. 'We are almost done. Please, follow me.'

She opened a door Rachel could have sworn would lead them back into the doctor's office. Instead, there was an anteroom with a large, padded visitor chair, the table beside it laden with a steaming teapot, delicate handle-less cup and a platter of the same dried berries served on the plane. 'Make yourself comfortable,' Ana said. 'The doctor will review the results and we will speak with him soon.' She left through the ultrasound suite.

Rachel didn't want the powdered berries—her slacks were still smeared grey from her taste-test at thirty thousand feet—but she drank the tea quickly, then refilled it. The brew was milky and sweet, warming but not too hot to swallow, with a vague lavender aftertaste. When she'd finished, she got up from the chair, afraid of nodding off. There was a high, thin window that Rachel could just see out of if she stood on tiptoe, but the view was unremarkable: a bland sky sitting low, nondescript buildings collected beneath it. The sun was threatening to set.

But she hadn't come here for the scenery.

'Mrs Mather? We are ready.'

Rachel was too weary to be surprised when she was led into the doctor's office, not back into the ultrasound suite. 'Mrs Mather.' His smile was to die for. 'I hope we didn't keep you for too long.'

He went through the findings of the scan, laying out possible scenarios according to what the blood tests might reveal of her hormone levels. Rachel wanted to know about the thinness of her endometrium, but the doctor was focusing on the size of the follicle that was growing. It meant nothing in the grand scheme of things. The egg was only there to set off a chain reaction, not because it was useful in itself: it would end up as weak and thin as all the others. Its destiny was to drift, unused, down her fallopian tube, then wait in her plumped womb for the donor blastocyst to take its place.

'And my lining?' Rachel interrupted. 'Is that okay?'

The doctor exchanged a glance with Ana. Rachel tried not to be paranoid. 'We won't know for proof until your blood tests come back, but everything seems fine, Mrs Mather.'

Emotion bloomed in Rachel's chest. Ana touched her shoulder.

The doctor murmured, and she translated: 'Please do not worry.' Her voice was gentle as a feather. 'We will do everything we can to make this work. You must only let us help you.'

***

The hotel they'd booked Rachel into was in the New Town, one street back from the waterfront. The building had originally been one of the communist-era apartment blocks, Ana explained, then transformed into a hotel when they reopened to the West. The ceiling of the lobby was adorned with cornices so ornate and artificial that the edges seemed wadded with spit balls. The carpet was a deep, verdant green, and the car-sized chandelier overhead dripped with aquamarine crystals.

Ana showed Rachel the private dining room, cool-water pool and yoga space, then took her to her room. It was a nice suite with a waterfall shower and kitchenette, the window capturing shards of Castle Hill that were visible between buildings. Ana unfolded a map and circled some landmarks: the castle, the central park, a fountain, the cathedral. 'There's a nice cider stall here, at the base of the bridges.' Ana tapped the southern side of the river. 'Ask for plain pear. It's alcohol free and low sugar.' Looking sympathetic, she clicked off the pen. 'It's good it's getting warmer. In winter, only the straight cider will do.'

Rachel longed for Ana to leave, but she didn't want to seem ungrateful. Sitting at the foot of the bed, she nodded as the chaperone took out a pamphlet in the pale purple hue of the clinic. 'This is the schedule,' she said. 'Things may shift by a day or two, but we'll take that as it comes.'

The two-week calendar had the days and dates pre-filled, with hourly slots from seven a.m. to seven p.m. Breakfast was at eight and dinner at six, with at least one appointment in between: blood tests, scans, massages, acupuncture, counselling. Overwhelmed, Rachel closed her eyes and the paper slipped from her hands.

'You are very tired.' Ana squeezed Rachel's shoulder until her eyes dragged open. 'I will leave you now and return at dinnertime. You may nap, but I recommend not for too long. It is best to sleep deeply overnight and have gentle activity during the day.' She flipped the pamphlet over and placed it on the bed. 'There is some advice, if you would like it.'

Finally, Rachel was alone. She was so exhausted it was like being made of dense sludge; she couldn't even drag herself up the mattress towards the headboard. Her palms sweated into the bedclothes as she realised how small the room was. Two weeks in a thirty-square-metre box. Looking out the window didn't help; she was too high up, the other buildings crowding around, as if trying to spy on her.

Her exhaustion warped into dread. This was a mistake, a grave one. For weeks she'd had stress dreams of being stuck overseas and needing to get back to Perth for a meeting or to stop her bathroom from flooding. Now those nightmares were coming true. She was in the wrong place; she needed to go home.

Well, okay, she realised, her heartbeat beginning to slow. If she wanted, she could blow this all up. The schedule for the next day included an appointment with Olga, from the video call. Rachel could use it to announce the truth: that she was single and would raise any child she conceived without a father. If the laws Olga had recited were real, she'd have to cancel Rachel's treatment and send her home.

The thought gave Rachel a bizarre sense of peace. At last, she was able to relax enough to roll onto her front, crawl up to meet the pillow, and sleep.

Jess
Saturday

Instead of sleeping late like she usually did when she had the morning off, Jess caught an early tram towards a suburb on the city's outskirts, near the airport. In the distance, faint smears of particulate over the roofs of warehouses tinted the white sky. She wondered if Elpis's enormous solar panel factory would soon join them.

The tram wound its way slowly along near-empty streets, coming to a complete stop at every station, though no-one was waiting to get on or off. Jess's leg bounced with impatience. In the six days since she'd learned about Elpis and the expo, an energy had built up in her that was now so strong she wondered if she shouldn't get off at the next stop and sprint. Potential glimmered on the horizon for the first time in forever.

Normally, Jess wouldn't have cared that Cassandra Caspie was coming. She wasn't in business, didn't know anything about solar power or batteries. But Viktor had told her more about the meetings that would take up his time over the next few weeks. A group had formed to lobby Elpis to build their mega-factory on the vacant site outside the city, and Viktor, with his broad connections, had been asked to help negotiate.

She wasn't too surprised. Her boyfriend had fingers in various pies—few, if any, of which she understood. He proudly called himself a 'fixer': knew everyone, was across everything. Solar panel manufacturing was just the latest area of expertise.

'It should not be hard,' Viktor had told her. 'We want the factory built; they want to build it. But if I impress, there is the potential to get in on the ground floor. To work with them further, on other projects.'

So this was what Radu and Boris meant when they joked that Viktor would be Caspie's lackey. 'Are you going to meet with Cassandra Caspie?' she asked.

'I would hope to.'

She wondered if he knew how long it was since the billionaire had been seen in person. 'If you do,' she said, running a finger over his collarbone, 'will you introduce me to her?'

'Sure,' Viktor had laughed. 'I will make you the best of friends.'

An international celebrity, a woman famously inaccessible, would soon be within her reach. Jess was ready to do what Viktor was doing, what the others would do if they had the same opportunity: monetise it.

The tram finally rolled to her stop, and she disembarked. The area was typically suburban, each block hosting its own stretch of apartments with shops on the ground floor, the structures' original cement painted over in a pastel yellow or green or pink. The view wasn't particularly depressing from the main road, but turning into side streets revealed the less pleasant aspects of such buildings: low-ceilinged parking garages, aluminium playgrounds bolted to bitumen, household waste bursting out of unattended skips. This was the kind of place she and Viktor had considered moving to in the past, where they could get two bedrooms and lift access for less than their one-bed in the Old Town, though Jess had argued that the cost of taking the tram in every day would soon eat away whatever was saved. That was true, but the main reason she didn't want to live in the suburbs was the crowded feeling: even a top-floor flat would have a view straight into the flat over the road. If Jess couldn't live somewhere scenic, then at least she could see it from her kitchen window.

After a few blocks, the surroundings transformed into low-rise industrial: car yards, wholesalers, discount warehouses. A canary-coloured building came into view, two-storeyed, with a rickety, disused balcony cinching the upper level and a flat shingle roof. Jess passed it and turned at the next corner, breathing in the welcoming smell of baking bread.

The café's dining space was two ice-cold aluminium tables in an annexe, with thick plastic sheeting hung in the entryway to guard patrons from the elements. Yara was there already, coffee steaming in front of her, typing on her smartphone. She wore fuchsia fingerless gloves and an ankle-length white puffer jacket with silvery faux fur trim. Her hair was scythed into a bob like Uma Thurman's in *Pulp Fiction*, but with streaks of neon blue in the black.

Yara was the editor and sole salaried employee of an English-language street paper that came out on Tuesdays. It was owned by a woman even more ruthless and stunning than Yara, but twenty years older, with greying hair buzzed to her scalp and earlobes pulled long by paperweight earrings. She was either Yara's adoptive mother or sugar-mama; Jess had heard both rumours. Despite owning a paper that published in English, the owner didn't speak a word of it and seemed dismissive of the whole venture, bankrolling it just to please Yara. It was probably a front for something, but Jess wasn't sophisticated enough to know what. And anyway, Yara ran the paper just like a real editor: without pity.

The previous leader of the English program, a man who'd since gone back to Ireland, was the first to put Jess in touch with Yara, though Viktor and the others knew her too. Yara liked hiring expat ESL teachers to write for her: the young people the paper was aimed at might've understood English, but they also knew what jobs were worth the pay. Whether because her budget was miniscule or she enjoyed being cruel, or both, Yara exploited her contributors. In three years, the most Jess had earned was two crowns, or enough for half-a-dozen pretzels from Sandy's cart, for a quarter-page report on a dance troupe's upcoming tour of Germany. Mostly Yara offered reviews that paid only in tickets to the show or copies of the book. Jess took Yara's assignments mostly to fill time when Viktor was working, but today she wanted a pay rise.

Jess ducked under the plastic and sat down. 'Thanks for meeting me.'

Yara completed her email before responding, 'You talk like we are plotting something.'

As Jess's cheeks pinkened, the baker ambled out. She wore bright orange earmuffs and didn't touch the notebook stuffed in her apron. 'Coffee?' she grunted.

'With milk, please, and sugar. And a pretzel twist.' She nodded at Yara's cup. 'You want more? Something to eat?'

Smirking, Yara shook her head. She waited for the woman to leave before commenting, 'Aren't you getting fluent.'

'I told you, I plan to stay here.'

Yara smiled, charmed like a mother whose toddler is going to be a superhero when he gets big. 'And I say, I've heard it before.'

Feeling a draught, Jess fitted her scarf more securely into her collar. 'I have a proposition for you.'

'You said so in your email.'

'It's about the expo next weekend.'

'Oh, wonderful.' Yara's voice was toneless. 'The famous expo.'

'I have a contact you might be interested in.'

Yara's façade shifted at last. 'Do you?'

'Well,' Jess backtracked, 'I might.'

'Again you talk in code,' Yara sighed. 'Are you a spy perhaps?'

'Cassandra Caspie's coming, right? Well, I want to interview her.'

Jess expected Yara to snort, or look surprised, or frown, but her only reaction was to shrug and go back to her phone. At first Jess thought the determined tapping was her contacting Elpis's media people to make the request, but by the time the baker came back with Jess's coffee and pretzel, she'd realised Yara was just ignoring her.

'Is that so crazy?' Jess asked, keeping her tone light. She sipped her drink, which had milk but no sugar, and thanked the baker emphatically.

Yara didn't look up. 'I thought you were a serious person, Jessica.'

Jess took a sugar packet from the other table.

'Cassandra Caspie does not do interviews,' Yara continued. 'If she did, it would be with the *New York Times* or the *Washington Post*.' She offered a crafty smile. 'You can interview the Polish Minister for Digital Affairs, maybe.'

'I know she hasn't spoken in public for a year or two, but—'

'A year or two? Try never.'

'She's never spoken in public?'

Yara watched her with bright eyes.

Jess tried to hold off the doubt creeping up her chest. She was determined not to back down. Viktor wouldn't. 'Well, she's coming to the expo, right? Or is that just a rumour?'

'Yes.'

'Yes, which?'

'Yes, she is coming. Yes, it is rumour.'

Jess tore a hunk off her pretzel. It was warm and salty and eased the rough edges off her irritation with this country and the way things were done.

'We love rumours,' Yara said. 'Cassandra Caspie has many. You know about the secret babies? The horrific face-melting? The jewel heist?'

'Jewel heist?'

'You haven't heard this? The solar business runs out of money, so Cassandra Caspie herself conducts a robbery in the centre of Wellington.'

The two women smirked at one another.

'No, seriously,' Jess argued. 'I want to write about the real her, whatever that means. She's an enigma, right? But she's coming here, after years in hiding.'

'Unless she's a robot. Or appears by hologram.' Yara sipped her coffee and pouted. 'Or they send a man in a suit, as always.'

'If she doesn't come, I won't write anything.'

'Of course you won't.' Yara was scandalised. 'I don't pay for stories about things that didn't happen.'

Tearing off another piece of pretzel, Jess felt brazen. 'And how much will you pay if I do interview her?'

Yara chuckled with delight. 'My budget is chained to the bottom of the ocean, you know this. But perhaps royalties from all the copies I sell.' She sat back, laced her fingers, and asked, 'How do you propose to hook this fish?'

Jess cleared her throat. She was at the limit of her ability to bluff. 'I guess, if you put in a request with her media people, say that while she's in town—'

'You said you had a contact, though.'

'Viktor's having meetings with Elpis. He said if he meets her in person, he'll introduce me.'

Yara gazed at her for a moment, her expression unreadable. 'Is that so,' she murmured.

'Surely she'd talk about the project.' Jess tried to sound knowledgeable, scraping together everything she could remember from the communications units that had padded out her undergrad degree. 'They want to set up a factory, don't they? Well, here's an opportunity to outline her plans for locals. And the wider world, since, you know, we publish in English.'

Yara lifted her chin. 'A puff piece.'

'I'm very fair,' Jess objected, her face warm. 'I won't go that easy on her.'

'Well, well. You are an investigative reporter now. Have I wasted your talents?'

Twenty minutes later, Jess was on her way back to the tram, skin just as cold or even colder than earlier, but feeling warm on the inside. Yara had been so amused by her bravado she'd agreed to give her a page in the edition that came out just after the expo, complaining at the same time that it would be too late for people to care. The paper was split into fractions of a page rather than lines or word count, and Jess had never been offered over a quarter before. The payment they agreed on would roughly cover Viktor's missing earnings for the next couple of weeks.

A page was a lot, especially with Yara's insistence that Cassandra Caspie didn't talk to the media, but Jess knew she'd come up with something. If Caspie wanted to make good with Viktor's group, how hard would it be to give Jess a few lines about how much she liked the country and how well the talks were going? She could pad it with stuff on Elpis, maybe details from Viktor about their meetings and whatever else Caspie did while she was there. The main thing was to have a story different from the daily paper's, if they had one at all.

It would be, like Viktor's meetings, an investment in their future. If she did a good job, Yara might ask Jess for more articles. If the Caspie interview was substantial—a scoop—other publications might buy it, which meant money and contacts. She could use her newfound credentials to pitch features on the tourism potential of the eastern hills. Holding the strap as the tram scraped around a bend, Jess imagined being commissioned to write about the cloudfall for *Natural Geographic*. Surely that kind of money would last months here.

She got off the tram outside their building and jogged up the stairs in excitement. Approaching the flat, she heard a voice declare, 'I *am* doing my part.' There was a quieter response as she fit her key in the door, then, as she swung it open, the first voice said, 'There is a lot more at stake for me here.'

In the hallway was the smell of coffee, slightly burnt, and she went into the kitchen without removing her coat. Viktor stood in front of the stove, facing Boris. Both men had their arms hanging slack by their sides to show they weren't fighting, but the coffee maker was hissing on the burner.

'Have I interrupted?' she asked, stretching to kiss Viktor's forehead. It felt cool. 'I think the coffee's done.'

'Ah, yes.' Viktor shut off the gas. 'Sorry. We were carried away.'

'Are you alright?' She leaned into Viktor but looked at Boris. Their friend's nose was red, the skin folded between his eyebrows. His had been the voice she'd heard.

'A disagreement,' Boris said. His tone was flat and he looked out the window. 'They would build out there, Vika. Disrupt your lovely view.'

'It will take years if they even develop at all. The tech moves fast, you remember. How soon until they move on to something else?'

Boris's frown deepened. 'Then why consult for them?' He was speaking louder than he needed to, but not shouting. 'Are you going to sabotage?'

'Just the potential of a factory brings energy that empty land does not. Think of Penthouse.'

'There are other ways to use it. As I said—'

'More ideas! I can count on many fingers the number of ideas for that site. And what happens?' Viktor shook his head. 'Nothing.'

'But you think the factory may not happen, either!'

'At least they come here with a detailed plan. Who would you rather get into their bed, a politician?' He jostled Jess, trying to seem cheery. 'Not literally, of course, darling.'

Boris was unamused. 'If you show interest, it pushes the project further. They can say, look, the public is on board.'

'The public will be on board, with or without me. You heard the crowd last week.'

Uneasy, Jess stepped between them to pull bowls down from the shelf and fill them with coffee. She sipped at one, decided it wasn't too burnt, and stirred in sugar. Viktor took his and went to sit in the window without offering the other to Boris.

Jess handed it over instead, trying to smile. 'How's Lena?' she asked.

'Fine, why?'

'We were talking about her last weekend, after the tavern.' She nodded at Viktor. 'I didn't get it when she said she was donating babies. I didn't know the word means eggs too.'

It took Boris a moment to understand. 'You thought she was giving away children?'

Jess laughed. 'I was so confused! Especially when she said she'd get paid for them.'

'We do not sell children here,' Boris said humourlessly. He sniffed his coffee and took a sip, then placed it back on the bench. 'We have not sunk this low, not yet.'

Viktor turned around. 'Bory, don't be dramatic. This isn't a lecture hall.'

'I'm showing my feelings.'

'Yes, but you don't need to get completely naked.'

Boris tapped the bench. Jess was surprised he was still there.

'Now, my love,' Viktor said indulgently, reaching for her hip to pull her closer. 'Where have you been this morning?'

She told them about her coffee with Yara, the commission to write an article. Viktor squeezed her waist and gave a distracted smile, but Boris was attentive.

'What will you write?' he asked.

'I'm going to write about Cassandra Caspie and the expo.'

Viktor frowned. 'What about her?'

'Ideally, I'll ask her about—'

'Ask her? What do you mean, ask her?'

Jess looked at Boris, who stared out the window. 'You said that if you met her, you could introduce me,' she reminded Viktor.

'Oh, my Jessie, that was a joke.' Viktor patted her shoulder apologetically. 'I'm sorry. She may not even come.'

Jess groaned, pulling away to tip her too-sweet coffee down the sink. Her excitement went with it. Why hadn't she run her idea past Viktor before going to Yara? Because, she realised, she hadn't wanted him to talk her out of it. She wanted to impress him by saying a deal had been done without him needing to hold her hand.

'I promised Yara I could talk to her. She's going to pay me fifty crowns.'

Viktor whistled. 'Stingy Yara, fifty crowns? When did you become a hustler?'

'If I don't meet her, maybe I can make that the focus of the story instead.' She wasn't sure Yara would accept the substitution, but there was a page to fill. 'Try to get to the bottom of why she's so private.'

'An article about not getting an article?' Viktor looked doubtful. 'I think this is too postmodern even for Yara.'

'Maybe you can do a simple profile,' Boris suggested. 'Miss Caspie is the big thing at the expo, whether she comes or not. People may read about her out of curiosity.'

Jess chewed the inside of her cheek and looked at the mountains. 'Maybe.'

Viktor waved dismissively. 'Darling, forget it, the uncertainty is too great. I doubt she will even come. In fact, I am sure she will not.'

Jess sighed with frustration, 'I feel like the public will be more excited if she doesn't show up than if she does.'

Her boyfriend's tone was fond. 'No-one ever comes.' He jostled her like she was a sulky child. 'Don't worry, we will find you something else to write about.'

'But Yara—'

'Yara needs a story, fine. The content is not so important to her.'

'Too bad you can't write an article in one year's time,' Boris said. He no longer seemed glum. 'When your boyfriend runs her factory, you get all the access you want.'

To Jess's surprise, his eyes met Viktor's, and both men smiled. 'You can have a job too, Bory,' Viktor promised, finishing his coffee.

'Just pay for my political campaign, please.'

They boomed with laughter, the tension finally gone.

***

The sun was setting when Jess set off for the bar. She enjoyed the city in pink light, the streets full of people heading out for the night's first act in a variety of costumes: leather trench coats buttoned to the chin, heavy furs, denim jackets lined with real shearling. It was like a fashion shoot from the end of the last century. A few years ago, the rest of the world had enjoyed a nineties fashion revival: here, fabrics like corduroy and chenille never went out of style.

Walking along the Promenade on the south side of the canal, Jess breathed in the Saturday night aroma of roasting chestnuts and marijuana, crowds of teenagers in baggy pants swigging from flasks as they hip-bumped one another across the open space. At the foot of the Twin Bridges was a small café table draped in a black cloth and topped with a lit candle, a woman in a blood-coloured dress holding the back of a chair with one hand and texting furiously with the other. A narrowboat sounded its horn as it prepared to depart the Old Town dock. A few blocks north, a firework sputtered from the roof of one of the communist-era buildings and petered out without showering sparks, chased by dismissive hollers from a bored audience of block-dwellers.

Jess started work at five, when the bar was picking up. Their signature cocktail meant they got busy early. The legend was that if you drank the Love Potion on an empty stomach you'd meet the man of your dreams, or at least get laid.

The drink was basically a vodka cranberry, but with a powder made of freeze-dried berries sprinkled across the surface and a sliver of strawberry, like the outline of a vulva, balanced on the rim. There was a way of drinking the whole thing through the membrane of the strawberry that Lena and Carolyn had showed her, the group cheering when Jess finished her glass to reveal pink-tinged incisors. 'Lucky you met the man of your dreams already,' Viktor announced, kissing the strawberry juice off her teeth.

It was early March now, technically springtime, and hens' parties from the UK and Ireland were ramping up. Jess poured cocktail after cocktail, using her own story to reassure tourists that the legend was true. There was a shortcut on her phone to two selfies with Viktor, one from the night of her first cocktail and another more recent, proving its magic. If her customers thought she'd met Viktor here, well, that was fine. The biggest tips came from making fantasies seem possible.

Because of the need to drink Love Potion on an empty stomach, the bar was the hens' first destination. By nine o'clock they'd moved on and the number of patrons was down to its usual dozen, so Jess put the uneaten strawberries in a plastic container, screwed the lid back on the berry powder, and switched the TV above the bar from the old MTV feed they played for the hens to the Hungarian news channel the business travellers preferred.

On the screen was a picture of Cassandra Caspie. It was the old publicity photo from the Elpis website and Caspie's short Wikipedia entry. The young woman's arms were folded so each long hand lay elegantly on the opposite upper arm, her smile Mona Lisa–like. Her outfit was almost the same as Jess's bartending garb, a collared white shirt and black pants, though surely Caspie's was cleaner and much more expensive. Over the shirt she wore an argyle vest with her thin orange braid trailing down one breast and a silver brooch on the other. A lot of futile investigations had been launched into the nature of the brooch, with many people sure it symbolised a plan to take over the world.

The TVs in the bar played without sound, making the switch to music videos pointless, and the news subtitles were in Hungarian, which Jess couldn't read. After a while the stock picture faded to a film clip, also old, of Cassandra draped in a poncho stepping from a private jet into a limousine, cameras flashing around her. Leaning on her elbows, Jess tried to guess what the next piece of footage would be: the time Caspie made a speech at the United Nations? The footage of the woman alleged to be Caspie, aged twenty-one, swigging from a wine bottle before holding her hand to block the camera? The blurred yearbook photo from a New Plymouth high school that showed Caspie with bad hair and pre-orthodontist teeth, with the personal motto *Do what you must to change the world* inscribed beneath it?

It turned out to be B-roll of several buildings with the Elpis logo. Disappointed, Jess straightened and wiped a cloth over the bar, struggling to suppress a yawn. After Viktor and Boris burst her bubble that morning, she'd spent the day looking up information on Caspie, only to find the same stuff over and over. Yara was right: the billionaire hadn't spoken to reporters in a decade.

When they were alone and she asked him directly, Viktor had been regretful that, in the unlikely event he did end up meeting Cassandra Caspie, it wouldn't be right to introduce them. 'It looks opportunistic, do you think? She is very careful. She does not schmooze.' He pronounced it *smooze*, offering a cheeky, apologetic grin. 'How can I say, *Here, Miss Caspie, please speak only to my girlfriend about a deal that is not final?* It would not be right.'

She didn't want to ask Yara to make first contact in case the editor decided to cut out Jess and do the interview herself. All she could hope was that if Caspie did end up attending the expo, there'd be some way of bumping into her. It was a small city. The CEO was single, allegedly; maybe she'd come in and order a Love Potion.

The news channel replayed the segment every twenty minutes or so, making Jess feel like Caspie was watching her. The story must have been about the expo for the nearby station to recycle it so often, but Jess still hadn't heard any customers mention it. Maybe the whole thing was called off.

Just before midnight, when the bar was almost empty, Jess crouched to open her phone's translator app and plugged in the Hungarian phrases scrolling across the chyron. Exhibition to take place next weekend, the first read, but the second had no results.

Above her, a glass rattled and clinked, about to fall. Jess stood.

'Sorry!' a customer on the other side of the bar cried in English, grabbing the stem.

Jess went for her cloth, but only a few spots of pink had spilled out. 'Don't apologise,' she said, leaning into her British accent the way she did with visitors, letting them know she understood them and should be tipped well. 'It's fine. Do you want another?'

'Oh, no, no, no,' the woman said, 'it's not my glass. I don't know what it is.'

'It's the Love Potion,' Jess explained, putting it on the rack with the other dirty glassware. 'Well, it was. Hopefully the drinker's off stumbling into her one true love.'

The patron was middle-aged, with brown hair brushing her shoulders and deep frown lines etched between her eyebrows. The IVF women were never in the bar this late. In town for work, Jess guessed, taking in the navy trench coat worn inside, the dry lips and lack of makeup. First time here, if she didn't know about Love Potion—it was on TripAdvisor, but not always in the professional debrief. Wary eyes suggested the woman hadn't quite believed her business development team when they said the city was modern and fairly safe.

Jess gave her most welcoming smile. 'What can I get you?'

'Just sparkling water with lemon. Is that okay?'

'Of course.' Trying to hide her disappointment, Jess put ice cubes and two lemon slices in the bottom of a glass, then drowned them with the soda gun. Passing it over, she shook her head as the woman fumbled in her waistband. 'It's free. No charge.'

'Really?' The woman's eyes shone. Was she getting emotional? 'That's so kind.'

It was illegal to charge for water here, even when spruced up with carbon dioxide and lemon. This was also in the travel guides. 'Don't mention it.'

The woman lingered, holding her water but not drinking it. She looked around as if bewildered, though the space was no different to a million other business hotel bars with its dark wood floor, small sticky tables and walls lined with mirrors. Maybe she'd expected exoticism, not the same low-grade capitalism as everywhere else.

Jess wandered away to top up a frequent flyer's whisky and prepare Irish coffees for a man and woman in nightclub wear. Seeing the woman with the fizzy water hold up a hand, Jess returned to her. 'Everything alright?'

'I wanted ... Can I ask you something?'

Not allowing her face to drop, Jess steeled her stomach. She'd been propositioned by tourists before—not as often as some of her colleagues, but enough. Viktor got the same in his customer-facing work. Men, women, a range of ages and passports, all thinking the pick-up line *I don't see you on the menu* was impossible to resist.

When Jess nodded curtly, the woman continued, 'Do people give tips here? I'm from Australia, and I don't want to offend anyone.'

Jess was relieved. 'Any gratuity is subject to the desires of the customer.'

After a beat of silence, the woman said, 'I'm sorry, I'm very jetlagged so I don't know what you mean.'

'It means you can tip if you want to.'

'Right.' Her features sank into pure exhaustion. 'How much, though? Like I said, I don't want to be insulting.'

Anything, Jess wanted to tell her. Just fling a couple of crowns whenever you see a local; you won't notice the loss, and it could do wonders for them. 'Whatever you give, no-one will be offended. Really.' Too late, she wished she'd hinted at big numbers.

'Oh, thank you.' The woman patted the bar as if it were Jess's hand. 'I sound like an idiot, I know.'

'I've heard that if you're jetlagged you should try to get on the local sleep schedule.'

'Yes.' She stared glumly at her water, which remained untouched. 'I've already messed that up.' Groaning, she dug in her waistband, pulled out some money and dropped it on the bar. 'Thanks for the drink. Can I take it to my room?'

'Of course. Good night.'

Holding the glass in both hands, the woman weaved around the abandoned tables and entered the adjoining lobby.

When she was out of view, Jess picked up the cash and inhaled. A day's pay. She wondered whether the woman understood the currency conversion or if she'd be back soon, claiming a mistake. Jess's manager had a rule: when it touches the bar, it belongs to the bar. Too bad. And anyway, the equivalent in pounds or euros was piddling. Probably Aussie dollars as well.

She put the notes in her apron pocket with the rest of the night's tips and zipped it closed. If only everyone was as generous, Jess wouldn't need to write for Yara at all.

Rachel

CD11

On her first morning in the city, Rachel was woken by a doorbell almost as soon as she'd dropped off to sleep. Her opening eyes met darkness: the room had thick block-out drapes, leaving her with no idea what time it was. The bell chimed and chimed. Knocking a shin against the corner of the bed, Rachel made her way to where she thought the door was, scrabbling her hands against what she remembered to be delicate seagrass wallpaper until she found the handle.

Ana was in the hallway, wearing the same soft purple blouse, hair pulled neatly off her face. 'Good morning, Mrs Mather. Did I wake you?'

Rachel was sure her flattened features and electric shock hair answered the question. 'What time is it?'

'Half-past eight. Breakfast is being served.'

Rachel slumped in the doorframe, desperate to go back to bed.

'You must eat,' Ana said gently. 'Today you will have a massage and acupuncture, then your consultation.' She touched the light switch and Rachel was ashamed of the clothes spread on the floor and the yeasty odour of the room. 'I will see you downstairs in twenty minutes. We leave for the clinic straight from breakfast.'

Rachel spent most of the time Ana had given her under the powerful jet of the shower, holding her face to the spray. She'd managed to limit herself to a short nap after Ana dropped her off, fighting tiredness through the evening by doing circles around the suite while blasting podcasts through her earphones. At eight she'd finally let herself sleep, only to jerk awake a couple of hours later. After an interminable amount of time lying in the dark, she'd given up and gone down to the bar, hoping that being around other people would calm her nebulous anxiety. Instead, the bar had been mostly empty, its few patrons turning and hunching their backs. Even the bartender had responded to Rachel's attempts at conversation with undisguised wariness, like she could be running a scam. Returning to her room, she'd turned the TV on low in the hopes that the soft, foreign voices would make her feel less alone, but that had taken a very long time.

Just before nine, she entered the private dining room they'd toured the day before. Ana rose from one of the small tables and gestured to the place setting opposite. The half-dozen other tables were all unoccupied, bare of cutlery and plates, and Rachel guessed she was the last person to eat. As she settled in, an older waiter with a hairnet covering his thick beard brought her a plate of food and a teapot, then shook out a napkin so it draped across her lap.

Remembering the phrases that she'd looked up on the flight over, Rachel tried to say 'thank you very much'.

The server just nodded, but Ana gave Rachel a bright smile as he returned to the kitchen. 'How nice of you to learn!'

'Well, it's nice of you to speak English,' Rachel said, then felt a hot bolt of embarrassment at the stupidity of that statement. 'I mean, it's the least I can do.'

Ana nodded at the plate. 'Eat whatever you like, as long as it's something.'

It was the same kind of stuff she'd been eating since her fertility treatments started: a bowl of grainy porridge with berries, fruit salad topped with Greek yoghurt, an egg-white omelette with spinach. 'Is this what you usually have for breakfast here?' Rachel asked, tugging her knife and fork from their protective serviette.

'It is nutritionally balanced,' Ana said. 'The hotel chef works with the clinic.'

By 'here' Rachel had meant the country, not the hotel, but she was too tired to get into it. As she cut into the omelette, Ana pulled a tablet from her carry case. There wasn't any food in front of her, just a tall glass of water she hadn't touched. The night before had been the same: Rachel ate a plate of protein and vegetables while Ana stared into the middle distance to make it clear she wasn't watching. But she had to be, in a way, or else they'd let Rachel eat by herself.

'Your results from yesterday are through,' Ana said, nodding at the device. 'The doctor is happy. Very happy.'

Rachel grinned like a child receiving praise. 'Really?'

'The follicle size is good, hormone levels good.' Ana's finger brushed the screen. 'He says to increase the injection by fifty, starting from today.'

Rachel swallowed her mouthful. 'I've done my injection.'

'This morning? Already?'

'I was trying to make up for the time difference.' Her previous needle had been deployed in a Dubai toilet cubicle, the airport's security personnel surprisingly unconcerned about the thick plastic pen and portable sharps container in her hand luggage. Rachel's chest burned with anxiety. 'Should I give myself a little bit more?'

After a pause, Ana shook her head. 'No, do not worry. Start from tomorrow.' She gave a pained smile. 'I will tell the doctor you made a little mistake.'

***

Around lunchtime, after her massage and acupuncture treatment, Ana led Rachel to the room where she'd have her meeting with Olga. 'I'll bring through some tea,' Ana said. 'Would you like anything else?'

Rachel would have preferred coffee, Diet Coke or Red Bull pumped right into her veins. The massage in combination with lack of sleep had left her completely enervated, slumped like a drunk in the chair. All she wanted was bed.

Olga came in before Ana returned. In person, the clinic manager was even taller than Rachel expected, and quite thin, with purple eyeshadow to match her silk shirtdress. 'Mrs Mather, hello. It is good to meet you at last.' She touched the back of the other armchair. 'May I sit?'

Rachel nodded. Olga sat with her knees pressed together and angled to one side, ankles crossed like a duchess.

'How are you feeling?' Olga asked. There was no trace of an accent; instead, she sounded like a Sky News presenter. Rachel wondered if she was from here, then worried that it was xenophobic to care.

'Okay. Tired. The massage was nice.'

Olga pouted. 'Just nice?'

'Very nice,' Rachel amended. 'Really good. The therapist was very skilled.'

'You found the massage relaxing?'

'Yes?' Was that a trick question? Surely it was the point of a massage.

'Have you found yourself very tense during this process, Mrs Mather?'

'Well.' Rachel sucked her teeth. 'I mean, I suppose, relatively.'

'Relative to what?'

'Relative to …' She cleared her throat. 'Not undergoing this process.'

Ana came in, balancing a tray with a teapot and two cups. She slid it onto the coffee table between their two chairs, nodded her farewell and left again.

To Rachel's dismay, Olga resumed her questions. 'What do you do to manage your tension usually?'

Rachel wanted to say that she got massages, but that seemed needlessly sarcastic. 'I suppose, go on long walks. Do yoga.' She didn't take drugs or drink much alcohol, but even if she did, she wouldn't have confessed it to Olga. If her coping mechanisms sounded bland and milquetoast, that's because Rachel was both those things, and she knew it. She hoped it would be a good trait in a mother. 'I cry, you know, when I feel particularly bad.'

'And that relieves the stress?'

'A bit.' Again, Olga was silent, inviting Rachel to continue. 'I mean, it's a stressful process, isn't it? All the appointments, the hormones, not knowing if it's going to work. The money aspect. It's just stressful. There's nothing that can be done about that.' She coughed. 'I messed up the injection this morning. That's made me a bit stressed.'

Olga took a small notebook and pen from her breast pocket and began to write. 'Please, Mrs Mather, help yourself to tea.'

Rachel passed the first full cup to Olga, in case this was a covert assessment of her character; a test to see if she was good enough for their precious embryos.

Olga stopped writing and held the notebook on her lap. 'Is your husband attentive to your stress, Mrs Mather?'

Rachel's hand stiffened around her teacup. 'Is he …?'

'Is he attentive to your stress?'

'He …' She swallowed, feeling hot along her hairline and under her arms. She put the teacup down and pretended to think. 'He's okay,' she said finally, on the verge of tears.

'He is attentive to your stress?'

Rachel nodded mutely, not trusting herself to say anything further. She'd thought they had an agreement.

Olga unfolded the notebook and wrote something down. 'Understandably, he can't be with you now. It's a long way to travel, and in this situation the embryo is already prepared. Men are lucky,' she said, capping the pen and tapping it against the rock of her cheekbone. 'Treatment so rarely involves their bodies that they can stay behind if they must. They don't always need to be by their wives' side.' Olga's eyes widened. 'We women, we are the strong ones, don't you think?'

Rachel's voice was hoarse as she said, 'Yes.'

'Yes,' Olga agreed, picking up her teacup and breathing in. 'We don't need them at all, sometimes. But it's good to know they're there.'

***

On the drive back from the clinic, Rachel tried to work out Olga's credentials. 'She's so impressive, speaking with her really made me think. Where did she get her education?'

'We have assembled a world-class staff,' Ana agreed.

The driver glanced in the mirror and said something, making the chaperone laugh. It was a different driver than yesterday, an older woman with slate-coloured hair under her cap, and Ana seemed to like her better.

Rachel turned back to the window. How ironic that her stress was higher after the massage and acupuncture than it had been before.

Instead of going up to her room, Rachel decided to stay out and walk. Meeting with Olga had upset her, though in the grand scheme of things, nothing had changed. The clinic was still holding up the image of Rachel as a married woman whose husband hadn't come with her but gave his deep and heartfelt blessing for what was happening. The notes from the meeting were surely just a box that had to be ticked; Olga's commentary about absent men all but confirmed that. The only thing that had really shifted was Rachel's fear. She'd changed her mind about hoping for an escape—it made her feel sick to contemplate being refused treatment now.

The air was frigid, clouded with a faint mist that made Rachel squint. She opened the map Ana had given her, got her bearings, then folded it back in the pocket of her coat to avoid looking like a tourist. It was a Sunday afternoon, and the footpath wasn't crowded, but you never knew who was watching.

She walked towards the river, the brine-and-cement odour strengthening as she got closer. The street ended at a dual carriageway, a thick white zebra crossing leading to the waterfront but no lights to signal when it was safe to venture out. After Rachel had hesitated on the footpath for a minute or so, there was a whirring sound over her shoulder and man wearing a lounge suit launched his Segway into the crossing without slowing down. Seeing the approaching cars brake, Rachel hurried in his wake, letting out a relieved sigh when she was on the other side.

A concrete boardwalk bordered the north bank of the river, the metal rail along the edge tinted green by the moist air. Despite the chill and flat sky there was a clump of people in the open space wearing either coveralls or high-vis vests, smoke or vapour or both streaming from their mouths.

Squeezing her arm against the passport tucked in the inner pocket of her coat, Rachel skirted the edge of the group. The workers' efforts were focused around building a marquee, its plastic skeleton half-erected and trembling in the weak breeze.

Two blocks west, twin pedestrian bridges spanned the water: the History Bridge and the Industrial Bridge, according to Ana's notes. Rachel took the Industrial Bridge because it was closer, the soles of her shoes clanging on the metal slats. The handrails along the ornate iron arch were wide and painted black, with gold domes like giant bullets at their highest point. At first she thought the base of one bullet was dirty but looking closer she saw a message had been scrawled around it in ink. A woman in a white ski jacket stood beside it, rubbing her head and frowning as she spoke into a phone. She turned away as Rachel passed.

The embankment on the southern, Old Town, side of the water was labelled on the map as the Promenade. Instead of the cement of New Town's Esplanade, the Promenade was laid with wooden planks, greying and soft with rot in places. This side had no rail to stop small children or drunks from tipping into the water, just a thicker wooden beam bolted perpendicular to the others and splotched with bird shit. Park benches were set at intervals along the centre of the boardwalk and buildings lined the other side, and the whole space was packed with stalls selling tat, and buskers with their instruments.

As she came off the bridge, Rachel passed an old man on a narrow stool who called out to her, waving a sketchbook. The scents of food and drink mixed with a damp mossy smell as Rachel passed a cart offering fresh bread twists and another selling cider, likely the same one Ana recommended, but she pushed on without buying. She'd brave the street food another time when she wasn't so jetlagged and tense.

There was a café a couple of blocks east of the bridge. Stepping inside, Rachel's scalp tingled under the dry roar of the heater, and she unwound her heavy scarf and shrugged off her coat. The place was packed but there was a table and chair in a corner. She weaved her way around the other customers and sat down, feeling as if she'd walked ten kilometres instead of one.

A waiter appeared beside her as soon as she caught her breath. He held out a laminated card. 'The English menu for you,' he said. 'I come back when you know what you want. Water?'

Rachel wondered what it was about her that marked her as foreign. Maybe it was how she'd shed her outer layers the second she stepped inside, unable to withstand the sultry air. The other patrons were still in their coats and gloves, faces red with amusement or the beginning of heatstroke.

The café had no counter or glass-covered cabinet, no visible coffee machine or fridge full of drinks. It reminded her more of a pub dining room, with a single swinging door through to the kitchen and the menu chalked onto blackboards hung from the walls. The floor was polished concrete, the legs of wooden furniture screaming against it. At last, Rachel felt the rush of a new place, the heady feeling of being surrounded by foreign sounds and customs, the elements that shift between familiarity and not. When she was younger, she'd liked to travel, to explore. She'd barely been anywhere since the divorce.

The café's tea menu was extensive, most of the names unfamiliar to Rachel. When the waiter came back, she asked, 'Are any of these caffeine-free?'

'They all have some caffeine,' he said, looking apologetic. 'But quite little.'

'Which has the least?' Rachel cringed and shook her head. 'Sorry, you probably don't know.'

He tilted her menu so he could read it, then tapped the last option. 'This has four percent the caffeine of a black coffee. You may have twenty and still be sleepy in the morning.'

Rachel wondered whether to believe him and his specific answer. Still, the variety he'd suggested was called Honey Morning Milk, which sounded nice and mellow. She handed back the card. 'A pot of that for one, please.'

His face fell. 'Ah, but Miss, so sorry. This is for a morning drink.'

She put her hand on the table where the menu had been. 'Oh.'

His worried look turned into a grin. 'I am joking, sorry, I am joking. You can drink the Morning Milk at any time of day.'

Usually, Rachel wouldn't have liked being teased, but the waiter's smile was disarming. He was extremely good-looking: dark, shiny hair in a short ponytail, silky eyelashes, a toothpick-sized gap between his front teeth. The skin on his hands was dark and his knuckles deeply lined, as if seamed with coffee grounds like a miner's with coal. He was probably in his mid-twenties; technically, he could be Rachel's son.

As she waited for her tea, Rachel people-watched. Four girls who looked about fourteen or fifteen years old had bunched themselves around the next table, the shoulders of their jackets rasping against one another. The three Rachel could see had loosened their zips and folded back the collars, the skin of their necks pink and shiny. Each wore a different pastel-coloured T-shirt with an English phrase inked in fancy lettering over their chests: *Frog in a Pot* against salmon pink, *Smile For Ever* on baby blue and *Feed Me Burgers Eat My Fries* across lemon yellow. At first Rachel thought the last one read *Eat My Friends*, which only made a little less sense. The girls had a facial piercing each and unstructured eyebrows, their hair long and piled lopsided on their heads like they'd slept that way. Their ice-white puffers were identical.

Rachel's tea came in a wide, shallow mug without a handle. Following those around her, she pinched the rim with her thumbs and forefingers, her other digits fanning out as she lifted it to her mouth. The liquid was the softest brown, like very milky coffee, and the heavenly scent that curled up was honey and caramel and a touch of pollen. It was thin, like water moving down her throat, cooled slightly by the wide mug to just the right temperature. The taste was identical to the smell, except for the faintest hint of something floral-sweet she couldn't put a finger on. Finishing quickly, she saw a pinkish sparkle left in the bottom. Sugar? She had a quick sniff but detected nothing.

'You liked it?' The waiter was back.

'Delicious.'

'You would like another?' Seeing her hesitate, he said, 'You can have twenty-four more before it is as bad as one coffee.'

'One more,' Rachel said, feeling unnecessarily wicked considering she was just drinking tea in public. The price was less than an Australian stamp. 'Can I ask, sorry, what's this in the bottom?'

'A little flavour only.' His eyes were the colour of the ocean. 'Wet your finger and press the granules.'

Rachel drew back in her seat, sure this was another joke.

'Look.' He tipped his head. The teenage girls at the next table were putting their thumbs in their own empty bowls and scraping off the grains with their bottom teeth. 'It is custom, okay?'

She waited until he was gone to run a fingertip across the damp granules and brush it over the tip of her tongue. There was the floral taste, strong but not overwhelming. She sucked her fingers, trying to work out the source.

The waiter brought her another cup. As he leaned over, she noticed the name tag on his vest: Dimitri. 'You taste? Nice, right?'

She nodded.

He looked pleased. 'Little bit of secret sauce.'

Rachel lingered over her second Honey Morning Milk, savouring it. When she was finished, all the leftover grains dug out with a fingernail, she rifled through her money belt. All she had was a large note. 'Can I—you don't need to give me all the change for that.'

His eyes were kind, but he was confused. 'What is this?'

'Can I tip you? No, just keep it all. Don't worry.'

'Please, this is too generous. I know.' He grinned, and she felt a dumb flutter in her chest. 'I will set up a tab. You come in any time, and I will serve you. Okay?'

'Okay.' Was this flirting? It had been so long. 'Yes, good idea.'

'I promise to remember.' He nodded solemnly, stepping aside as she stood to leave. 'Have a nice stay, okay. And good luck.'

She'd planned to walk further into the Old Town to see the cathedral and some other things Ana had circled for her but felt suddenly exhausted. It was bedtime back home, and Dimitri had been right about the minuscule amount of caffeine in the tea. Rachel dragged herself back along the boardwalk and over the History Bridge, the chill of the stone permeating through the gritty parapet and into her palm. On the other side, the marquee was fully constructed and the workers had gone.

In the hotel lobby, another woman was waiting by the lifts. They entered the arriving one together, and when Rachel pressed the number for her floor, the woman spoke.

'Level six? Let me guess why you're here.'

For a second, Rachel was going to pretend she didn't speak English, but the woman had clocked her look of recognition.

'I don't mean to be creepy,' she said breezily. 'I like to think we have a camaraderie, but not everyone feels the same.'

Rachel nodded, though she had no idea what the woman was talking about.

'I was beginning to think no-one else was coming.' The other guest gave a sunny smile. She was attractive and well cared for, brunette bob and dewy skin shining in the light. Even in her heeled boots, she was diminutive, and carried a heavy, expensive-looking coat. 'Usually there's loads of patients. The dining room is a ghost town.'

The lift doors opened for the sixth floor, and the other woman stepped out. Reluctantly, Rachel followed.

'Personally, we're frequent flyers. *Eighth* time. Suckers for punishment, apparently, but what can you do?'

She passed Rachel's room and continued towards the larger suites. Rachel was glad to be able to stop and touch the door handle. 'This is me.'

'I'm just going to change and then head down to the bar.' The woman rolled her eyes. 'Virgin piña colada. Care to join me?'

'I'd love to,' Rachel lied, 'but I'm really wiped. Jetlag.' This part was true.

'When did you get in?'

'Yesterday.'

'Where from?'

'Australia.'

'Oh, terrible! Yes, go and have a nap.' She patted Rachel's forearm, and it sent disconcerting sparks of electricity through her. Rachel was reminded, again, of how rarely she was touched. 'I'm Gabby.'

'Rachel.'

'Nice to meet you. I'm sure we'll see one another tomorrow.' She grimaced. 'And the rest of it.'

Rachel was surprised to feel such an aversion to Gabby. The woman seemed perfectly pleasant, if not a little intrusive, but Rachel was already calculating how to avoid her.

'Bye, then,' she said, feeling the rush of relief as she closed the door.

Jess
Monday

There'd been hints of the expo's appearance over the weekend, but overnight on Sunday it fully emerged from its chrysalis. By first light, both town halls and the parliament building were wallpapered with banners featuring the event's logo, a white squiggle topped with a star against a forest green background that looked a little too Christmassy. The official venue was the convention centre on the southern border of Old Town, a futuristic grey dome that resembled a crashed UFO, but larger outdoor spaces like the Esplanade and public squares were set up for break-out events with screens and portable grandstands. Cables wound through crevices in the cobbled ground, padded in some places with bright red duct tape to prevent people from tripping.

Jess walked the perimeter of City Square in the chilly morning air. The usually empty space had been converted to a social-media hub, with a black backdrop rigged up on the far side, the official expo hashtag printed on it in a font so darkly coloured it was difficult to read. By the fountain, six-foot-high plastic letters spelled out the city's name in lower case, ready for influencers to drape themselves over. In another corner, two men each pushed a trolley carrying a sheet of plywood with an angel's wing painted on it. A reporter trailed the workers as they set up the photo op, pressing a hand to her ear to speak.

Her senior English course had finished for the term, but Jess was heading to the library to look up information on Caspie and Elpis for her story. Wi-fi in the flat had been spotty over the weekend, leaving her more and more frustrated every time she had to restart the router. She knew it didn't work that way, but she wouldn't be surprised if all the upheaval from the expo setup was somehow sapping the city's internet connection. It could only happen here.

The other benefit of using the library was access to their database subscriptions, where Jess hoped to find something beyond the same threadbare material that appeared over and over in the public search engines. When she set aside her irritation, Jess found it fascinating that Cassandra Caspie had managed to maintain her privacy in an era of documentation and data. The Elpis website contained nothing but opaque business-speak: synergies, solutions, reinvestment, returns. The media page identified the head of communications, but the only way of getting in touch was through the generic *hello@elpis.com.* As for Caspie herself, after a couple of financial channel interviews, the only times she'd spoken publicly in a decade were in promotional videos, at product launches and in her famous address to the UN. Jess was beginning to wonder if Yara had offered the fifty crowns as a joke, knowing there'd never be an article.

Well, she was going to come up with something. She'd find some way in.

As she reached the library's top step, someone stepped away from a pillar and into her path, calling, 'Teacher!' It was Vera, the short-haired academic.

'Everything alright?' Jess used the local language. 'You know we don't have class today.'

'Yes, yes.' Vera rolled her eyes good-humouredly. They'd had the shop-bought sponge cake and sung a song, a sure sign that proceedings were over. 'I am at the library for other activities, you know. Where else would I learn of your class?'

'Okay.' Jess wasn't sure whether to continue into the building or not. Had Vera been coming out as she arrived, or going in?

'I am glad to run into you, in fact,' Vera said. She pressed both hands to the clasp on her heavy purse, as if afraid Jess would reach out and grab it. 'The expo is this weekend. Are you leaving?'

Jess was surprised to hear Vera bring it up again. After all the chatter on the Friday before Boris's speech, none of the nannas had mentioned the expo during the final week of classes. Their talk during the breaks was back to the weather, the government and grandchildren.

'Actually, I'm doing a report on it.'

Vera's face darkened so comprehensively that Jess wondered if she'd mistranslated a word, like with Lena and her babies. Did 'report' mean something more sinister? Secret police, that kind of thing?

'For whom?' the older woman snapped.

'The arts paper. The English-speaking one.'

Vera relaxed. 'Oh, Yara's paper, yes? No-one cares about that.'

Jess was stung.

'Report on the expo, you will say what?'

Jess wasn't about to mention her proposed interview with Cassandra Caspie in case Vera laughed in her face. 'I don't know. It hasn't happened yet.'

'I suppose crowd numbers, types of booths, yes? Previously Yara has gone into great detail about food and drink at these events. You can investigate the origin of the teabags.' Vera grinned, inviting Jess into the joke.

'I think Yara does a good job on a tight budget,' Jess said formally.

The older woman waved a hand. 'Of course, no-one has money. This is why I suggest renting out your apartment.'

Jess wanted to ask Vera if that was why she was doing the same thing but didn't think it would go down well. Instead, she glanced pointedly at the library entrance.

Vera ignored the signals. 'Well, if you wish to stay, fine. But it will be bedlam. The German chancellor flies in. Russian president is almost confirmed. Can you imagine the security that will be needed for such people? You cannot move on the streets.'

'That's fine, I don't have a car.'

'If Russia will come, then America must. China. Perhaps not leaders, but important people. None have ever been here, so they must give gifts, unveil plaques. I used to live in Vienna. *That* is a real city, one that dignitaries visit. They bring chaos. It would be better to leave.' Her top lip was sharp when she smiled, like the Grinch. Jess couldn't believe this spiteful-looking old dame was the same sophisticated, intelligent woman from her language class. 'You can still write your report. Yara won't know you aren't there.'

'You mean, make it up?'

'The crowd will be large. The food will be bad. The beer will be watery.' Vera dusted her hands. 'There, the story is written. Some crowns in your pocket and you are at ease in the countryside.'

'That's not right.' Jess lifted her chin. 'Even here, journalists don't do that.'

'Yes, well.' It was Vera's turn to be offended. 'Fine. Stay. I try to help, but you don't want this.' She sneered. 'Good luck. I look forward to reading your little story.'

Pushing her hands deep in her coat pockets, Vera stomped down the steps to the street. Jess watched, rattled, as the older woman turned at the corner with Avenue Centro, her bright white head joining the crowds heading in the direction of New Town and the canal.

When Vera was gone, Jess took a deep breath and tried to collect herself. She'd lived here long enough to know that behaviour she found weird was just as likely to have a benign interpretation as a sinister one. It might seem like Vera was hell-bent on getting Jess out of the city so someone she'd never met could take up residence in her desirable apartment, but there was every chance the older woman was just pissed off at not being taken seriously. Or maybe she thought expats like Jess were dumb as blocks.

Inside the library was hushed, dotted with older people reading newspapers in overstuffed armchairs. As she headed to the study area, Jess passed an aisle where two women held one another as they wept. She slowed, concerned, but kept going once she realised that theirs were tears of laughter.

A metal box like a parking ticket dispenser took coins in exchange for computer access. Jess's crown landed with a clang and a white slip with a long code printed in landscape came out of the slot. She took it over to one of the spare research stations, joining a handful of university students flipping through textbooks and surreptitiously sipping coffee.

This time Jess started with Caspie's company, Elpis. She knew some of the history. As an engineering student in Australia, Caspie had been part of a solar-powered vehicle design competition when she had an idea for a slimline panel with its own in-built battery. Her teammates didn't want to risk it, so she quit and started over on her own, and was awarded with a commendation for innovation despite being unable to finish in time. From there, an investment fund offered seed money, and she returned to New Zealand to develop a prototype in her parents' garage.

In the end, the hybrid panels didn't work for cars, but when adapted for rooftop solar they'd sold well in Australia and New Zealand. The first profile of Cassandra that Jess found was fifteen years old, a PDF of an article called 'The Battery Queen' published in an antipodean business magazine, complete with the original publicity still of Cassandra in her sweater vest and brooch. The male author didn't try to hide his bemusement that a young woman had come so far in a competitive market and expressed concern that she'd never marry and have kids if she kept up her eighteen-hour days.

Jess wasn't surprised the experience with *Oztrepreneur* had put Caspie off engaging with the media. ('The engineering graduate is twenty-four, but looks much younger', the original profile negged. 'Her long ginger hair steals attention, eliminating the need for makeup, nail polish or even perfume.') A handful of other stories followed, all strictly company-focused, with no reference to Caspie's looks. Even so, her quotes got shorter and shorter. By the time she was on the *Forbes* list of billionaires under thirty, she was a full-blown hermit.

There were plenty of stories about the fact that little could be found out about Caspie. Reporters described trying to locate her parents, her friends, former employees, anyone. The few who went on the record would only say that Cassandra was kind, a workaholic, and trying to save the world. 'She's really very funny when you get to know her,' another young entrepreneur was reported to have said, and Jess got excited for a couple of minutes before she discovered the retraction in the next issue: the entrepreneur denied making any such comment. She hadn't even met Caspie.

After finishing with the business publications, Jess looked for some of the bigger Caspie rumours. There was a good story in *Wired* from a few years before that explored the theory Caspie didn't exist. They traced its origins to a tweet from some Aussie shit-stirrer who claimed that no Cassandra Caspie had graduated with an engineering degree in the year given on her Wikipedia page and a mate who'd gone to the same uni had never heard of her. A follow-up said no official documents connected Caspie to either Elpis or the mansion on Tamaki Drive where she was alleged to live.

A techie podcast had picked up the story and interviewed the Twitter user. Jess couldn't play the episode without her headphones, but it was transcribed in full on their website. The podcasters had clearly goaded the Aussie but told *Wired* they were just trying to get the guy to shoot himself in the foot. In another episode, they played a voicemail from someone claiming to be the engineering mate who'd said Caspie wasn't real, although as *Wired* pointed out, the original voice and the whistleblower's sounded pretty much the same. 'You'd think her college would advertise the hell out of it, particularly if this so-called genius is female,' one of the podcasters said. 'I don't know, man, it's like, if there's shit, there's fire, y'know?'

Wired showed there'd been pushback the whole time, with engineers tweeting at the shit-stirrer and podcasters that Caspie had been in lectures with them and was identified as Elpis's CEO on the Australian Securities & Investments Commission website. The graduation date was wrong because Caspie reduced her course load after the solar car competition and took an extra year to finish. But the truth was boring, and mainstream media picked up the original story in a 'just reporting what's goin' on' kind of way, pretending to focus on how stupid the claims were but instead strengthening them with attention. The result was that people who tuned out after an opening paragraph or soundbite were aware that Caspie's existence had been questioned, but not that it was a disproved project of three tech trolls. In the final paragraph of the *Wired* article a spokesperson for Elpis commented, 'If they wanted to know if she existed, they could have asked for an interview.'

Will you make Cassandra available for comment? the *Wired* reporter had asked.

The answer from Elpis was, regretfully, no.

Jess's two hours of access ended, and the system logged her off. She could have paid for more time but figured there was little left to find. Caspie existed, and she was almost certainly still head of Elpis, but otherwise, she was an enigma. A misunderstood genius who just wanted to help the world convert to greener tech, or a rich-bitch brainiac who didn't even use perfume. The longer Jess gazed at the determined face staring out of the publicity shot, at the childlike orange plait and too-big vest, the more she wanted to speak to her. Not just for the article, either; she longed to figure out what made Cassandra Caspie tick. How to become the kind of person who felt passion and commitment and who could advocate for herself.

Outside, the air was just as frigid as it had been when she arrived at the library; colder, even. Though the winter sky was always white, the air often tinted with it, the fashion was to wear padded jackets in ivory or cream like clouds sucked down to earth. This was the only place Jess knew of where wearing dark colours was unusual. Even artsy people like Yara didn't dress in black.

Jess headed to City Park for a warm pretzel, but when she got there Sandy's cart was folded up, its work surfaces and signs packed away. Hearing Jess's greeting, Sandy stood up from where she'd been crouched over a crate of water bottles, face clouded with irritation.

'Are you closing?' Jess asked, checking her watch. Not even midday.

'Been told to clear out.'

Jess looked around. The only others in the park were a couple of toddlers swinging in the playground, their mothers sharing the nearby bench. 'Why?'

'Permit suspension's been extended.' Pressing her orange-painted lips together, Sandy rolled her eyes so hard that flakes of mascara shed onto her cheeks. 'Starts today instead of Thursday. We were supposed to get a letter, they said.'

Jess breathed in the warm bread. Sandy had transferred the portable oven to its protective bag, but there was a paper sack of fresh pretzels lying on top. Jess glanced around for the gold uniform of the municipal police. 'Can you still sell me one of those?'

Sandy frowned. 'Not allowed to sell, but I can give you one. They'll only go in the bin otherwise.'

'In that case, could I take a few?' Seeing Sandy's sceptical look, Jess promised, 'I'll pay you back when you reopen.'

'Pretzels on credit,' Sandy clucked, using a serviette to hand Jess half a dozen from the warmth of the sack. 'What is this world coming to?'

Jess put the pretzels in her shoulder bag, wondering what the municipal officers would do if they saw her. Were the goods contraband if Sandy's permit was suspended? If they confiscated the pretzels from Jess, they'd just hand them out back at the police station. She was surprised whoever was enforcing the suspension hadn't taken the stock themselves.

'Are you going to be alright if you can't work for a week?' she asked.

'We'll manage,' Sandy said gruffly, sliding the oven bag onto its shelf and latching the door. 'We're flying out to see family on Wednesday, anyway. Got an offer to rent the flat.'

'Lots of people are leaving, I guess,' Jess said, taking a pretzel and unwinding its plaited end.

'You're staying?'

'I've got work.'

'Oh, you work at the hotel, don't you.' Sandy's lips thinned. 'I suppose that's the one thing they can't shut.'

'I heard the president of Russia will make an appearance.'

She waved a hand. 'He cancelled days ago. But the lady billionaire is.'

'Cassandra Caspie?'

'The redheaded Kiwi, right? She flies in tonight.'

Excitement prickled along Jess's hairline. 'I thought she wasn't going to come.'

'She is.' Sandy was pleased to have intel that Jess didn't. 'Staying at Penthouse, of all places. On the top floor.'

Jess's fingers sweated tackily onto the paper bag. 'Who told you that?'

'I hear everything.'

'Wow,' Jess murmured.

Sandy sneered. '*Wow*? She's a bloody stupid woman. Wants to build on the empty site off east, doesn't she?'

'It could be a good use of the space.'

'Oh, they've come up with a million uses for that black hole. Nuclear waste disposal, they reckoned a couple of decades ago. Then carbon-requesting, what is it, putting the carbon back into the earth. Both of those fell over. The whole thing's a colossal waste of time.'

'The Elpis plan?'

'The whole expo!' Sandy gestured at the near-empty park. 'Suspending permits, putting up solar panels, crying about the weather. I've been here forty years, you know. It hasn't changed. *It has not changed.* There never was any rain in March.'

Stunned, Jess tried to be diplomatic. For the sake of the pretzels, if nothing else.

'You don't think we need new technology? Even if the climate isn't—if the weather's the same?'

'We don't need to disrupt how businesses work. Not just mine.' Sandy breathed more quickly. 'There's a lot of coalminers in this country. What are they meant to do?'

'The expo's about alternative industries, creating different jobs. The factory that Elpis wants to set up—'

Sandy shook her head. 'Jobs for robots.'

'But the coalmines are closing anyway.' Jess was parroting something she'd heard Viktor say. 'The economy's changing.'

'I'll tell you something,' Sandy said. She was speaking loudly, as if to a crowd, but when Jess glanced around, she saw even the mothers with their children had gone. 'I've been here a long time. Do you know what coalminers do when their jobs disappear?'

Jess felt nervous. 'Go on public assistance?'

'Public assistance,' Sandy snorted. 'Thank God they're too proud for that. No,' she continued, giving Jess no time to reflect on how much Sandy's ideology must have changed over the past forty rainless years, 'I'll tell you what they do. They come down from the mountain and buy pretzel carts and steal my customers.'

Rachel

CD12

On her second day, Rachel woke in time to be ready for Ana.

'Lovely!' the chaperone proclaimed when Rachel opened the door wearing jeans and a loose jumper, hair scraped off her face. Though she knew the response was exaggerated, like everything here, Rachel warmed a little in the sun of it. The only other person who really praised her was Jamie, and he was her boss.

Entering the breakfast room, Rachel worried she'd see Gabby, but again there was no-one else there. Ana chatted as the waiter brought over Rachel's tray. 'What did you do yesterday? Did you see the cathedral? Walk up Castle Hill?'

'Not yet,' Rachel said. 'Maybe today.'

Ana looked rueful. 'You can walk, but the castle is closed. I think also the cathedral.'

Rachel assumed the closures were because it was a Monday, but on the drive to the clinic she noticed how empty the streets were, like half of the population had vanished overnight. Business after business had darkened windows and chains on the doors. 'What's going on?' she asked.

'There is an event this weekend,' Ana explained. 'A lot of people are coming in, so it seems many others are going out.'

Rachel recalled the marquee she'd seen on the Esplanade. 'What kind of event?'

Their driver was the older woman from the previous day. Her eyes were strong in the rear-view mirror. 'Trying to save the world,' she said in clear English.

'It's an exhibition on technology,' Ana corrected, her tone as jolly as ever.

'What, like artificial intelligence?'

The driver made an indecipherable sound.

'Climate technologies,' Ana clarified. 'We are going green. The talk is that we become the biggest solar panel manufacturers in Europe.'

'That's great,' Rachel said politely.

The driver muttered something to Ana, who offered a poker face. Rachel shifted in her seat, wanting to ask what had been said.

'She is worried about jobs,' Ana explained. 'A domestic issue.'

Rachel nodded, pretending to understand. She was embarrassed to admit to a sense of hopelessness and wilful avoidance when the climate crisis was discussed; the issue was too big, impossible, and yet it had to be fixed. But there was nothing she could do, so she felt it best to stay out of it. She'd help when someone told her how to do it right.

At the clinic, Rachel had her blood drawn and a second massage, then a session marked on the schedule as 'group therapy'. The counsellor was Ian, a middle-aged expat in dusky chinos and a thick cable jumper, his grey hair slicked off his forehead. The other attendees came in: two American women, one with dark hair and freckles and the other a wispy blonde with large eyes, followed by Gabby and a tall, older man. Gabby nodded at Rachel as they took their seats.

Ian gave a quick preamble: this was a safe space to share feelings and experiences with people who were going through the same thing; the only ones who could truly understand. The five of them shared grim looks. The others had been there longer than Rachel and introduced themselves at Ian's invitation, familiar with editing their lives into a quick biography. Harper, the brunette, was to be a gestational carrier for blonde Meg and her partner, while Gabby and her husband were trying for a daughter. Warwick already had three sons.

Rachel longed for more. Was Harper being paid by Meg, or doing it out of the goodness of her heart? She'd said she already had a two-year-old, and that the pregnancy had been easy, but surely it would take more than that to carry a child for someone else. Meg seemed stranded on the verge of tears and kept clutching Harper's upper arm to gaze at her in wonder and gratitude. Was that because she was paying Harper, or because she wasn't?

Then there was Gabby and Warwick and their gender selection. It was allowed here, but not in the UK, where Gabby and Warwick were from. No-one from the clinic had ever asked Rachel if she wanted to know the sex of the three embryos she'd bought. Maybe it was a perk for those who could prove they were married.

When Ian invited her to share, Rachel crossed her legs to the left, then the right. 'It's fairly basic,' she apologised. 'I tried at home for a couple of years, meanwhile my eggs got older. I'm forty-two,' she explained to Harper, who seemed to be the youngest one there. 'Now I need an egg donor, and I felt the program here was— was more comprehensive.' She wondered if the others would understand she meant cheaper.

'Rachel's husband is unable to be here,' Ian added. 'Like Meg's.'
Meg wiped her eyes.

'I'm happy to be surrounded by beautiful women,' Warwick said.

As the others released awkward chuckles, Gabby pressed her monogrammed handbag into her stomach and shook her head.

The conversation was loose, directed by Ian, who could have played a therapist in a movie: *How did you feel about that? What emotions did that bring up for you?* Several times Meg pushed her chair back and went to grab wads of tissues from the console table by the door, and Rachel wished she'd just bring the box back with her. Harper, by contrast, was dry-eyed, her manner languorous, leaning back in her seat and cupping her hands around the base of her belly like she was already pregnant.

Ian wanted them to talk about the image of a family they'd had when they were younger. Did the women brush dolls' hair and put them to bed? As Meg emoted her way through her childhood dreams of four kids, Rachel compared herself to Harper. Both would soon have an unrelated embryo transferred into their womb in the hope it would develop and continue to birth. If each worked, however, Rachel would keep the baby, while Harper handed hers back to its parents. Georgi and Nadya would have no idea who their embryo had turned into, where it had gone, while Harper would presumably fade from Meg's child's life. Both scenarios were apparently fine and valid, and though Rachel agreed in theory, there was something about the surrogate that filled her with an emotion she couldn't name.

Four years ago, when Rachel first started this process, the concept of using a donor egg had never once crossed her mind. Of course she'd intended to be biologically related to her child. But as each step took her further and further, that expectation had fallen away, like so many others. If she carried a baby in her womb, it would be hers. But the child Harper carried would be different.

'And you, Mrs Mather?' Ian asked. His eyes were the glassy green of wine bottles. 'Did you think you'd have kids when you were younger?'

'No.'

'Not at all?'

'My mother says I was against it.' Rachel laughed with embarrassment.

'When did you change your mind?'

'I don't know.'

Ian waited for her to continue.

It was difficult, not only because she couldn't mention the divorce. Whenever she thought about it, Rachel couldn't pinpoint the moment she'd decided to try for a baby; only that it was after her separation from Ben. 'I guess—I was getting older, and I thought about the future. I wasn't sure I wanted to be alone.'

'You shouldn't have a baby for company,' Meg said in a low, wet voice.

Rachel was annoyed. 'That's not it. I don't mean for company. I don't know what I mean.'

'Do you feel it's a deep need?' Ian asked.

'Yes,' Rachel said, but that didn't quite cover it. 'I feel like it's something I need to try to do. It's my last chance.'

The room was silent for a moment as everyone contemplated this, and then, to Rachel's relief, they moved on.

***

Olga intercepted Rachel after the session, resplendent in a lavender pantsuit and white blouse. 'Mrs Mather!' she greeted loudly, causing the other couples to look around. Ana was nowhere to be seen. 'How did your first group appointment go?' Olga turned side-on to Rachel and touched her elbow. 'Come through and let's chat.'

Rachel felt sick as she followed Olga into the sparse office. The blood results from the morning must be back; her levels would be falling, or skyrocketing, whichever was most unfixable. All because she'd done her injection too early the day before. Or perhaps a freezer had unplugged somewhere and her embryos were in a puddle on the floor. She swallowed back bile, shaking her head at Olga's offer of tea. If they brought out the dried berries, she might scream.

'Now, a slight hiccup, Mrs Mather.' Olga opened a manila folder that was waiting on the desk. 'We have just been reviewing your paperwork, and your husband's signature is not where we need it.'

Rachel peered at the form she was pointing to, knowing the signature line was blank. On the video call Olga had assured her that, while there were most certainly two Mathers, only one of the prospective parents needed to sign the contract.

'It must be an oversight,' Olga said. 'There is a lot to do before travelling. Elements are overlooked.'

'I almost left my passport at home,' Rachel agreed. This wasn't true, but she wanted to offer a connection if she could. Olga was all smooth surfaces, nowhere to get a grip.

'You will contact your husband to get a new copy signed? For tomorrow?'

'Tomorrow?' Rachel pictured Ben on a sofa with Melissa or taking an evening jog around the block with her son. It was almost dinnertime where they were; she'd have to be in touch soon, before they went to bed.

Except Ben wasn't her husband. No-one was.

'It shouldn't take long,' Olga said. 'Some people sign as just a squiggle, you know.'

Rachel nodded, heart thunderous. She checked her watch but didn't see the time.

Olga closed the folder and stood up. 'It's very straightforward, Mrs Mather. Someone needs to print the form, mark the line and send a scanned copy back.'

Her teeth glistened as she opened the door, revealing Ana in the hallway. Rachel lifted herself from the chair with shaking legs.

'Oh, and also,' Olga went on blithely, 'this morning's blood test shows very good numbers. Your oestrogen is rising nicely. Everything is on course.'

***

Later, Rachel sat dumbstruck in the back of the town car, wondering how she was going to get Ben's signature in the next twenty-four hours. She tried to remember the last time they'd been in touch. A year ago? Eighteen months? He didn't know she was trying to have a baby. No-one did. How surprised would he be? He liked to pretend he knew everything, even—especially—what he couldn't possibly have known. After fifteen years together she could summon Ben's voice like her own conscience, and she imagined the manufactured weight in his words as he said, 'I was never *really* convinced you didn't want kids.' His pretend serious face. 'I'm kind of proud, Rach. You're being so brave.'

The thought made her angry, not because of the studious sympathy that he'd deny up and down was pity, but because she knew what would come next: he was sorry, it pained him badly, but he wouldn't be able to help.

They'd met in the humidity of a nightclub, Rachel's too-long hair dripping as she shook and stomped across the dancefloor. She had no rhythm, but that wasn't the point: her on-off boyfriend had just moved to Japan, and she needed to sweat him out. She was twenty-three, drove a Hyundai with a back seat as deep as a bathroom drawer, and, at that moment, was four cocktails in plus pre-drinks at her friend Mandy's.

Ben had been on the periphery all night. She bumped into him as she carried her first lot of drinks from the bar, and when she went for the next round, he stood next to her. He was going into the men's toilets as she came out of the ladies. Ben began to smile when they passed, greeting her in a more pointed way each time. He had expressive eyes, and she could see the dark hair of his chest through his light-coloured shirt. He seemed nice, perhaps a bit dim. She showed playful contempt for the beer in his hand. 'Drink a whisky!' she shouted as she swept into the loos. 'Act like you mean it!'

Ten minutes later she was half-heartedly twisting a few metres away from Mandy and the man she could only meet up with while they were out, because he lived with another woman. Ben came up.

'Whisky,' he announced, holding up a glass. 'And Coke.'

She curled her lip to disguise her endearment. 'I suppose that'll have to do.'

'What're you drinking?'

She tilted her cocktail in his direction and cried out when he snatched a cheeky sip.

'Fruity. And what's that, gin?'

'I don't know!' Sweat ran down the valley of her spine. 'It tastes good, that's all I care about.'

They kissed sloppily at the end of the evening, and Rachel wanted it but not so much that she felt embarrassed to have him stroke the damp mess of her hair. She tasted the whisky in his mouth. It was why she'd told him to switch: she couldn't stand beer on a man's tongue.

How had their relationship unfolded? It was so boring to think of now, which was its own little tragedy. He'd been the keener one at the start, she was sure of that, though later his line was that she couldn't get enough of him. After a few months, she'd been convinced that he wasn't flighty like the boy in Japan (who was already engaged to someone over there); also, he was fun, easy, good-natured. She liked to explore his chest hair. He was a teacher, which surprised her: she would've guessed carpenter or plumber, some type of tradesman, but he taught Year Five and physical education. He was a year younger than her, which wasn't important and grew to be even less so as time went on. She felt stable with Ben. Their problems were trifling: one or both of their mothers being difficult, him buying season tickets to the footy when they were saving for a deposit. They got engaged when she was twenty-eight and married soon after, but they'd both known it was permanent from early on and marriage was just for proof. They'd been wrong.

The reasons for their separation were just as mundane: each thought they'd stayed the same while the other had changed, and those changes, or not-changes, meant they no longer spent time together. They grew far enough apart that it felt impossible to come back together. It brought real pain—pain and uncertainty and fear and resentment—but to Rachel it was so unspecial that she found it hard to share the deep emotions with other people.

Ben's loyalty was one of his greatest qualities, a brilliant foundation, but it couldn't support the weight of a collapsing marriage. As things went bad, his allegiances shifted. He left her when she had shingles to go for a weekend with his mates, for example. He sided with his mother when she criticised Rachel. When they were together Rachel could feel how he no longer cared about her in the same way, and it made her despise him. They only just escaped with their first impressions of one another intact: Rachel thought Ben was dumb, and Ben thought Rachel was kind of a bitch.

That loyalty would be back to full strength in Ben's new relationship. He'd put Melissa's feelings before his own, and far ahead of his ex-wife's. He'd decide that signing the form for Rachel would be disrespectful and say he just couldn't do it.

The shame and disappointment burned so hot it was as if the rejection had really happened. Rachel put her head in her hands.

Glancing in the rear-view mirror, the older driver made a comment. Ana asked, 'Are you feeling alright?'

'Oh.' Rachel rubbed a hand down one side of her face. 'Just nervous.'

Ana's eyes were gentle. 'Your numbers were very good. Everything is on track.'

'Olga said my husband's signature needs to be on the paperwork by tomorrow.' She waited for a response, but the chaperone's expression didn't change. 'It's going to be very difficult. Impossible.'

'Nothing is impossible,' Ana said lightly.

The driver asked a question, and there was a quick back-and-forth. Finally, Ana sighed. 'What did Olga recommend?'

Rachel tried to remember. 'That he needs to print off the form, sign with the original date, and send a copy back.'

For a while all three women were quiet. Outside, the white and grey of the city flashed past. Rachel couldn't understand why this trip seemed to be taking so long when there were barely any other vehicles on the road. She supposed they could be driving in circles for some reason. It would make as much sense as anything else.

At last, the car turned onto a street Rachel recognised. Ana said, 'It's true, someone will need to sign the form.'

The driver nodded. 'A signature on the paper. By tomorrow.'

She looked in the rear-view mirror. 'That is all. Easy.'

Something released in Rachel as she understood. 'Yes. Of course. Easy.'

The older woman smiled as they pulled up to the kerb. Setting the brake, she turned around. 'Don't worry, Miss. Everything always works out.'

***

Yet again, Rachel was too emotionally exhausted to take the tourist route Ana had drawn up for her. Instead, she wound a scarf around her neck and walked towards the river, craving the chill air on her prickling face.

Just like the roads, the area around the Esplanade was largely deserted. The people who passed by walked at full speed in sharp business-wear, talking into earpieces. Crossing over onto the Promenade, Rachel noticed the stallholders from the day before had gone.

To her relief, the café was open. Two tables were occupied, both with the same official-looking types she'd seen on the way. Rachel sat down and scanned a menu but knew just what she wanted.

After a few minutes, Dimitri came out from the kitchen and stood by her chair. 'Hello again.' He touched his fingertips to the table. 'More tea?'

'That would be amazing.'

He smiled and Rachel reminded herself that Dimitri worked in hospitality; he was there to make money. Maybe he liked talking to customers, to tourists, and that was why he'd opened a café. Whatever it was, he had no particular interest in her, a woman twenty years older, swollen with drugs and monolingual.

He brought out the Honey Morning Milk in its bowl, the warm scent and steam making Rachel relax. She'd have to find this tea in Australia, she thought. If she did become pregnant, it would honour where the miracle occurred. If not, she'd drink it to console herself.

Dimitri dropped in on the other customers, switching languages easily. By the time Rachel was halfway through her tea, both groups had gone, leaving crumpled banknotes behind. Now she and Dimitri were alone.

He cleaned the tables, then wandered back to her. She was savouring the final mouthfuls of tea, swirling the bowl so a whirlpool picked up the last of the flavour. Dimitri gave a distracted smile, then yawned. 'You probably want to go home,' she said.

'You don't have to hurry. Full, empty, we are open until late.'

Glad for the excuse to chat, Rachel asked, 'Where is everyone?'

'The news reported that an event on the weekend would cause bad traffic, so everyone left town to avoid it.'

'I expect that caused some traffic jams, too,' Rachel said. 'Everyone going at once.'

Dimitri looked amused. She noticed his hips were moving slightly from side to side. There was music in the café, a faint background buzz, but the rhythms didn't match.

'What's the event? Something about technology?'

'Exactly so.' He continued to sway. 'Lean, green energy.'

'So, it's just a display? Booths and things?' Rachel could only think of the world's fairs that'd been staged decades before, but surely those had long since been superseded. They had the internet now.

'A chance to display, yes, and also to network. From nowhere it has all of a sudden become big. There are rumbles about the future, politicians need to be seen doing something. This is how they show it.'

'Like what?' Rachel asked. 'I suppose you don't know yet.'

'One project has been mentioned. There is a vacant site where they will make solar panels.'

'That sounds good,' Rachel offered. 'I've got panels at home.'

'Opportunity is what we need. It is a hungry place.'

She wasn't sure whether he was being literal or figurative. 'Right.'

'The untapped energy is large. What we can make of business when we put our minds to it, amazing.' He shook his head proudly. 'This building was an old horses' stables. Now it is a bustling café.'

'Yes,' Rachel agreed, looking around at the empty tables.

In the lull, Dimitri stepped towards her. She was flustered until she realised that he was reaching for the dirty bowl. 'If you wish to see some of the tourist sights, may I recommend to do this tomorrow or the next day. Before they are crowded with visitors.'

He turned in the direction of the kitchen. 'Anyone interesting coming?' she asked, trying to keep him there. 'Or just politicians?'

'Maybe everyone,' Dimitri said, tapping a finger on his lips, showing their softness. 'You will see.'

***

One her way back along the avenue to the hotel, Rachel passed a small shop selling toiletries, magazines and souvenirs. It was open. Catching a glint of metal in the window, she went in.

The jewellery was cheap, cased in clear plastic with a pink foam backing. There were some earrings and bracelets in dark silver sourced from a small mine in the east. They were oddly shaped, especially the earrings: a tight twist that looped at one end and finished in a flat point, like the tip of a sword, at the other.

In a small bin on the bottom shelf, under a rack of postcards featuring a puff of smoke at the base of a hill and the dark spire of the cathedral, were rings in egg-shaped canisters. They reminded Rachel of the machines that used to be in shopping centres, where you dropped in a coin and turned the key and a random one fell through the slot. She picked one up and looked through its domed lid. The band was slightly uneven and thick, more like a man's ring than a woman's, but it didn't cost much and looked like it would fit.

Back in her room, she popped the top off the egg and tipped out the ring. The wedding bands she and Ben had chosen were gold, fairly slim, with words etched on the inside. Slipping the cheap silver over her ring finger sent a train of wistfulness charging through her. It'd been a long time; she no longer remembered what the inscriptions had said.

This ring was a size or two too big, but if she was careful, it wouldn't slip off. She held her hand out to look. It would have to pass.

Jess
Tuesday

The luxury apartment building called Penthouse had a long and storied history. The ultra-modern, smoke-grey cylinder by the river at the south-eastern corner of New Town had been completed a few years before Jess first met Viktor. A faculty of the university had been the original occupant of the site, their building constructed around a central theatre that replicated Shakespeare's Globe. Peacocks had roamed the grounds, cawing blithely as they passed by student rallies and speakers on soapboxes. Then, in the seventies, the communist leader had it knocked down overnight, a week before the end of summer break. A press release declared that the arts were an indulgent mode of study unworthy of such a great nation, and so the source of such depravity had been razed for the protection of the national character. The students' degrees were cancelled, and their professors fired; if they wanted, they could take up positions as high school teachers. Otherwise, too bad, get a blue-collar job like everyone else.

The location was extremely desirable: on the canal, within easy access of town but beyond the hustle, with a beautiful outlook to the east. The leader wanted a residence built over the rubble in time for the following summer, then just nine months away, and his architect hurriedly produced plans for a façade in the style of Vienna's Imperial Palace, with thirty bedrooms and forty bathrooms. It would face the mountains, and the recently built concrete apartment blocks in the vicinity would be torn down so the leader's preferred trees could be planted, offering a forest view from every east- and north-facing window. As for the southern aspect over the canal, a long brick wall the height of the palace would be constructed along the Old Town Promenade, onto which was to be painted a collage of the leader's favourite things.

'But he hated the arts,' Jess had objected, confused. 'Why would he want a mural?'

'His nephew was to be commissioned,' Viktor explained. 'Luckily, the nephew's French girlfriend was a famous muralist. The pay would be generous, of course, and last many years.'

The leadership was overthrown before the palace could be finished, and for years its skeleton stood on the riverfront. The new democratic government put fencing around it, but it was flimsy, and the site was covered with graffiti, the foundations of forty bathrooms shat on by students angry that, though the arts faculty had been reinstated, their new premises were a mission-brown office block three streets back. At the time of the coup the wall overlooking the Promenade had been finished but unpainted, so it was dismantled one brick at a time and the materials used to construct an education centre in the same spot, directly opposite where the leader's bedroom window would have been. According to Viktor, there'd been debate about whether a similar thing should be done with the half-built palace, or if it should be returned to the university, or demolished in favour of a new park or public square.

'They took two decades to make a move,' he said. 'This was

the beginning of our national indecision. A million meetings, town halls, open comments, and every week the newspaper full of opinions. There was paralysis.'

If the new government commandeered the site for their own use, the people would believe nothing had changed. If they turned it into open space, with a plaque to commemorate what happened, it would be too melancholy; a desirable location held hostage to the past. And they didn't want to give it back to the university because it was too nice. The shitting students could have their ugly new block, though the peachicks they were trying to reintroduce kept on dying.

In the end, they had their cake and ate it. A cheeky MP proposed using the site for something the deposed leader hated. He'd denounced the Art Deco style, abhorring curves, so the government's new architecture office drew up plans for a cylindrical apartment tower, far taller and grander than the palace would have been. The fifty apartments would be sold at cost, and citizens from all over could go into a ballot for the right to buy. The old leader had not wanted his people to live in luxury, but the new government did. There was enough symbolism in the plan that consensus was reached at last, and ground was broken for Penthouse.

The project had run years behind schedule and over budget, and there were stoppages as issues arose and fell away like tides. The head architect wanted to be granted an apartment without having to enter the lottery. So did the owner of the building company. Labourers asked that there be a special lottery for them, to increase their chances. A scandal arose when it was discovered that members of the ruling party, technically prevented from entering the lottery, had arranged to have their under-age nieces' and nephews' names added so they could sign the apartments over if they won. Parliament was dissolved and reformed in almost the same configuration, and then, when the party was caught fixing the lottery to reward key donors, dissolved again.

By the time the building was finished, the public lottery was no longer trusted, and anyway, the costs had skyrocketed. The new planning minister proposed selling the properties at market rates, and the people were so sick of the whole thing that they agreed without debate. (Without debate! In this country! Jess couldn't believe it.) Selling the apartments to overseas investors with no idea of their cursed history was a fruitful move: the debt was covered, the university compensated and no locals had to live in the building, which had gone from a Shangri-la to something groaned about.

'It is funny,' Viktor had mused. 'The building has done what it was meant to. It unites the city.'

Though Jess was familiar with Penthouse, she didn't have much to do with it. It was in a part of town she didn't visit, and it wasn't visible from their apartment. She hadn't been to the education centre, either. The only mark of the former leader's folly that impacted her at all was the stadium-sized area between the city and the mountains that had been razed to maintain clear views from the planned palace. Jess and Viktor could see this from their kitchen as well; it was the place where Cassandra Caspie wanted to set up her factory.

Midmorning on Tuesday, Jess bundled herself into a coat and set off for Penthouse. It was only half a kilometre due north of their apartment, but she had to travel in a C-shape, detouring along Avenue Centro to cross the canal. The Old Town felt muted, with fewer people than she expected on the Promenade or crossing the Twin Bridges. On the New Town side, Jess passed a group of workers setting up barriers around a marquee. Two men dressed in black and wearing earpieces stood with conspicuous posture nearby, but while they watched Jess pass, they didn't say anything. From there all the way to Penthouse, Jess didn't see a single person.

A courtyard of brilliant green grass ran between the Esplanade and the curved front of the building, cut through with a path of white stones. At the entrance a guard in a navy suit sat on a stool, scrolling through his phone.

Jess greeted him. 'I'm here to meet with Miss Caspie.'

He looked up slowly. 'Who?'

'Miss Caspie. Cassandra.' She knew from heist films to feign confidence. 'She's in town for the expo.'

The guard's face was soft and ruddy, all cheeks and forehead. 'Staying here?'

Jess nodded. 'On the top floor.'

'No,' he said gruffly, eyes sliding back to his screen.

She shifted her weight. 'She might be in a different ap—'

'Not here.'

Not sure what to do, Jess waited until the man glanced at her again. His affect was so flat she could have ice-skated on it. 'Believe me, I know all who sleep in this building.' He released a dry chuckle. 'No Caspie. No lady.'

'She might be arriving later.'

Lifting his eyes to the colourless sky, the man took a deep, thoughtful breath. 'Many things are possible.'

'So I should come back.'

'You do what you must,' he said, returning to his phone.

Straightening her shoulders, Jess crunched back to the Esplanade. There was a metal bench on the far side of the boardwalk, facing the water. Jess took a seat at one end and turned so her knees pointed east. With an arm slung over the backrest, she could twist enough to gaze back over the courtyard. The guard raised a hand in greeting and she nodded stiffly.

The breeze along the canal was a few degrees colder than the ambient temperature, and Jess shivered in her thick coat. Every parent who booked her for conversation classes had cancelled for the week, blaming the upcoming expo. Her funds depleted and the next few days empty aside from bartending shifts, Jess had decided to chase the story, and Caspie, all by herself. The billionaire's opinion of Viktor couldn't be affected if she didn't know Jess was his girlfriend. She just hoped that what Sandy had heard was right.

The prospect of a stakeout felt bleak without a pretzel and coffee. Walking over, all the usual carts were gone, the kiosks shuttered. Here, food sellers didn't even close on Christmas. Jess wondered if Sandy and Novak were at home, mute in matching armchairs, not sure what to do when they weren't working. Maybe they'd left early to see their kids, who lived in the UK, not far from where Jess had grown up and her family still lived.

In the three years she'd been away, Jess had gone back only once. Her parents asked her to take the coach in from Stansted so they didn't have to pick her up, which should've been a sign. The bus trip took almost as long as the flight had, and Jess was alarmed at how detached she felt from the passing landscape. It was like a businessperson returning to a place they'd been to before: familiar, but meaningless. The window could have been a TV screen.

The house itself still hit her where it hurt, the smell of Keith's hair cream and the washing liquid Rosalind used; the porridge they stewed to sludge every morning. Her sister's kids' drawings on the fridge where hers and Amy's used to be, her parents' wedding photos in the hallway, the portraits above the fireplace of all the labradors they ever had. The current labs, Missy and Betsy, were curled up on the good armchairs, leaving the broken old sofa for the humans.

Keith and Rosalind were formal with Jess, even awkward. Hers was the only room that was different: Rosalind's sewing machine was on the desk and her yoga mat underneath the window, the single bed replaced by an Ikea futon. Rosalind asked Jess to sleep on it in the couch configuration so she could still do her sun salutations.

Jess knew her parents weren't thrilled by Viktor, and that they disapproved of her moving away, but she hadn't expected this cool a reception. They barely glanced at her pictures of their flat, the hotel bar, the library. Their silence led Jess to talk more than she meant to about life there: the ancient plumbing in the flat, the toxic humidity in summer, the impossibility of finding full-time work. With each complaint her parents' expressions grew more rigid, and their responses devolved into grunts.

On the last day they watched TV for hours while the dogs snored. Jess, desperate, started describing the shows she watched with Viktor. She was trying to make them laugh, or something.

'—I don't know how, but every family that goes on the program has a dad with a bushy moustache and a three-piece suit, and he's always the one they put on the platform in the third round. If the rest don't get the answer right, he gets dunked in a pool of jelly, and there'll be a little kid who ends up shouting the wrong—'

Rosalind let out a creaking sigh and widened her eyes at Keith. He shook his head.

'What?' Jess asked. 'What happened?'

'I don't know what you expect us to *do*,' her mother snapped. 'Frankly, it all sounds terrible.'

'Have you had jack of it?' Keith asked. 'Are you wanting to come home, or what?'

'I'm just talking,' Jess whined.

'Everything about the place is awful.' Rosalind rolled her eyes. 'Even the shows on telly. It's hideous. We get the picture.'

'It's not hideous.'

Keith laughed. 'Could've fooled me.'

'I'm just talking,' Jess had repeated, eyes stinging with tears.

'You've made your bed,' her father said. 'You lie in it.'

'I am—'

'You made a decision,' Rosalind interrupted. 'You face the consequences.'

'I know what "you made your bed now lie in it" means.'

'Too clever by halves,' Rosalind told Keith. 'Can't tell her a thing.'

Jess had fought tears all evening, and on the coach and plane the next day, not letting herself sob until she was in Viktor's arms. He stroked her hair with his long fingers. 'What is it, darling? Are you alright?'

She pushed her head into his neck. 'I'm just so glad to be home.'

Jess was still in touch with her parents, but not often, and their conversations were brief and without depth. They didn't ask her home for Christmas or suggest coming out for a visit, and she was careful to only say neutral things: work was busy, the weather was okay, Viktor was fine. Often, while Rosalind talked, Jess tried to imagine asking her for money. A hundred quid would cover Viktor's shortfall during the expo, and even her parents could afford that. But she'd lost the language to tell them she needed help.

The Penthouse guard was still in his seat. Jess squinted up at the building's curved windows, trying to make out any movement within. Radu had once worked as a night concierge there, but they let him go because there was nothing to do. He claimed less than five of the fifty apartments were occupied, all of them by housekeepers on standby in case the wealthy owners swung into town.

Only a handful of people in the building: ideal for the privacy-loving head of Elpis.

After two hours, Jess had seen no-one enter or exit Penthouse through the front. Barely anyone had passed on the Esplanade either, just workers in coveralls or dog owners with their heads down, the animals hurrying as if they too knew something was up.

At midday, one of the municipal police's gold hatchbacks pulled into the closest parking spot and two figures in uniform emerged. Heart sinking, Jess stood up and glanced over at the Penthouse guard. He nodded calmly back.

The officers were female, one with a solid build and the other narrow-shouldered. Both had soft, youthful skin. Jess guessed the larger framed one was in her early twenties and the other younger, maybe nineteen. Their heavy boots clunked on the cement.

Policing here was complex. There were four different, often overlapping, branches: national, regional, city and municipal, the gold-coloured squad being least threatening but the most finicky. Their role was a mix of parking officer, traffic cop and petty claims judge. Often when Jess lined up at one of the few ATMs in the Old Town, a municipal officer or two would approach, wanting to chat. They were mostly toothless, probably bored, but still the cold fear of being questioned would descend.

She'd tried to suggest to Viktor once that the municipal brigade was an inversion of the former secret police: deliberately visible, remembering nothing. He hadn't liked that very much. 'I lived in the time of secret police,' he countered shortly. (He'd been a year old when the communists were overthrown.) 'They are nothing the same.'

That had been her point, but Jess knew better than to push it.

'Hello!' the younger officer greeted, as if they knew each other and were meeting by surprise. She spoke fluent English, which was more likely to be a display of power than a sign they knew Jess was foreign. 'Can we talk for a minute?'

Jess didn't think it was a fineable offence to sit on a bench for two hours, but it was best to be deferential. 'Of course.'

Close up, the policewomen were beautiful. Their badges bore only their officer numbers; Jess knew she was allowed to make a note, in case she needed to lodge a complaint that would go nowhere.

'Nice day, do you think?' the younger one asked.

'Yes,' Jess agreed, though it wasn't particularly. 'Cold, though.'

'It is to warm up at the end of the week. There is to be rain.'

Jess was surprised. Rain in March was a big deal. 'Will it affect the expo?'

'You are going to the expo?' The younger woman sounded excited, like Jess had tickets to a sold-out concert.

'No, I don't think so.'

'But you stay in town.'

They were playing with her, the way they could. Jess looked past the officers' shoulders. The Penthouse guard looked pleased.

'I work in hospitality.' Viktor had told her she didn't need to give precise details to gold police; generalisations were all they could ask for. 'We're open over the weekend.'

'So are we,' the younger policewoman joked.

Jess faked a smile.

The older officer came to life. 'You like it?' she asked, gesturing at Penthouse.

'The architecture's nice. The curves.'

'This is famous. Beautiful apartments.' She smirked at her colleague. 'So they say.'

The performance was tiring, but Jess could only wait. There was no such thing as excusing yourself from the attention of the police, even the gold ones.

'You know someone staying here?' the younger one asked.

'I thought so,' Jess said. 'Looks like I made a mistake.'

The other officer nodded at the Penthouse guard. He sat back on his stool.

'You have something else to do?'

'I'm going to the university,' Jess said, making it up on the spot. She didn't want to return to the flat empty-handed, and the campus was close by. Surely they wouldn't object to her visiting a place of learning.

'You are a student?'

'Meeting a friend.'

'Another friend, huh?'

The words could have been pointed, but the younger woman sounded tired. She let her bored gaze drift across the canal.

'You know where to go?' The older officer pointed up the avenue. 'About ten minutes. Walking is faster than waiting for a tram today.'

It was true that public transport had been reduced to a skeleton service, but Jess knew they really meant, *Scram!*

'Good idea.' It felt safe to shoulder her bag; the performance was winding up. 'I could use the walk.'

'You sat down for a long time,' the young one acknowledged. 'Well. Have a good day.'

'Maybe get your Penthouse friend to call you first,' the older one sniggered. 'Let you know he is actually there.'

'I will,' Jess said. 'Thank you.'

The officers turned and strode up the path, white stones crackling under the soles of their boots. Jess headed for the avenue as she'd promised. Any other route would have invited the officers to abandon the guard and follow her, asking more questions.

She didn't mind leaving. The municipal officers showing up meant Cassandra Caspie wasn't there or coming anytime soon. If she was, the security guard would have called the city cops in sky-blue, or even the national force in purple. The blue police had prison vans and the purples had AK-47s.

The university's central building was two storeys tall and built in a basic neoclassical style, allowing it to avoid the arts faculty's fate. Instead of knocking it over, the dictator had shown his distaste by changing the institution's name to the generic 'school' and covering any ornate insignia with cement squares. On some of its façades, iron panels with the word SCHOOL were still welded over the original carvings.

The main gate was open, but like the rest of the city, the grounds were almost empty. Jess stood outside, wondering if the municipal policewomen would know how long she hung around.

A figure in a greatcoat walked around her, then stopped.

'Jessie?' It was Boris. They gripped arms and kissed on the cheek, but when Jess went to step back, Boris kept hold of her sleeve. 'What are you doing here?'

'I don't know.' Jess tried to laugh. 'I told the gold police I was heading this way, so here I am.'

'Come inside. You would like coffee?'

The cafés and food vans were closed. Boris led her to one of the rooms the sessional staff used, an odd space that dog-legged around the back of some stairs, with brown carpet and no windows. Two postgrads were in there, side-by-side on a narrow sofa, each staring at a laptop with heavy earphones arced over their heads.

'Don't worry about them,' Boris said from the kitchenette, putting coffee bags into mugs as the kettle boiled. 'They basically live here. We are in their house, so to speak.'

She and Boris sat at a table with their instant coffees and a bowl of dried berries. When preserved, the fruits were said to last forever, but these ones seemed to be rapidly approaching that date.

When they travelled to the east, Jess and Viktor sometimes

foraged for berries. She enjoyed them fresh, the tart meatiness, but in the city they were served with the essence sucked out and sugar sifted over the top to replace the stolen flavour. Wondering if there was some deeper meaning there, Jess politely declined when Boris pointed at the bowl.

She'd assumed Boris wanted to talk about something, but he just sipped from his mug and whistled. Jess glanced at the pair on the couch, trying to work out if they'd swapped places while she wasn't looking, then said to Boris, 'All my English conversation sessions got cancelled. Are your students coming in this week?'

'It is a study break anyway, thank goodness.'

'Has everyone left?'

'Most are still working. As ushers and things.'

'So, the expo *is* good for the economy.'

Boris gave her a wry smile. It made her proud.

'Viktor's been flat out for days,' she said. 'Too bad they aren't paying him.'

'Wheeling and dealing, our Vika.'

His tone sounded tender enough for her to ask, 'Are you two okay?'

Boris furrowed his brow.

'You disagreed about them building the factory,' she reminded him.

'Oh, we disagree on many things.'

She trusted Boris not to judge her when she confessed, 'I don't really know what the issue is. You don't want Viktor to get involved with Elpis?'

'Elpis is not a problem in themselves. I just have other ideas.'

'I know you made a speech about it, but I didn't totally understand.'

Boris was happy to repeat his talking points. 'I think a factory is not the best use of the site. Elpis has much automation, meaning that few jobs are created, and mostly blue-collar. I propose a technological innovation hub for the location instead. Why slave away for a foreign company when we can build business for ourselves?'

'Hmmm,' Jess said, thinking of the solar car competition that led Caspie to create Elpis in the first place.

'There is great brain drain in this country. Our best and brightest go elsewhere.' Boris plucked a dried berry from the plate, put it in his mouth, and winced. He spat into a yellowing serviette and licked the tartness from his lips before continuing. 'In the engineering faculty, over fifty percent of graduates have emigrated within five years.'

'Why can't they do both? Have the factory, and the innovation stuff?'

'That would make too much sense. No, the government must do one thing at a time, and extremely slowly.'

Jess was reaching the limits of her understanding. 'But if Elpis buys the land and pays for the factory, couldn't the government afford to support other industries with that money?'

'Most likely Elpis pays a pittance. The government gives a subsidy to have their factory here and not in another country.'

Jess chewed her lip. 'Are they really that bad?'

On the couch, one of the students ripped the headphone jack from his laptop. 'Fuck this,' he commented to his companion, then stood and stalked from the room.

Her only reaction was to shift so that she was sitting in the middle of the two cushions before continuing to type.

'Are we bothering them?' Jess asked.

'It's not us. Look. Help!' Boris called in the direction of the young woman. 'Help, there is a shark, I am being eaten alive.'

She didn't flinch.

Boris nodded at Jess. 'What was it you were saying?'

'Are Elpis's factories really terrible? Is Viktor doing a bad thing, trying to help win the deal?'

His eyes softened at her worried expression. 'Of course not. Solar panels are good, creating jobs is good. Vika looks out for his fellow man.'

She was confused. 'But you're so opposed.'

'I have a different idea.' He patted her shoulder heartily. 'Despite what many think, Vika and I don't agree on everything. That is healthy, do you think?'

Jess smiled, but she was still troubled. She couldn't remember ever disagreeing with Viktor.

***

Viktor was still out when Jess got back to the flat. She rang to check if he'd be home before her bartending shift but got his voicemail. Soon after, her phone pinged twice. Lena was sending messages to the group chat.

Vika, your boss arrives tomorrow. Be prepared! the first said, followed by an out of focus photo of a sheet of paper. Zooming in, Jess made out the words KING SUITE – CASEY, C. – AIRPORT PICKUP & EARLY CHECK-IN.

She waited for someone else to respond, but there was nothing. They must all be working. Bracing herself to sound dense, she phoned Lena.

'Is that a joke, in the chat?'

'What do you mean?'

'Who's C. Casey?'

Lena clucked. 'It's fake, Jessie. You know from your own hotel that wealthy guests never use their names.'

'But how do you know it's Cassandra Caspie?'

'King Suite. Airport pickup in the limo. Who else do you think?' She heard Lena exhale. 'Especially since the politicians have all dropped out.'

A shiver of anticipation ran through Jess. 'Can you let me know when she gets there?'

'Why?'

'I want to meet her. I'm writing a story for Yara.'

Jess was prepared for Lena to scoff, but her mild tone didn't change. 'I work again in the morning. You can come in with me.'

Jess hummed at the back of her throat, nervous. Would that be stalking? Okay, she'd tried to do the same thing at Penthouse earlier, but it hadn't involved entering the building.

'Otherwise, what?' Lena asked. 'I tell you she arrived, and you try to phone up to her room? She will ignore you.'

Jess knew Lena was right. Her emails to hello@elpis had received boilerplate responses with links to press releases. Besides, if Cassandra Caspie was at the hotel, Jess wouldn't have to talk to her right away. She could come up with a plan. She just needed to know Caspie was there in the flesh.

'Do you know what time she'll arrive?' she asked Lena.

'It's a private jet, so the time is not set. Midmorning is the window,' Lena said. 'My shift starts at ten. I will collect you on the way.'

Rachel
CD13

The acupuncture felt particularly needle-y that morning; the therapist, whose name Rachel hadn't yet caught, digging under her skin as if unearthing rows of splinters. Rachel gasped and sweated, thinking of the email attachment she'd sent to Olga before leaving her hotel room: a loose squiggle above the line for HUSBAND backdated to two months before. There was no space given for a name.

'You are tense,' the therapist murmured, placing the final two acupuncture needles below her belly button. 'We will fix this.'

Rachel knew her tension was mental and emotional, muscular if anything. Surely she didn't have a tense womb. She hated the idea that a woman caused her own infertility by experiencing stress, a claim that ended up being self-fulfilling: I am stressed because I feel stressed. Instead, she tried to tell herself that it couldn't be terrible to relax.

When the only blastocyst that ever developed from one of Rachel's eggs failed to implant, Dr Leonard had no explanation. Or rather, he had several different explanations, which indicated to Rachel that he had no idea what was wrong. Maybe her lining hadn't been receptive, maybe there'd been something wrong with the embryo. Maybe the egg, though more resilient than any other she'd been able to produce, had been deficient. (*Or maybe the sperm was crappy,* Rachel had wanted to suggest. *Maybe it's not always my fault.*) 'Of course,' the doctor added, 'up to fifty percent of embryos just don't implant. It isn't always possible to know why.'

He was always reducing her chances. When the blastocyst reached day five and was ready for transfer, Dr Leonard called her himself; when it was bad news, the embryologists had done it. 'We have reached the final hurdle,' he said. Rachel remembered, because she'd written the words in her journal and underlined them. She'd taken it to mean that all the hurdles were now behind her, but apparently there was one still looming ahead.

When the acupuncturist returned, she turned the lights up very slowly, to transition Rachel out of the meditative state she hadn't been in. 'How do you feel?'

'Very relaxed,' she replied. 'Thank you.'

If she did feel that way—and Rachel was so disconnected from her stupid body that she didn't know whether she was or not—it wouldn't last, because her next appointment was with Olga.

Dressed, she waited alone in the small office, so hungry she could have eaten the desk. She'd had the usual breakfast—egg-white omelette, fruit salad and yoghurt, porridge with dried berries, a cup of mint tea—and her stomach was full enough, but there was something missing: fat, carbs, pleasure. There was an emptiness that only the fragrant bowls of Honey Morning Milk tea came close to satisfying.

This sense of hollowness was probably psychological; she was definitely aggrieved. Other women didn't have to eat like monks to have a chance of getting pregnant. They just went and fucked men. Some of them only ever had to do it once, a concept Rachel was finding more and more unbelievable as time went on.

Today Olga wore a jumpsuit made of dark purple silk, pointed mauve shoes peeking from the hems. Her skin shone bronze like she'd spent two weeks on a beach. 'Mrs Mather. How are you today?'

'Anxious,' Rachel confessed. She wondered if that made her sound guilty, so she clarified, 'About the results of my blood test.'

Olga's eyes searched Rachel's: for weakness, she couldn't help thinking. 'Can you tell me why that is?'

'I like to be able to plan. Not knowing exactly when the transfer will be makes me nervous.' She paused. 'If there's going to be a transfer, I mean.'

'Well, as you know, we have a guarantee.'

This was all over the website and printed materials: if for some reason an embryo transfer could not take place, the cost of treatment was refunded in full. It was one of the things that reassured her, after so many cycles had ended in a waste of time and money.

'Yes,' Rachel said, 'but I'd rather have the chance than the money.'

Olga's face finally registered approval. She reached beneath the desk and pulled out a folder. 'I'm happy to tell you, Mrs Mather, that your hormones and scans are perfect. Ana will administer the injection for ovulation tonight and the transfer will be on Monday.'

The news relieved Rachel's tension more effectively than an hour of acupuncture. She sank back in the seat. 'Oh, that's great.'

'Also, I received the updated signature on your paperwork.' Olga patted the folder with splayed fingers, each perfectly set with lavender nail polish. 'Just in time.'

Rachel decided not to respond, though under Olga's gaze she thought it might be a good idea to wipe under her eyes. It could impress her.

It didn't. Instead, Olga's gaze cooled and set. 'Your husband. I realised I don't know his name.'

It was best for one's lies to be built on a strong foundation of truth. Rachel's brother Antony had taught her that with the stories he told their mother during his bad times.

'Ben,' she told Olga. The squiggle she'd drawn on the form could begin with a B.

'And what does Ben do?'

'He's a schoolteacher. Primary school.' Not sure if the term would translate, Rachel explained, 'Younger kids, around ten years old.'

'A noble profession,' Olga said crisply. 'At least you know, if you do become pregnant, your husband will be so good with children.'

Rachel's throat burned. It was his job that had made Ben not want kids of his own. He was brilliant with them, but he said he knew all too well what kids needed to thrive. He could supply it for thirty hours a week and that was it.

'He's very good with children,' Rachel confirmed. 'And babies.'

Towards the end of their marriage, when she truly couldn't stand Ben, the only thing that softened her towards him was his tenderness with Conrad's twins. In the last weeks she'd stared at a picture of Ben with a boy in the crook of each arm, trying to force herself to love him again. He could be tender. He could be vulnerable. Just not with her.

'He must be sad not to accompany you,' Olga commented.

'He can't get time off during the school term.'

True, true, all of it was true.

'And you couldn't wait, I suppose.'

'No,' Rachel said honestly. 'I couldn't wait.'

Again, respect glinted in Olga's eyes. She swept the folder off the table and back into the slot under the desk without having opened it. Rachel wondered if it really contained her results or was just a prop.

'As I say, your chaperone will administer the injection this evening. Please discontinue with the other medications. Ana will explain the next steps.'

Olga stood, pressing her palms to her thighs, and Rachel noticed a slim gold band on each of her ring fingers. In response, Rachel put her own hands on the desk, hoping Olga would register the thick silver ring from the souvenir shop.

'Good luck, Mrs Mather. I wish you and your husband well.'

***

For the last few days, Rachel had taken dinner as room service, the tray brought up by hotel staff and set on a table by the window so she could eat while looking at the view. That night, in celebration, she met Ana in the private dining room instead, where they were again the only guests.

Unlike at breakfast, this time Ana accepted a plate of her own: vegetable soup, chicken breast, string beans and carrots, with a raspberry rice pudding for dessert. The food of a well-regarded hospital.

Afterwards, Ana accompanied Rachel back to her room. Slung over her shoulder by a long strap, like a jaunty little purse, was a cold pack containing the trigger injection, which had been stored in a hotel fridge while they ate.

'It's not that we think you can't do this yourself,' Ana told Rachel as they came out of the lift. 'It's just part of the program, to have a chaperone do it.'

Rachel didn't mind. She was tired of administering drugs alone, sweating and urging herself to plunge the needle in her belly. It wasn't that it hurt—usually, anyway, though sometimes there was a quick bee-sting sensation—but that it seemed so unnatural. It *was* unnatural, not only because she was forcing sharpened metal into soft skin, but because there was no-one keeping her company. The information video she'd watched during her first ever cycle featured a male partner who stood beside the woman as she stamped herself, patting her arm afterwards and giving her a chaste hug. Like they needed IVF because they'd never learned the concept of sex.

Ana asked her to lie on the bed, tummy up, and lift her shirt to her ribs. Rachel was embarrassed at the pillowy white flesh this revealed. She imagined Ana's stomach to be flat as a plank, peach-coloured and hairless, her navel a perfect innie.

'You would like to count, or just do it?' Ana asked.

Rachel closed her eyes. 'Maybe a countdown?'

'Okay, wiggle your toes.' Surprised by the instruction, Rachel did. 'Three, two, one, and—there.' The pain was mild and momentary, a quick flick with a fingernail. 'Well done.'

Rachel went to sit up, but Ana put a hand on her shoulder. 'Wait, please, there is a little more.'

Ana recapped the injection pen and pushed it through the jaws of a portable hazardous waste container, then dimmed the lights until the room was a cool grey. Returning to the carry bag, she took out a sphere the size of a juggling ball and put it on the bedside table. It was a portable speaker: when Ana touched the top, soft music filtered out.

'This is a stressful time,' Ana said. 'It can help to meditate for a moment, to re-centre.'

Rachel wanted to scream. The acupuncture was bad enough, and the therapy. She didn't want to know her innermost self, she wanted to have a fucking baby.

She jerked as Ana's cool fingers slid around one of her hands. 'A massage,' the young woman explained. Sensing Rachel's reticence, she said, 'It is short.'

Ana worked her knuckles into the meat of Rachel's palm and squeezed along the length of each finger. The music was pleasant. Rachel considered following the instructions and meditating, but she was never sure what that was meant to involve. Instead, she told herself that what would be would be. The injection was done, and soon she'd ovulate the egg that had been carefully grown on both sides of the world. It was in the hands of science now.

As promised, the music slipped into silence after a few minutes and Ana delivered the final bit of pressure to Rachel's left thumb. Rachel took a moment to open her eyes.

Ana stood by the door with the cooler bag and waste container. 'That's all for today,' she said gently. 'We advise a quiet evening and an early night. No medication tomorrow.'

'I have the day off?' Rachel asked, groggy.

'We will leave at ten o'clock for your appointments, but there will be no injections.' Ana gave a stunning smile. 'Your body can rest.'

Saying goodbye, the chaperone let herself out.

Rachel lay on the bed for a minute, then dragged herself up and went to her window to look down at the hotel forecourt. Soon a streetlight illuminated the top of Ana's head, dark hair streaming behind her as she crossed to the waiting town car. As soon as the passenger door closed, the driver released the brake, completed the arc of the slip lane, and turned into an almost empty street.

Rachel closed the curtains and got into the shower, gentle with the soap on her bruised belly. When she was dry, she changed into the most attractive clothes she'd brought, slim jeans and a leather jacket, then set off for the Old Town café.

It was her fourth visit in three days: she'd been there only a few hours earlier, after the clinic. She really had meant to go to the cathedral that time, but a block away from the bridge she saw a road closure sign ahead and lost heart. The Honey Morning Milk had been calling her, and so had Dimitri. When she arrived to find another woman there, Rachel felt a sharp pinch of jealousy. She sat in the café for far too long, hoping Dimitri would show he preferred her company, but he'd divided his time between tables equally. Sensing it was becoming a stand-off between her and the other woman, Rachel had given up and left.

Now she thought she might have sex with Dimitri.

She had an ovum in the chamber, ready to launch. It was a stunning outcome when she thought about it. Over three years of treatment, she'd needed higher and higher doses of hormones to produce fewer and fewer eggs. Now, somehow, she was back on a regimen Dr Leonard had first prescribed when she was thirty-eight and offered intra-uterine insemination, only this time it had produced a textbook result: a ripe egg at day fourteen.

It might be the last ever. If this transfer didn't work, she wouldn't try with the other two embryos.

Her feelings of envy at the café had sparked an idea that solidified during her meditation with Ana. The egg was supposed to be a means to an end; ovulation would push her into the next stage of her cycle, her uterine lining becoming receptive to an embryo. No-one at the clinic cared about the egg. It could have a shitty shell, too tough or too weak; it might be missing chromosomes or have too many. Maybe, if pierced, it'd be hollow. But it was also a lottery ticket, one Rachel may never have again.

It was close to nine o'clock as she crossed the History Bridge, emotion pushing in a big bubble against her diaphragm. IVF patients weren't meant to have sex: all the clinics she'd been to said so. Aside from the fact that it could result in a twin pregnancy, which was higher risk, Rachel was meant to be resting, not engaging in any physical activity that could upset the delicate equilibrium the medications and acupuncture and massages and therapy had brought about. She was supposed to relax.

Wishful thinking was trailed by self-loathing. Propositioning Dimitri and having second thoughts about it were both pointless, because it wouldn't work. If cycle after cycle of medical intervention had failed, then surely a mystery egg and ten minutes behind the swinging kitchen door had no chance.

But what if? The story she'd planned to tell if she returned home pregnant, the one about a mystery man and one wild night: it could be the truth. Other women got pregnant the same way. This was something she told herself all the time. Other people got pregnant. It was possible to get pregnant at forty-two and single.

The café was empty; the other woman had gone. Dimitri was on a stool by the counter scrolling through his phone when the door clinked, and he seemed pleased to see her. 'Are you still open?'

'Yes, of course.' His eyes glittered and she felt a pull in her pelvis. Was the injection working already? 'Another bowl of tea?'

'Please,' she said. A sudden rush of bravery led Rachel to mount the stool beside him. 'I thought we could keep one another company.'

***

Later, Rachel took a book and went down to the hotel lobby. If she watched another subtitled rerun of *Friends*, she'd lose her mind. But the open space was too distracting—not because it was busy, but because it wasn't. She was the only one sitting in any of the artfully angled lounge chairs, and the reception staff had nothing to do. They stood in a semicircle, murmuring, one leaving the desk every so often to refill Rachel's water glass.

'Quiet night,' she commented when the third clerk came over. They were taking turns. She'd seen another lift a silent phone from behind the desk and hold it to his ear, then replace it and shrug at his colleagues.

He gave an uneasy smile. 'Perhaps the planes are delayed.'

After twenty minutes, Rachel couldn't stand it anymore. She felt the wistful eyes of the workers on her as she went into the bar.

To her relief, there were a handful of people at tables, drinking and eating snacks. There were too many staff here too. One, the English girl who'd been on duty the night Rachel arrived, brought a drinks menu over. 'What can I get you?'

Rachel hadn't intended to switch from water; all she wanted was a change of scenery. 'Um—'

'Oh, sorry.' The woman took the menu from Rachel and flipped it. 'We also have non-alcoholic.'

Frowning, Rachel turned it back and scanned the options, suddenly dying for a big glass of rosé. A bowl of it, like the tea Dimitri had served her. Or, given the chill outside, a fragrant cider with nutmeg and chunks of boiled pear. Or a beer, or Coke. Anything unnatural, devoid of nutritional benefit. Something to wet the bottom of the deep cavern of need that was cracking open within her.

She couldn't decide.

'We do mocktails. Or cocktails.' The bartender raised her eyebrows. 'How about a Love Potion?'

'What's that?'

'Give me a second,' the bartender said, taking the menu with her. In a couple of minutes she came back from the bar holding two martini glasses with zigzag stems. Both drinks were pink, with pink sugar dusted on the surface and a slice of strawberry hooked over the rim. 'Lefty is the regular one, righty's the non-alcoholic version.' The bartender squinted for a second. 'My right, that is. So, your left.'

Not wanting to waste weeks of sobriety on something that tasted terrible, Rachel took the one without alcohol. When she tipped a little into her mouth, it was delicious.

'That's fantastic,' she said, smacking her lips and feeling the sugary granules. The faint tartness of the powdered berries took the too-sweet edge off the drink. Giddy with determination to be a bad girl, or her version of it, she put down the mocktail and lifted the alcoholic one.

'Let me show you something,' the bartender said. She nodded towards the drink Rachel had abandoned. 'Do you mind—?'

'Go ahead.'

The bartender positioned the glass so that the strawberry sliver covered her mouth like a rosebud kiss. She demonstrated how to bite through the flesh and suck shallowly so that the pink liquid filtered into her mouth.

Rachel did the same. Whether it was the addition of the mushy fruit or the alcohol, it tasted even better. When she'd finished the whole cocktail she chewed the soggy remainder of the strawberry, warmth filling the pit in her gut. 'That's just what I needed.'

'It's a good luck charm, too.'

'What?'

'It can bring true love. Did you have an empty stomach when you came in? That's part of the legend.'

It took Rachel a moment to respond, her mood sinking. 'I was drinking water in the lobby.' Wanting to pierce the bartender's good humour, she added, 'And I had dinner earlier.'

'Oh.' The bartender looked unaffected. 'I mean, it's just a story.'

The taste was souring in Rachel's mouth. 'How much alcohol is in this?'

'Not much.' She glanced back at the bottles stacked behind the bar. 'I did offer you the mocktail.'

Rachel put her forehead in the crook of her thumb and forefinger and sighed.

'Hang on,' the bartender said, leaving the table for a second time. A little while later, just as Rachel was about to go back to her room, she reappeared with a woven basket of fries. 'If you're going to cheat on a diet, this is probably better.'

Rachel pushed a handful into her mouth, not caring what she looked like. The warm, salty greasiness hit the spot almost as much as the cocktail and brought less regret.

The bartender watched. 'It's all on the house, by the way,' she said. 'Sorry. It's been a weird night.'

Rachel wondered for a second if the woman knew about Dimitri. Maybe she'd passed the café on her way to work and saw them through the window. Not that there was anything to see. After Rachel climbed onto a stool and made her weak attempt at flirtation, he'd brought out her third Honey Morning Milk of the day wearing a gold band on his ring finger she was certain hadn't been there before. She had to finish the tea while they pretended that she hadn't made a sad, obvious little come on, Dimitri holding out his phone to show pictures of his wife and newborn daughter as she drank. Just when she thought she was free, he went out the back and got her another bowl. 'I told you, the caffeine is nothing,' he said brightly, as if that's what made her face so red.

By the time she finished her final bowl, she knew she'd never drink that tea again.

Jess
Wednesday

The Palace Hotel, where Lena worked, was, in Jess's opinion, the most beautiful building in the city. It had been the residence of the royal family, much loved rulers whose reign almost extinguished itself after the king and queen's only daughter died of the flu in 1919. When the Second World War broke out, the ageing royals loaned the property to the army and went to Switzerland. In the void between the end of hostilities and the monarchs' return, the communists had assumed power, declared them exiled and put their heir, a nephew, in prison. To show their disdain for the divine right of kings and royal profligacy, the leader claimed the palace for 'administrative use', or so he called it. When democracy was reinstated forty years later, it was revealed to contain the libraries of the secret police.

Unlike Penthouse, which took decades to construct, the palace was converted into a hotel quickly. It was the capital's only five-star accommodation: the New Town Hotel where Jess bartended had four-and-a-half. She and Viktor couldn't afford a single night in even the most basic room, but she'd seen pictures on social media of the clawfoot bathtubs, lush carpets and goose-feather pillows. It made sense that if Cassandra Caspie wasn't in Penthouse, this was where she'd stay.

Jess waited for Lena on the Promenade, at the base of the Twin Bridges. The area was even more deserted than the day before, the boardwalk picked clean. Some work group or other had left crowd control barriers lying on their sides, so the bars touched the ground and the feet stuck up, ready to trip whoever passed too close. The area was so quiet Jess could hear the tinkle of love padlocks on the Industrial Bridge shifting in the breeze. Overhead, the sky was the palest blue, with a thin line of white cloud in the east. Jess wondered if the policewomen from yesterday really had heard rumours of rain, or if they were trying to mess with her head.

Lena arrived dressed in her pearlescent white puffer, black skirt, thick tights and sneakers. Her work shoes were in one gloved hand, and she took Jess's elbow with the other. 'Quick. If you slow down, you'll freeze.'

The Palace was on the Old Town side of the canal, across the perimeter road from Castle Hill. They saw no-one on their walk, and Jess could almost convince herself there'd been an apocalypse. Banners for the expo clicked against flagpoles, met only by the distant moan of metal on metal as a tram rounded a curve in the distance.

Lena led Jess around the back of the hotel, where half a dozen cleaning staff sat on a narrow service patio waiting to start their shift. Each held a styrofoam cup of black coffee, and, like Lena, wore polyester skirts and dense stockings beneath their heavy coats. Though Jess's civvies showed she didn't belong, the circle opened to accept her. One of the younger women filled a cup and passed it over.

'Bryna!' Lena greeted her. 'Have you heard about Miss Caspie? Has she arrived?' To Jess, she explained, 'Bryna's brother works night shift.'

Bryna re-capped the large thermos. 'Who?'

'Caspie? The solar panel lady? She is coming in by private plane.'

'Oh, yes.' Bryna extended her neck and tipped the last of the coffee into her mouth, then rubbed her face with the back of her glove. 'Sergei didn't say.'

'They're putting her in King Suite,' Lena prompted.

An older woman broke off her conversation to interrupt. 'There is a man in King Suite.' Her eyebrows danced. 'A man, and someone he claims is his secretary.'

'No, the man and his secretary left,' Lena said. 'The solar panel woman comes today. They have her down as Casey.'

'Left?' the older woman scoffed. 'No-one leaves this week. Just more and more checking in.'

'I heard there were cancellations,' Bryna said. 'Sergei got some calls overnight.'

Jess was mildly alarmed at this, but no-one else reacted. 'So, the man hasn't checked out of King Suite?' she asked the older woman. 'Who's coming in on the jet, then?'

'The man may leave today,' Bryna interrupted. 'Or they put her in Queen Suite. More suitable, I think. And it is empty so far.'

'Queen, please!' another of the cleaners interjected. Her left ear was crowded with silver rings, while the right one was bare. The unevenness made Jess itch. 'She is silly to show her face. Nobody wants her here. If she comes, there are protests for sure.'

Concerned, Jess looked at Lena.

'She is a shapeshifter,' the earringed woman continued with excitement. 'I saw her lizard eyes on the news.'

'Natalya,' Lena admonished. 'Really.'

'No, the woman is dangerous in a different way,' the older cleaner corrected. 'Her plans affect us negatively.'

'You mean the big government subsidies to build the factory?' Jess asked.

The cleaner blinked at Jess, who wondered if something had been lost in translation.

'Who is in King Suite, then?' Bryna asked. 'Is the man Casey?'

The older cleaner held up her empty cup and squeezed until the styrofoam cracked. As if responding to a bell, the others started filing through a staff door into the hotel.

'Wait,' Jess said. 'Is she coming, or not?'

'I have to go,' Lena said. 'Enter the lobby, order a drink. Watch the door. If I hear anything, I will try to let you know.'

It wasn't until Lena had disappeared with the others that Jess realised Caspie might come in through a private entrance like this one, avoiding any media or protesters. But if Jess loitered around the staff entrance the municipal police might come past again; the note of their encounter the day before could mean even more scrutiny. Waiting in the lobby would draw less attention, so it'd have to do.

The hotel lobby was ballroom-sized, dotted with overstuffed armchairs from which visitors could order hot drinks in the morning and cocktails later. Jess chose a spot where she could see both the front entrance and the bank of lifts, and a waiter took her order for a coffee with milk. This was a venue for tourists and socialites, notoriously overpriced, and Jess winced as she signed the bill. It was an investment, she told herself. Investment. Investment.

Doormen in waistcoats moved quickly, greeting people as they entered. Jess wondered where everyone was coming from, since the Promenade had been deserted when she and Lena arrived.

Some guests went to check in and a few took seats in the lobby, but most headed straight for the pair of gold-plated lifts at the far end. When their doors slid open, they were always empty. No-one appeared to be leaving the hotel.

Jess sipped from her bowl slowly, not wanting to have to buy anything else. She was down to a cold puddle when a man and woman came in and took seats near her. They gave their coats and scarves to the waiter and ordered tea in English, then pulled laptops and tablets from their shoulder bags. Jess's heartbeat quickened when she saw the logo of an American news channel on the flaps. She flipped a notebook from her pocket to lie on the seat beside her and held her pen in a fist by her hip.

'Did you get the schedule?' the woman asked her companion. 'How many private planes is that, I wonder?'

'Private plane travel to discuss climate solutions.'

The woman tilted her screen towards him. 'Look at that, though. Even if half of them don't end up coming, it's completely fucked.'

The waiter interrupted with their drinks and as she turned to say thanks the female journalist's eyes met Jess's. Realising it was too late to look away, Jess smiled, the lid of the pen digging into her palm.

The woman's attention slid back to the laptop, her expression unchanged. 'These press releases are nuts. Did you get the one from that town action committee saying the factory's going to destroy their land? The proposed site isn't anywhere near them.'

'It's that grandfather conspiracy crap,' the man said. 'You know the one?'

Grandfather conspiracy, Jess wrote, stiff-wristed.

'No?' the woman asked.

'Something about how his farm was stolen from under him so she's back to get revenge.'

'Why does she care? She should be bowing at their goddamn feet. No way she'd be a billionaire today if her family still lived here.'

The man's phone tinkled, and he took it out to read the message. 'Well, the farmers don't need to worry. Apparently, Elpis is scaling back.' He slid the device back into his trouser pocket. 'Continuing to explore synergies, blah, blah.'

'The first domino,' his colleague mused, sipping her tea. 'What'd I tell you? Fucking small fry. I don't care what she's trying to avenge, no way in hell was Cassandra Caspie going to make *this* her grand appearance.'

'Can't blame them for getting excited. They'll probably never make the world stage again.'

Stretching, the woman looked around the lobby, her eyes again meeting Jess's. This time she grimaced.

'This fucking country,' she told her colleague. 'At least the tea is good.'

***

A couple of hours since her walk along the deserted Promenade and the streets were already filling up again. There were half a dozen passengers on the tram Jess took from the Palace to the suburbs. As it rattled along the track she called Viktor, who was able to answer for the first time all week. Another bad sign.

When she reported what the journalists had said, he sounded distant but certain: Elpis was just streamlining. They were still dedicated to the project.

'Are you going to be able to squeeze in any work?' she asked. 'Maybe at the buffet?'

'The meetings continue, my darling. And anyway, the buffet remains closed.'

Alighting near Yara's building, Jess wound her scarf around her head like a mummy and drove her fists into her pockets. Shrubs trembled as she stalked past. At the corner she took a moment to square her shoulders, using the window of a closed dentist to check her reflection and give herself words of confidence.

A shadow stopped behind her. 'There is no need to impress me, of course.'

Jess turned in greeting, but Yara shook her head. Her face was long and gloomy. 'Come up. The coffee shop is shut, like everything else.'

The newspaper office was contained in a narrow room half the size of Jess and Viktor's apartment. The end with windows was given over to Yara's desk, with a disused flatplan and overstuffed shelving units in the centre and trestle tables along the far walls that freelancers could use as a workspace if they relocated piles of papers. Yara had papered the ceiling in old front pages, making the space darker than it had to be. Several hung by a couple of corners, threatening to detach and deliver a papercut to the skull of anyone below.

Jess dragged a stool over. There was a kettle sitting on a dirty plate on the carpet, and Yara bent down to switch it on. At first Jess thought the intermittent groans were part of the machine, then realised that they were coming from Yara.

'I hope you don't want milk,' the editor said, lifting teabags from a clouded glass jar and sniffing them. 'There isn't any.'

'This is fine.'

The kettle switched off with a springy sound. Yara dropped two bags into chipped mugs and poured water over the top, then passed Jess one. The hot liquid within had turned mauve, indigo threads spooling up from the sunken teabag.

Sitting back in her chair and lifting the liquorice-smelling brew to her mouth, Yara commented, 'You know the expo is off.'

'It's cancelled?'

'Of course not *cancelled*.' Yara rolled her eyes at this foreigner, unable to understand nuance. 'It will go ahead to empty rooms. Mostly empty,' she amended, in case Jess took her literally. 'But all the big guests are out.'

'Like Cassandra Caspie.'

'So I heard.' Yara put her elbows on the desk and leaned closer. 'And Viktor? Will he speak to her directly?'

'They're still working with Elpis, but he said he probably won't meet her,' Jess admitted.

'So. No article.' Yara sat back and looked out the window. 'Another blank page.'

'I could write about the cancellations?'

'I will do that. It takes five minutes; just google the names of those who promised to come, copy and paste.' She pouted. 'Perhaps this is good news. The list may fill the whole paper.'

'Could we explore why, though?' Jess used the pronoun purposefully, and Yara's frown showed she'd caught it. 'The public might want to know the reasons they decided not to come. What does it say about, about—' She was falling apart under Yara's severe stare. 'About the state of the world?'

'Jessica.' Yara spoke clearly and precisely. 'The reasons why things fail to happen do not make a story. Why the man did not get hit by the tram: he was not on the tracks. Why the building did not fall over: it was built securely.'

'But this is different.'

'We are a street paper, arts focused, yes? I'm writing about the expo because nothing else is happening. Now even the expo is barely happening.'

'Why, though?' Jess was aware that she sounded naïve. 'What made it all fall over?'

'What do you think? They called it a final attempt at solving the climate crisis. Through the innovation of business, we would escape what business innovation had caused. The fact that we believed even for a moment shows desperation, do you think?' She clicked her tongue. 'You saw the editorial in the tabloid this morning?'

Jess hadn't. It was hard for her to read the language even without the formal style the daily paper adopted. Usually, Viktor read out the most important articles, but he'd had back-to-back meetings for days.

A copy lay on Yara's desk. She opened to the inside cover and handed it over. The first thing Jess noticed was the by-line: Boris. 'Expo must be boycotted if we are serious about the planet', urged the title. Why hadn't he mentioned this yesterday? 'He's a friend of mine.'

'Yes,' Yara said, unimpressed. 'Mine too. And Bory is right, not that it matters.'

Jess skimmed what she could. His argument seemed to be that holding an expo on green tech was just more faffing about; they needed to start implementing solutions right away. This didn't mean building the factory, he went on to say. To put all their efforts into producing solar panels would be like swimming in place while the ship sank. They needed to create radical solutions for themselves. Build the innovation hub.

She passed the paper back to Yara. 'What happens now?'

Yara looked amused. 'Nothing. The expo takes place with no guests. The government says it was a success. The daily news reports both sides: success, failure. They discuss whether to build the factory until the technology is out of date, and the café reopens next week.' She frowned at her inky tea. 'Thank God.'

Jess didn't know whether to be relieved or upset. The article had been getting away from her, but they needed the fifty crowns. Especially with what she'd just wasted on coffee at the Palace.

'Okay,' she told Yara. 'Well, thanks for the opportunity.'

'You will need something else.'

'What?'

'For the page. Do you have an idea?'

'I—well, I said I could write about the reasons why the expo—'

'No.' Yara shook her head, perfect bob staying in place as her features moved beneath it. 'Boring, I said. Another idea.'

'I don't really ...' Jess tried to think. It was great to keep the assignment, but now she'd have to come up with something else to fill a whole page. A profile of Sandy and her pretzel cart? The secrets of the Palace Hotel cleaning crew? An investigation into Vera's conspiracy theories? Yara might like the last two, though not as newspaper articles.

'There is so little happening this week, I am like a snake who swallows its own head. My usual writers have left. They knew better than to write about the expo.'

Jess tried not to feel more insulted than she should.

'If I have to fill another page myself...' Yara's features shadowed. 'And anyway, I think you may need the thirty crowns.'

Jess's heart dropped. 'I thought it was fifty?'

'It was fifty for a billionaire. Do you know another billionaire? No,' Yara said before Jess could respond. 'Because Viktor would not introduce you to the first one.'

Rachel
1 day post ovulation/1DPO

Rachel was collected before breakfast and taken to the clinic for an early ultrasound to confirm ovulation. If for some reason the injection hadn't worked, there was still the chance to try again without wasting the embryo.

As Ana touched Rachel's shoulder to guide her through the doorway and a nurse stepped forward to take her arm, it occurred to her that patients were never allowed to wander alone in the facility. If they weren't confined to a small space, a chaperone or nurse or receptionist was there to lead them. Like a baby passed from arm to arm, unable to look after itself.

She put on the mauve paper gown and pulled back the curtain. The three nurses stood in a line, smiling, then one broke away and brought Rachel to the examination table. Learned helplessness, Rachel thought; after all, she'd stood there in the open cubicle waiting for direction.

She assumed the position, legs splayed below a sheet scented with lavender. As with all her other ultrasounds, one nurse narrated in English while the second guided the probe and the third made notes in Rachel's file. One or two of the nurses were different each time she saw them, and they performed different roles on different days. Most, if not all of them, must know English then. Having worked this out, she tried not to be suspicious when they chatted in their own language during scans. It would be for precision, not so they could say things about her that she couldn't understand.

'So, Mrs Mather,' the day's translator said. Her hair was cut into a short, punky style and her nostril had an indent where a ring had been removed. 'Today we have a brief check to make sure the egg has left the ovary.'

Though Rachel was sure it had—very early in the morning she'd been woken by a sharp ripping pain along the left side of her abdomen, a sensation she only had on follicle stimulating hormones—she still felt anxious.

The nurse raised the top half of the table so Rachel could see the screen more clearly. 'Do not worry, Mrs Mather. We have never failed.'

The other nurses nodded.

'Don't let me be the first,' Rachel said.

The nurse with the ultrasound wand held it up and said something. The punky nurse translated, 'A slight pressure, please.'

Rachel held her breath. The device went in.

'Please do not worry,' the nurse repeated. 'Look. You see.'

Her ovary had been found, and the crater of the follicle rose up on the screen. The third nurse used her forearms to hold the clipboard to her chest and clapped with delight.

'You are on your way, Mrs Mather.' The wand slid out of Rachel with a rush of heat, and she gasped. The punky nurse squeezed her arm. 'I will help you get dressed.'

Rachel let her.

***

After the scan they took Rachel to yet another small room, where her usual breakfast was waiting. There was meditation afterwards— thank God a masseuse didn't touch her right after she'd eaten— before she went into another session with Olga.

Rachel had grown to dread meeting with the clinic manager. She preferred group therapy, which was held on alternate days, though it was painful in a different way. The day before, Ian had asked them all to articulate why they wanted to be parents. Rachel was envious of Harper, who was able to sit back, stone-faced, while the others shared. Meg had sobbed through her explanation and Ian made encouraging noises, pretending to understand what she was saying. Warwick wanted to sit out because he already had kids, like Harper, but Ian made him confess that he wanted a legacy of children of both sexes.

Gabby was next. Instead of answering the question, she described one of her earlier trips to the clinic, a peer group meeting just like this one.

'There was a mother and daughter who'd come together. The mother was in her seventies, maybe eighties. She was the daughter's support person. The daughter was trying to get pregnant on her own.'

Surprised at the indiscretion, Rachel had looked at Ian for signs of alarm, but he just nodded Gabby on.

'The mother was single too, and always had been, so they only ever had one another.' Warwick wasn't reacting to the story. Had he been there? Rachel wondered. Did he remember them? 'Now, the mother was getting older, and she realised she was going to leave her daughter alone. She wanted her to have a child, so she could experience the same companionship.'

Rachel was appalled. She imagined growing up enmeshed with her mother like that; Jean being here for her treatment, for her therapy. She felt lucky she could lie to her mother.

'And what does that story mean to you?' Ian asked.

Gabby shrugged. 'Just that it's not what I want. I don't want to be a parent like that.'

'Well, you won't be,' Warwick had said gruffly.

Rachel wondered if he knew the other way that statement could be interpreted.

As soon as Ian finished yesterday's session, Gabby had risen from her seat and gone to Rachel. 'Could I go back to the hotel with you? Warwick's having our driver take him to the airport.'

'He's leaving?' Rachel asked, shocked. They didn't seem to be getting on very well, but she didn't think it was bad enough for him to leave her in the middle of treatment.

'Just for the night. He's got a meeting in Frankfurt tomorrow, then he's coming right back.'

Warwick joined them, kissing his wife on the top of the head. He had a small rolling case with him and held a suit bag. 'You'll be alright without me?'

'I'll pine, of course,' Gabby said drily, looking at Rachel.

The gathering drew the attention of Meg and Harper, who floated over. 'What's up, guys?' Meg asked, forcing casualness. Despite its aim of bringing them together, after the previous group session the five of them hadn't interacted at all, just lowered their gaze to the floor and filed out.

'I'm heading off overnight,' Warwick said. 'My flight's at four.'

'Are you going straight to the airport?' Harper asked, spotting his luggage. 'Gabby, do you want to come back in our car?'

With the driver and the chaperone, their vehicle would be full. Gabby looked at Rachel again, but she took the excuse to drift towards the door, smiling apologetically. She heard Harper suggest 'Maybe we could go into the Old Town together—' as she slipped out and cancelled her own loose plans to see the cathedral.

She couldn't say why she didn't want to get close to Gabby. Rachel had friends at home, though there were issues there, too. Her closest girlfriends, Devan and Mandy, each had an eight-year-old daughter and a son two years younger, the boys born in the same week, even. Their husbands were now best mates, and it was natural for the eight of them to do family things together: community events for kids, early weekend breakfasts, messy play, junior soccer. There was a standing invitation for Rachel to come to any of it, and sometimes she did, but she found it both tedious and stressful watching little ones discover the world. She ended up wanting to parent them but knew she couldn't and shouldn't. Instead she had to watch Dev's oldest ruin books that didn't belong to her and Mandy's son get teased on the playground because his mother thought he'd develop resilience by working things out for himself. It smarted that Dev and Mandy were so different in how they approached things but still shared an understanding so deep that Rachel could never dig all the way down to it. Even if she became a parent herself, she'd always be years behind; the others would see her as following their guiding light.

She'd probably done something similar when her friends were in new couples and she'd been with Ben forever. They'd been the first to get married, after five years together, and when Dev and Mandy each did it after three years it annoyed Rachel a bit, like they hadn't put in the work.

Mandy and Wen wanted kids quickly, and before they even got married, they'd ditched their Mount Lawley unit for a family home in the suburbs. At the housewarming, Rachel couldn't relax, like a bad fortune she'd been warned of was on the verge of coming true. Then, when Mandy was six months pregnant, Dev showed up to lunch with a strange, dizzy expression and told them with her face in her hands. She and Patrick had been putting off having kids until some magical day, and the day was now. After Dev finished giggle-weeping at feeling Mandy's daughter kick, they'd turned to Rachel and insisted that nothing would change. She'd had no choice but to believe them.

The day she told them about the divorce Mandy and Dev were mirrors, each cradling a toddler in one arm and inverting a bottle over his soft little face with the other, their expressions concerned but distant. Despite the trials of having young kids, neither of them could imagine splitting up with their partners, Dev because she adored Paddy more than ever now and Mandy because she needed Wen's income, and it was better the devil you knew.

Her friends who didn't have children were hard work in a different way. There were two ex-colleagues she sometimes went for drinks with, Anouk and Danielle, both in their late forties and proudly childfree, but when they'd tried to get together in sober daylight, they had nothing else in common. Her single neighbour had a story more awful than Rachel's because Bridget was *desperate* for a baby—she used the word herself—and often cried about how she'd missed her chance and should have stayed with one or another toxic ex long enough to get knocked up.

Rachel's yearning didn't feel as naked as Bridget's, but she couldn't identify with Anouk and Dani either. It was why she hadn't told anyone what she was doing: she'd never get the right reaction, because she didn't know what that reaction was. Gabby was the person who might understand her best, and Rachel didn't want that to go wrong, either.

Today in Olga's office there was a large unframed canvas propped up against one wall, pink and purple splashed across it in a way that reminded Rachel of a Rorschach test. Her gaze drifted until she noticed how, in one corner, the brushstrokes formed the pear-like shape of a uterus; in another, pink curves with a puce oval between them became a swaddled newborn in a mother's arms.

Though in a way she was closer to motherhood than ever, Rachel still felt the immeasurable distance between her and the reality of holding her own baby. It was still as impressionistic, as abstract, as the painting.

Olga had chosen darker purples today, down to the mottled suede of her ankle books. Sitting, she cupped her hands on her knees. 'Mrs Mather. I hear you have good news.'

'Yes, I ovulated.'

Olga's smile was a few millimetres too wide. It was a witchy smile. 'We have never had a failure there.' She appraised Rachel. 'But you were worried.'

'I feel like I have bad luck.' Rachel's throat thickened. 'Nothing's gone right so far.'

'I know it is difficult. There are many unlucky cases here. People travel as a final step when nothing has worked. And though we cannot guarantee a child, we can give patients the peace of mind that they've done everything possible in their attempt.'

They sat quietly for a moment, absorbing that.

'You and your husband,' Olga said. Rachel dreaded the resumption of the topic. 'What will you do if you aren't able to become parents?'

Rachel could only shake her head. For now, her future stopped in two weeks' time, when she learned the outcome of the transfer.

'If you aren't successful this time, you may wish to transfer the remaining two embryos together. The doctor would approve, due to your age.'

Two embryos could mean twins. Like the risk she took trying to seduce Dimitri. Rachel inhaled sharply.

'Others explore surrogacy. Adoption, either from here or

elsewhere. Fostering a needy child.' Olga paused. 'Some decide to make their peace with being childless. They focus elsewhere. Have you and your husband discussed this?'

'We—we're taking things one step at a time.'

'It must be difficult, being here alone.'

Rachel couldn't admit she was used to it. 'It's not ideal.'

Olga took Rachel's file from beneath the desk, opened it and began to write.

Rachel looked at the art again. Maybe the pear was just a shape, the pink curves and the puce-coloured bean accidents of brushwork.

Olga paused with her pen to the paper. 'When does your husband arrive?'

Coldness pierced Rachel's solar plexus. 'Pardon me?'

'When does your husband arrive?'

'He …' she faltered under Olga's gaze. There was no ambiguous response to this. 'He isn't coming. He has to work.'

'He isn't coming,' Olga repeated. She didn't write this down. 'Mrs Mather. Unfortunately, Mr Mather will have to be here.'

Mr Mather was Rachel's dead father, or her two brothers. Ben had never been a Mather, just as she'd never taken his last name. She'd never been a Mrs anything. Mrs Mather was Jean. This was all roleplay, bullshit. Rachel's heart thundered in her chest. She pictured Ben at the whiteboard, kiddies watching from their desks. Even if he'd take leave for her, even if she could afford another airfare—for what, forty-eight hours? Twenty-four?—it was ridiculous, impossible.

The chill was replaced by heat, anger. 'Well, he can't. I told you that from the start.'

Olga shuffled through the file as if being filmed. 'This has not been noted anywhere,' she announced.

Rachel wanted to scream. If there was a camera in here, there'd be proof they had this fucking conversation two days ago.

'Of course, we only provide services for married opposite sex couples who need assistance to conceive.'

'Of course,' Rachel mimicked, trying to keep the sarcasm out of her voice.

'We expect both parents to be present during treatment, for the embryo transfer at least. It is, after all, a kind of conception.'

'Not really, though,' Rachel snapped.

Olga's eyebrows went up.

'The conception occurred in the lab, didn't it? When the egg was fertilised.'

'If you and Mr Mather wish to become parents, the psychology is very important. Yes.' She closed the file. 'Your egg reserve is low. Mr Mather has no sperm count. You cannot conceive on your own. But it is an important stage in the process for you to be together when the baby'—she shook her head—'the *embryo* becomes one with the body of the mother. This is the closest to natural conception you will get, but it helps to set the idea in your minds that the baby is yours.'

'The embryo *is* mine,' Rachel said. *I paid for it*, she added silently. Her fingers gripped the chair. 'I'm sure that would be a magical experience, but Ben has to work. He can't come.'

Olga sighed. 'All I can say to you, Mrs Mather, is that the law of this country states that fertility services are only available to opposite sex married couples. Both members of the couple are required to be present at the time of service, barring extraordinary circumstances.'

'Aren't our circumstances extraordinary?'

Olga didn't respond.

A hot, sick layer settled over the top of Rachel's stomach. 'But Ben signed the form.'

'It was just preliminary, of course.'

Rachel put a hand over her eyes.

'I am not trying to upset you, Mrs Mather. I am only reminding you of the policy. I do not wish for this to come to nothing. For you to be out of pocket with nothing to show for it.'

Rachel couldn't speak; if her mouth opened, she'd either cry or be sick.

'Mrs Mather.' Olga's voice softened. 'You will understand. The expo begins tomorrow, and this is a time of great attention in the city. You see how things must be done the correct way.'

'But I told you,' Rachel insisted. 'I told you from the beginning that it would just be me.'

'Again.' Olga tapped her pen. 'We do not have this in writing.'

'I don't know what I'm supposed to do. I thought it was okay. You said—'

Olga interrupted coolly. 'If it is not in my notes, then it was not said, Mrs Mather.'

'Can Ben—' Rachel attempted to draw her hand from her face, but it was like staring into the sun. 'Can he write you an email, a statement to say that he'd love to be here but of course he can't, he's got work, he has to earn money to pay for the treatment and for the upkeep of our future child, embryo?'

Chair legs rustled against the carpet. 'Unfortunately, this cannot be accepted. I'm sorry for the confusion, Mrs Mather.'

When Rachel uncovered her eyes, Olga was gazing down at her.

'I don't want to cause you unnecessary stress at this vital time. I'm sure you will be able to work things out with your husband.'

***

In the waiting room, things were subdued. The receptionists wouldn't meet Rachel's eye.

'Are you alright?' Ana asked, not waiting for an answer before leading her out.

The traffic had picked up a bit. The driver stayed below the speed limit, her hands tight on the wheel, mouth set. A limousine cut across them and she sucked air through her teeth but said nothing.

Rachel's panic was growing. There was no question of being able to get Ben here in the next four days. If they refused her on the day of the transfer, as Olga had implied, an embryo would've been thawed for nothing, wasted. She should cancel now, eat the cost, but at least leave the embryo on ice for another chance.

Another chance, like she'd be able to find a husband in a couple of months. And anyway, she'd already resolved that this was going to be her last try; if she left, there was no coming back. She couldn't put herself through this again.

The driver turned onto the street that led to the hotel, but said something to Ana and kept heading west, passing it. Rachel wondered if they were taking her to the airport, kicking her out.

'You need a break,' Ana commented. 'We would like to take you somewhere.'

The avenue ended at the dual carriageway that ran along Castle Hill. They parked. 'Have you seen the view?' Ana asked. Rachel shook her head. 'Now is a nice time, maybe.'

When they got out Rachel noticed the weather was the warmest it had been. The air was soft on her cheeks and brought the smell of grass, like it really was spring.

Cobblestone steps had been cut into the hillside. The incline was steep, and Rachel had to take off her coat and carry it. The youngest of them, Ana, moved pixie-light, and the driver was somewhere in between, her own jacket still zipped when they reached the top.

The castle was compact, with tiny windows set high on the sheer stone walls. Around it was an elegant garden of intersecting paths, shady trees and wooden seating. An older woman sat with a dog on her lap, gazing out at the city. A couple of joggers passed, their breathing noisy in the quiet afternoon.

The driver touched Rachel's back, directing her to a south-facing bench with a view over the high-rise apartments. The ones closest to Castle Hill and the Old Town had colourfully painted balconies and murals on their windowless sides, but beyond the ring-road they scaled out to uniform grey.

'It is a steep climb, but a nice vantage point,' Ana said. 'You can see all the way to the mountains.'

Rachel looked to her left. She'd glimpsed the mountain range from ground level, but from here she could see how expansive it was, how grand. In the afternoon light the peaks were like folds of emerald-coloured velvet.

'It's lovely,' she said. 'I should have come up earlier.'

'Oh, everything is closed,' Ana said, waving her hand. 'The castle galleries, the museum, even the kiosk.'

'And so cold at the top, usually,' the driver added. She hunched her shoulders together and rubbed her hands. '*Brrr*!'

Rachel smiled despite herself.

'You had bad news today,' Ana said. 'It is nice to get fresh air, a pretty view, a little exercise. It can change our perspective.'

Of course, they knew what had happened.

'My husband can't be here, I told them that from the beginning.'

The driver said something, and Ana responded in an admonishing tone. Irritated, the driver rolled her shoulders. 'It is ridiculous,' she told Rachel in English. 'It makes no sense, I agree with this.'

Exasperated, Ana tried to interrupt again.

'I don't work for them,' the driver snapped. 'I say what I like.' To Rachel, she explained, 'How things are done, that is nothing here. How they are *seen* to be done; this is the key. But now, oh, the eyes of the world are on us. For once!' She snorted. 'So, things must be done in the way we have said. We put on the show. Even if it makes no sense. Especially then!'

'Mama,' Ana said. 'Please.'

Rachel looked between them, only now seeing the resemblance. 'She's your mother?'

The driver hooted and clapped, her gloves making a hollow sound in the quiet park.

'Many people left town for the expo, as you know,' Ana said. 'Mama filled in at short notice.' She reached across Rachel to pat her mother's knee. 'Though she was hired to drive, not to philosophise about the functioning of the state.'

'Okay, well.' Though the revelation surprised Rachel, it made no difference really. She needed to know what to do about Monday. 'However your country runs, Ben can't be here. I'm going to have to cancel before they thaw the embryo.'

Feeling the tears rise, she pressed her lips together and looked out at the calm green peaks.

The driver put her arm around Rachel's shoulders and squeezed. She leaned into the hug, gripping Ana's mother's hand to draw strength from it.

'They put on a show,' she murmured in Rachel's ear. 'Well, you put on a bigger one.'

'I'm just so tired of this.'

Ana looked at her watch. 'We should get you back. You need to rest.'

With a sigh, the driver let go. Rachel held her own palms to her chest for a moment, trying to conserve the warmth and comfort.

The steps were set at different heights and treads, and the walk down felt treacherous. Ana and her mother were nimbler and soon went on ahead. Rachel heard the tones of an argument.

The sky was darkening; they'd been out for longer than Rachel thought. By the time she got to the bottom, Ana's mother had started the engine. Rachel asked Ana, who held the door open, 'Do you think if I had treatment another time, things wouldn't be so strict?'

'The clinic follows the rules.'

'Before I came, they said they understood if my husband couldn't be here. So maybe sometimes the rules aren't as—'

'Just think,' Ana interrupted. 'Think about what is best.'

'I can't waste an embryo.' Rachel's voice was hoarse, her face too close to Ana's. The younger woman was meant to be her helper, her advocate. 'I can't risk going for the transfer and having them say I can't do it by myself.'

Even close up, Ana's skin was flawless, her eyes bright with health and youth. She had at least fifteen years of her own luxurious fertility left, if not longer. She might have worked with dozens of Rachels, but could she really, truly understand?

Ana stood motionless, her eyes sad in a disappointed way rather than an empathetic one.

Ana's mother flashed the lights; it was becoming too dark, too cold. Rachel drew her coat around herself and got back in the car.

Jess
Thursday

The sky was swollen as Jess hurried down the Promenade, and there was a wetness to the air. But when she looked east for the telltale haze of precipitation, there was none: just the dark green of the hills.

Lena was waiting for Jess at the Palace Hotel taxi rank. She'd changed from her cleaning uniform into black jeans and a fluffy jumper, and she appraised Jess's outfit before greeting her. She'd said to dress like a happy, middle-class city woman, and though Jess had lived in the capital for three years, the description was lost on her. In the end, she'd chosen a sweater dress with leggings under her ankle-length coat.

'Very good,' Lena said at last, taking Jess's shoulders to kiss her.

A taxi crawled up and they slid inside. The vehicle was old, its back seats soft leather over flattened springs, and only Jess's safety belt worked. The air inside was cold and smelled of diesel. Lena gave the address and Jess checked the mirror for the driver's reaction, but there was none. He hit the indicator and peeled out into the light traffic on the avenue. There were pedestrians on the footpath and around the base of Castle Hill, and banners for the expo still fluttered on light poles, though they looked dulled, like the event had long since passed.

'How was work?' Jess asked Lena. 'Busy, or not?'

'A normal day, I think.'

'I thought all the guests would've left.' Jess amended, 'Well, lots of them.'

'There was some turnover.' Lena shrugged. 'Boring, boring.'

'Not Cassandra Caspie?' Jess was mostly joking.

'No,' Lena said ruefully. 'And Mr. C. Casey pulled out too, whoever he was.'

The taxi climbed onto the ring-road and accelerated, pushing the women into the seat. When the driver slowed at last, Jess spoke again: 'Thanks for letting me come with you.'

'It's fine.' Lena broke into a grin. 'If you sign up, I get a bonus.'

Jess had been surprised at how unbothered Lena was by her sudden interest in the fertility clinic. When she'd rung the day before, on her way home from meeting Yara, Lena told her the intake appointment happened to be the next afternoon, Thursday, and Jess was welcome to come. The clinic supplied cab vouchers, and there were lots of spare vehicles on the streets, their back seats empty of foreign dignitaries.

'What happens today, anyway?' Jess asked. 'For you.'

'Not so much. I sign a form to show my intention, speak with the clinic leader about the treatment. Of course, I know about it already, but it is a tick in the box.' Lena raised an eyebrow. 'They test my blood for hormones and diseases, then perhaps a look at my insides with a scan.' She frowned and chewed her lip. 'Or maybe not now. I was last here a while ago, so I don't remember.'

Jess wondered if Lena expected her to stay for the medical parts.

She probably should, if she could, to add detail to the story. Even the idea of seeing someone else's blood being taken made Jess feel uneasy, let alone whatever the scan was meant to involve.

After ten minutes, the taxi reached a grey building on the outskirts of town and dropped into its underground garage. Jess noticed the expensive models of the cars inside; how washed and shiny they were.

The driver stopped by a well-lit elevator. Lena thanked him and handed over her voucher, but when they got out, she led Jess from where they'd been set down towards a service lift and typed a code into the keypad. Inside, Lena pressed the button for the second floor.

As they climbed, Jess asked, 'Do people around here—what do they think of the fertility clinics?'

'How do you mean?'

'Is it a taboo subject, fertility and things?'

'If it were taboo, would I be taking you along?'

Jess was disappointed; how much juicier would the article be if she was blowing the lid off a secretive industry? 'I guess what I mean is, is there any kind of angst about women selling their eggs to wealthy foreigners?'

Lena was fluent in English, but she didn't seem to understand 'angst'. Jess couldn't think of an equivalent. 'Do people worry about it?' she rephrased. 'Is it something people think about, about what it means?'

The elevator doors opened onto a plain white hallway. They stepped out.

'We do a lot of things for wealthy foreigners, Jessie,' Lena said. Her tone was slightly patronising, which stung, though Jess figured she deserved it. 'Have you heard of a small thing called capitalism?'

'I know, but—'

'Besides, you are considering it, yes?' Lena eyed her. 'That's why you're here.'

Jess stayed quiet as they entered a waiting area, also white. In the centre of a ring of plastic chairs was a melamine coffee table with a jug of water and stack of disposable cups. An opening had been cut into one wall, behind which was an empty office.

Lena leaned on the ledge and looked through. 'Hello?'

A woman in mauve scrubs came in. 'You have an appointment?'

Lena gave her name, then nodded back at Jess. 'My friend will join me.'

The nurse went to a filing cabinet and pulled it open with a thud. 'Age?'

'Twenty-six,' Lena said. She was talking about Jess.

The nurse found a clipboard and waved it at them. 'You are applying, Miss Friend?'

'Oh,' Jess said, 'no, not right now, thank you. I'm just interested in what it's all about.'

The nurse shrugged, slammed the drawer shut, and handed the clipboard to Lena. 'You know what it is?'

Lena took a chair and Jess sat beside her, then regretted it, feeling they were too close. She'd never spent this much time alone with Lena.

There was a set of papers attached to the clipboard. Lena showed it to Jess, which meant she wasn't annoyed about the tasteless remark in the lift. A series of questions asked the respondent to rate aspects of their life on a scale from one to five: depression, anxiety, nutritional intake, water intake, physical movement, avoidance of smoking and alcohol. Jess watched as Lena drew a circle around 5 for each one, pulling a face at the final question.

Lena stood and returned the questionnaire to the nurse, who'd been leaning through the opening as she waited, her uncovered yawning making Jess do the same. The room wasn't overly warm, but it had no windows and felt stuffy. For a moment, Jess mistook the hum of the vents for distant rain.

The nurse left the office and appeared in the waiting room. Lena got up and said to Jess, 'Come on.'

'Oh, already?' It was a medical clinic, so she'd expected to have to wait.

They entered another clean white hallway, the nurse and Lena chatting so rapidly Jess had trouble keeping up. Her cheeks burned with embarrassment, though from what she could tell they were only talking about the weather and how stupid the expo closures were. Whenever Jess felt confident about her grasp of the language, this was what happened; some accidental proof that she wasn't as good as she thought. Egg and baby. She wondered if people ever thought she was a moron. She tried to translate *moron* and failed.

The nurse led them into an office with a desk and three chairs, an examination table fixed to one wall with a handbasin at the end. After a moment, Jess realised there wasn't a privacy curtain around it. There were no windows in this room, either.

They sat and put their handbags on the floor. Jess felt weird about asking Lena more questions. Something in the room suggested surveillance, though there was no sign of any electronics other than a tablet and corded phone on the desk—not even a smoke detector or sprinkler head in the ceiling, which was a different worry.

Lena said casually, 'Did you know that in the United States, they pay people to carry babies for them, too.'

Jess had read about female celebrities hiring surrogates. 'It must be expensive.'

'Well, it depends.' Lena stretched in her seat. 'Expensive to buy an American woman, but maybe not for one coming from another country.'

It was strange to talk to Lena side-by-side; it felt too intimate to turn and look at her as she spoke, but it was equally bizarre not to.

'Also,' she went on, 'they pay people for blood and plasma. For eggs, for sperm.'

'What about kidneys?'

'Kidneys.' Lena paused. 'I am not sure.'

'I know what you're saying. We're not the only ones who do this.'

'I mean, they would have their own people do it, so the difference is?' Foreseeing Jess's rebuttal, Lena went on, 'Our cost of living is less, so eggs come at a lower price. There are call centres based here also, for the same reason. Our flight attendants work for American airlines. Cheap.' She tipped her chin. 'Why else would Miss Caspie think to build her factory here?'

'I'm not judging you,' Jess said. 'I'm sorry if it sounds like I was.'

'Judging, not judging, I just tell you how it works.' Lena relaxed, sliding her thighs forward in the chair. 'I want to do this, and it pays well. Are you not chasing Miss Caspie to make money, too?'

Jess blushed. She hadn't told Lena that the story on Cassandra Caspie was dead in the water, and she was actually here to try to rustle up something else. Lena would never have let her come if she suspected any risk to her livelihood. And anyway, Jess knew the concept was weak. When she'd told Yara she wanted to write an overview of how the clinic operated, the editor was unenthusiastic but had given approval. 'Better to have the doctors make an advertorial,' she'd moaned to Jess. 'Then they could pay you, not me.'

The door clicked and a tall woman with sleek hair entered

wearing a soft eggplant-coloured turtleneck, purple slacks and suede boots. She carried Lena's clipboard. 'You are back, Leni, well done.' Seeing Jess, she said, 'You have a friend today.'

'This is Jessie. Jessie, this is Olga.'

Olga took the other chair. 'Are you considering donation, Jessie?'

Yara had told Jess not to mention the article at the clinic, not because they were planning some exposé, but because it'd be too much work. 'If you tell a business that you want a story, they will try to give you one,' she'd said. 'Or you get tangled in the tape. Approval must go to the next level and the next and the next until you are looking down from the clouds and can see nothing.'

'Kind of like going undercover,' Jess said with excitement.

'Jessica, please.' Yara had sighed. 'What is with you and spies?'

Now, Jess smiled at the woman in purple. 'I'm just here to see how it works.'

It was meant to sound innocuous, but Olga sat straighter, and her jaw tensed. She spoke as though to a camera, her eyes sliding past Jess. 'We are a professional outfit with many excellent reviews. Whether you wish to conceive, freeze or donate, *we change lives.*'

'Wow.' Jess nodded, hoping to calm the woman back down.

'There's a photo wall of all the babies born from the clinic,' Lena added. 'On the other floor.'

'Hundreds,' Olga barked. 'Perhaps a thousand.'

'That's wonderful.' Jess put both hands to her chest to emphasise her awe, and Olga's shoulders softened. 'Amazing.'

Here, people spoke with two distinct accents: a short, snappy form around the capital, and the countryside's more drawn-out version, with little flecks of dialect. In learning so much from Viktor, a proud rural boy, Jess had picked up a lot of his pronunciation. This could be a disadvantage, but today it was turning out to be useful. Olga seemed to think Jess was provincial and slow, probably uneducated in the ways of science.

'You must make families very happy,' Jess gushed.

'Lena's last family was thrilled,' Olga said. 'You produced ten, yes, Leni?'

'Eleven.'

'And the family has twins!' She clapped twice. 'Two boys. Wonderful. And three embryos left, if they wish to have more.'

Lena nodded. Jess wanted to glance across at her, see if she looked emotional, but she didn't like to move her gaze from Olga's. The others began to discuss Lena's proposed treatment, their speech getting faster and more complex. Jess could parse little of it. She gazed at her lap with a vague smile.

'Well!' Olga snapped after a few minutes, making Jess jerk in her seat. 'What do you think of all that?'

'Oh.' Jess shifted. 'It's all very complicated, isn't it?'

'We pay fifty crowns per egg. Not so complicated.'

As much for a single egg as an interview with Cassandra Caspie. That meant the last time she'd done this Lena earned over five hundred crowns. It'd take months of cleaning work to make the same amount.

'And the women who buy the eggs,' Jess said. 'Is it always successful?'

She felt Lena's head rotate towards her. Olga maintained her poker face as she asked, 'What do you mean?'

'Do they always have children?'

'The last patient had twins.'

'Eleven eggs do not become eleven children, Jessie,' Lena

explained. 'Some fail for reasons out of our control. This is why we need to grow many.'

Jess nodded, but it didn't answer her question. She wasn't completely sure what the question was.

'Lena got eleven eggs and she was thirty years old,' Olga mused. 'You are twenty-six, yes? In a different stage of life. Even more fertile.' As in English, the word for this was the same as describing soil quality. 'Remember, it is fifty crowns per egg. Would this kind of money be useful for you?'

Thinking the question was the stupidest she'd ever heard, Jess said, 'Oh, maybe.'

'You do not need to commit now. In fact, we do an inspection first. An ultrasound and blood exam will be administered for free, with a twenty-crown bonus. To see if you are'—Jess expected her to say *worthy*—'eligible.'

'I'm not sure.' Jess reapplied her dazed smile, hoping for pity.

'Well, you don't even know if you can, until you have the tests. You could do them today, with your friend.' Olga stared hard at her. 'Where are you from?'

Jess considered claiming Viktor's hometown but knew it wouldn't stand up to scrutiny. 'I live in the Old Town, so I can come back any time.'

Lena tilted to gather her bag. 'Thank you, Olga,' she said. The women stood and shook hands across the desk. Jess followed Lena's example, feeling the cool touch of Olga's fingers, the brisk efficiency in her wrist.

'Let us talk when your results come, Leni. And Jessie, please think about it.' Her eyes shimmered. 'Women your age may get eighteen, twenty eggs.'

The nurse from earlier was waiting in the corridor when Jess and Lena emerged. 'No tests today?' she grunted at Jess, then pointed back up the way they'd come. 'Please be patient.'

Jess's mind was crowded as she returned to the waiting area. There was no denying that a thousand crowns would be a massive windfall for her and Viktor. Viktor could do one of the pricy online MBAs he sometimes talked about, or she could quit her teaching and bartending jobs and find something she liked to do. Working for one of the tour companies was her dream, but there were more than enough guides to meet demand and where there weren't, the jobs were kept in the family. With a thousand crowns she could put a deposit on a people-mover and set up her own business running day tours to the cloudfall.

She'd do it, too, if she thought the eggs were just eggs. But, as the language proved, eggs really meant babies. Technically, Lena already had two, and Olga claimed there could be three more even before she did more treatment. Five kids! Jess was passionate about a woman's right to control her own body, of course she was, but *five*? It wasn't that she felt the twins or any other potential infants were really Lena's; that she'd given them up, sold them for cash the way Jess first misunderstood. All Lena did was provide the building blocks, and if she didn't feel like they were her children, then fine. Good. Jess agreed. Parents were the people who raised you, a family was what you chose, like she had chosen Viktor. But if Jess became a donor, if she met the clinic's expectations and produced twenty eggs (and she still didn't know what this involved, or how they got to them), could twenty kids be added to the world's population? Twenty kids raised in Western countries, draining fossil fuels and creating landfill?

When Lena came back she didn't look any different, though Jess assumed there was at least a plaster on the seam of her elbow. Lena waved the two ten-crown notes at her before slipping them in her pocket. In the lift down to the basement, Lena typed a message on her phone and Jess began to wish she'd recorded the meeting so she could work out what had been said. The only thing she was sure of were the numbers: Twenty crowns for having tests done, and fifty per egg. That was an ad, not a story.

Lena pocketed her phone and wound her arm through Jess's. 'We must go to the rank outside. Taxis won't pick up here.'

The temperature had dropped while they were inside, and the air felt frozen and hard to pass through. Jess leaned into it, though there was no wind. The heavy cloud from earlier had disintegrated, leaving a cold blue; in the east, the hills were grey.

The taxi stand was on the other side of the street. A long black car mounted the exit ramp from the garage, and Lena held Jess to the kerb while it passed. The rear windows were wound down despite the cold, and as the vehicle went by, Jess saw a single passenger in its spacious back seat.

It was the woman from the bar. The one who'd left the big tip one night, then drunk the Love Potion she wasn't supposed to have.

***

Back at the flat, Jess put the oven on and sat in the warm nook of the kitchen to dial the clinic's information number. When someone answered, Jess spoke in English, leaning into her natural accent. 'Hello, I was wondering how much your treatment costs?'

'I am so sorry that you are in need of our services,' a female voice said. Jess, who had no such need, felt a jolt of emotion at the sincerity. 'If it is okay, may I ask about your situation and diagnosis?'

Fuck. 'I'm, I've, we've been trying to have a baby for a while, but it's not working.' When the woman stayed quiet, Jess added, 'We're looking into our options, you know?'

'Of course. May I ask where you are based?'

'Uh, the UK. England.'

'I understand there are NHS services available for patients in your country. Have you explored those?'

'We just want to know what else is possible.'

'Of course. The need to have a child can be innate.' Jess heard the woman breathe gently. 'If you are able to give me your English mailing address, I can send a brochure for you and your husband to view together.'

Jess didn't think she'd mentioned a husband. 'Ah, well, we're here at the moment, actually, so we thought we might be able to get a consultation. Two birds, one stone.' She wondered if the woman on the other end of the phone knew enough English to grasp the aphorism. The equivalent phrase here was 'one skein, many scarves', but using it would blow her cover.

'You're visiting the capital?' the woman said, her pitch rising for the first time. 'That's unusual, if I may say. For how long?'

'For the expo. A week or so.'

The voice turned sombre. 'I am afraid we are not working with clients for the duration of the expo. Are you and your husband returning at any time?'

Jess suspected this was a lie—she'd seen the cars parked in the garage, the woman from the hotel being driven out—but couldn't say so. 'We'll definitely come back,' she said, realising this would sound weird. People didn't often come back. 'Because of expo stuff.'

'I can send the materials to your English address in the meantime. Perhaps you would choose to undergo treatment when you are next in town.'

'What if I came and got them?' Jess said. 'Since I'm here anyway.' So long as she didn't bump into Olga or that nurse. Maybe she should wear a wig.

'I'm sorry, but the office is completely closed,' the woman said smoothly. 'If you give me an address, I can have the materials couriered out for when you are home.'

Jess didn't want an IVF information brochure being sent to her parents' house. She considered giving her sister's address, but Amy wouldn't understand either.

'Maybe I should think about the best thing to do.'

'Yes, you and your husband should talk further,' the woman suggested. 'Please, have a nice day.'

***

Later, Jess walked through the darkening streets to her bartending shift. The crowds were thin, though not as bad as earlier in the week; most places were still shut, but at least one café on the Promenade was serving customers. Someone had put the Christmas lights back on the Twin Bridges, and they glowed bright white. On the Esplanade side, a couple of teenagers stood with signs protesting the waste of electricity: *You've had YOUR future, now think of OURS.*

Farther up, by the marquee, a small rally was underway, the leader standing on a milk crate wearing only a T-shirt, shouting about the immorality of the expo. The crowd of a dozen or so whistled in response. Jess squinted as she passed, but she didn't recognise any of the attendees, and the speaker wasn't Boris.

She wondered why they were bothering, with the expo shrunk down to almost nothing. Maybe, with nothing else to protest about over the weekend, they had to make do.

Turning onto the avenue that led from the Promenade to the hotel, Jess passed the same guest she'd seen leaving the clinic that afternoon.

The woman recognised her too. She stopped. 'You work at the hotel bar.'

'Headed there now actually,' Jess said. 'Out for a walk?'

'Oh, I don't know what I'm doing.' She held out an ungloved hand, skin grey under the streetlights. 'I'm Rachel, by the way.'

Her fingers were freezing when Jess shook them. 'Aren't you cold?'

Rachel kicked the toes of her boots against the pavement. 'I'm probably leaving in the next few days.'

'The city not what you thought it was?' Jess said, pretending Rachel was a regular tourist. 'I think if it weren't for the expo, you'd have had a better time.'

Rachel stared directly at her, eyes as bright and glossy as if they'd been frozen. 'No, it's not that. I'm here to do IVF, but they're going to cancel my treatment if my husband doesn't come.'

'What?'

'I'm halfway through the cycle. It'll all be wasted.'

'Are you pregnant?'

Rachel snorted, the syrupy sound of its aftermath letting Jess know she was holding back tears. 'No. I'm definitely not pregnant.'

Jess checked her watch: she was going to be late. 'You're not leaving tonight, are you?'

Rachel shook her head.

'This is going to sound weird, but can we catch up tomorrow?'

She looked surprised, then wary. 'I don't know. I'm busy in the morning. I think.'

'I'll buy you a coffee after lunch, then. Or some tea. There's a place that's open, over on the Promenade.'

Rachel shook her head. 'I know where you mean. I don't want to go there.' Just as Jess was beginning to think the suggestion was a bust, Rachel continued, 'I'll meet you in the hotel lobby. Two o'clock?'

'Thanks, great.' Jess reached out to shake her hand again, gasping a little at the iciness of Rachel's skin. 'Seriously, you should go back inside. Order a banana split from room service and eat it in bed.'

'I'm okay. I need to walk.'

'I'll see you tomorrow, then.'

Rachel nodded and wandered away, in the direction of the canal.

Jess broke into a jog for the last couple of blocks, relief spurring her on. Maybe she'd have something to fill Yara's page after all.

Rachel
2DPO

On Friday, after her massage, Rachel was led into the group therapy room for the third time. While she preferred talking to the couples and Ian to being in a psychological torture chamber with Olga, Rachel longed to skip both. The past two group sessions hadn't been helpful in any way she could identify, though there was always the chance that in a week or a month or a year she'd have a breakthrough that could be traced back to Ian.

She doubted it.

The clinic's group therapy program was designed to be repetitive, allowing patients to enter and exit in whatever way suited their treatment. In Rachel's cohort, Gabby and Warwick had started first, in the middle of February, then Harper and Meg, and now Rachel. No-one new had joined since.

'Today,' Ian announced, once they were settled and the chaperones had gone, 'we're going to talk about our fears.'

'We've done this one,' Warwick said.

Ian turned to him. 'Pardon?'

'We've done the name-your-fears session. Numerous times.'

Gabby put a hand on her husband's arm.

Ian's lips puckered in sympathy. 'You've completed several

cycles, I know. This may add to your fears.'

'Yes, but we did the fear one two weeks ago. I can't say mine have changed in a fortnight.'

Rachel couldn't tell if Warwick was angry or upset; he looked placid to her, perhaps a little exasperated, like there was something more useful he could be doing. He adjusted the heavy watch on his wrist.

'A fortnight ...?' Ian repeated, flicking through his notebook.

Gabby said, 'It was whenever you ran it last.' She lifted her chin and explained to the others, 'My body isn't responding to the drugs properly. We've been here longer than expected.'

'I'm so sorry,' Meg said. Her distress seemed genuine. 'That must be terrible.'

Looking at Rachel, Gabby said, 'It is what it is.'

For a moment Rachel felt put on the spot, then realised Gabby preferred to make eye contact with someone who could remain unemotional. She gave a single nod and was pleased when Gabby nodded crisply back.

'Ah, yes,' Ian said at last, tapping a sheet of paper. 'Well, I still think it's possible that your fears have evolved. Or perhaps you've thought about them more deeply.'

'No, I don't think so,' Warwick said.

Meg put a finger to the bridge of her nose and took a breath, like she was trying not to cry. Harper leaned over to whisper something, and the tenderness in the gesture made Rachel aware that there was more than a surrogacy relationship there: the women were close.

'You don't think you have any new fears?' Ian asked Warwick. 'Or you don't think that your view of them has changed?'

'Well, either, quite frankly.'

Ian cleared his throat. 'Would you like to talk about that?'

'About how I don't have any new fears or anything to say about them?' Warwick seemed amused by Ian's enthusiastic nod. 'No, that's quite alright.' His wife's small hand slid down his arm as he got to his feet. 'I think I'll skip this one. Darling?' he asked Gabby. 'Would you like to talk to Ian about your fears again?'

Gabby kept looking at Rachel. 'I suppose I'll stay.'

'Fine,' he said amiably. 'I'll see you outside. Goodbye, ladies.'

He took his briefcase, stooped to kiss Gabby's cheek, and went out one of the doors. Rachel wondered if he'd chosen the right one, though Warwick didn't seem to be the kind of man who'd admit to entering a cupboard or a strange hallway. He'd just march around the building until he got where he needed to go.

'Meg.' Ian's voice was a notch too loud, as if he was trying to regain control of the group. There was no need: the four of them sat meekly, stunned. 'You reacted quite emotionally to Warwick just now. Are you able to tell us about that?'

Meg nodded, pressing a second finger to her nose. The skin around her nostrils glowed red. 'He reminded me of my father. Dad was a very decisive man, too. Very snappy.' She took a breath. 'It makes me worry about parenting.'

'Because you're fearful of being short-tempered with a child?' Ian asked, eyes wide, like he wanted to drink up her response.

'I'm sorry, Gabby,' Meg said. 'I'm not trying to criticise.'

'It's perfectly alright.'

'I just, I worry about emotional needs, you know? Will I be like him?'

Both Harper and Ian were hanging on Meg's every word. Rachel, unable to bear it, stared down at her crossed arms.

'But then, did his personality give me a resilience I wouldn't have otherwise? It's so hard to find the balance.'

'It *is*,' Harper agreed, her voice rich. 'I've found that with our older child. When do I tell him yes, and when do I tell him no?

Sometimes I lie awake at night, going over everything I said to him during the day.'

Rachel was quietly appalled. That was parenthood? She knew that if she became a mother her sleep would be negatively affected, but she hadn't realised it would be so self-inflicted. Surely you just said *yes* if something was okay, and *no* if it wasn't? Or was she turning into Jean Mather already, without even having a baby?

Meg talked some more, then Harper shared how she was afraid the embryo transfer wouldn't be successful and that she'd fail Meg. Ian encouraged her to replace the word 'fail' with something that *honoured her intentions*, as he put it. The two women looked at each other with bottomless emotion and Rachel was again stirred by the depth of their friendship.

'I wouldn't blame you,' Meg said heartily, threading her fingers through Harper's. 'We'd just try again.'

'Can I ask a question, Harper?' Gabby asked. 'You don't have to answer, obviously.'

Harper shrugged. 'Go for it.'

'Are you afraid of not being able to give up the baby when it's born?'

Rachel exhaled with discomfort, but Harper's response was swift: 'Not at all.' Her voice reached all four walls, like she was acting in a play and knew an agent lurked somewhere in the audience. 'I know Meg will be the most amazing mother.'

Once again, Gabby caught Rachel's eye across the circle. This time, she winked.

***

Traffic on the ring-road was jammed, and after their conversation on Castle Hill the day before, Ana and her mother were circumspect. Arriving back at the hotel, Rachel wanted to lie down for a while before making excuses with the bartender, whose help she no longer needed. She was calmer than yesterday and had the beginnings of a plan to deal with Olga.

Gabby and Warwick's driver must have been better at getting through the gridlock, because the couple were talking by the entrance when Rachel got out of the car. Seeing her approach, Gabby stepped away from her husband.

'Hello, Rachel. I was wondering if you might like to have lunch?'

Hesitant, Rachel glanced at Warwick, who shook his head. 'I have a meeting. You ladies enjoy yourself.'

'Oh, well,' Rachel said, swallowing. 'Is there anywhere to go? I thought everything was closed.'

'I booked at table at the Palace,' Gabby said smoothly. 'It's a ten-minute walk. Is that alright?'

Before she could answer, Warwick leaned across to kiss Gabby goodbye. Rachel shifted her gaze to give them privacy and was startled when she felt Warwick's warm hand snake around her waist and squeeze it.

'Thank you,' he said, then strode off before she could respond, heading east. Rachel had never been in that direction; it was all offices and apartments, as far as she could tell.

'One of his business associates is staying in Penthouse,' Gabby said. 'Might be the first time ever.'

Rachel nodded, uncomprehending.

Gabby flicked up the collar of her coat. 'Shall we go? I apologise, I'm a brisk walker.'

She wasn't joking. Gabby was a small woman, but had speed and agility, dodging the bodies that crowded the avenue and the Esplanade. They power walked past the marquee, now ringed with security, a screen set up alongside it to broadcast the proceedings to those who couldn't fit inside. Dozens of people had clustered to watch, though there wasn't any sound.

Rachel followed Gabby over the steel bridge and west along the softly creaking slats of the Old Town boardwalk. Street artists performed in the open space: a caricaturist, a juggler, a woman winding yarn around wire to create earrings. Rachel wanted to look closer but had to walk fast to keep up with Gabby, who maintained her pace, eyes fixed straight ahead so the panhandlers and would-be scammers didn't bother with her.

A few blocks over, almost at the base of Castle Hill, was a grand building painted in pale yellow with white trim. A barricade had been set up at the top of the steps, but Gabby marched up and showed her phone to a security guard. When he nodded, Gabby turned and called to Rachel, who'd lingered at the bottom, 'This way!'

Rachel followed Gabby along the outside of the building until they reached a glass door. It opened into an impressive, old-style restaurant, with thick carpets and heavy white tablecloths. Portraits in gold frames covered the walls. It was warm inside, real candles ringing the chandeliers.

A waitress in a dark grey shift dress led them to the only available table. The other patrons wore suits, men and women alike, their wine glasses full and sweating. The waitress offered to take Rachel's coat, but she declined. Despite being overheated from the walk, she was reluctant to reveal her jeans and shapeless knit top in such a fancy place.

'Soda water with lemon, please,' Gabby requested, sliding into a velvet-upholstered chair. 'We'll see the vegetarian menu.'

When the waitress left, Gabby twisted her lips theatrically. 'I eat meat, but the veggie options are a better match with the clinic's stupid diet. Promise me you'll come back some time and eat the real cuisine. The roast pork is to die for, and they do these little cheese squares.' She rolled her eyes to demonstrate ecstasy.

'I've tried the tea,' Rachel said. Honey Morning Milk, the Love Potion and dried berries were the only local delicacies she'd had.

'Thank God for tea,' Gabby said. The waitress reappeared with menus in red leather folders. 'Thank you.'

Rachel pretended to read hers, knowing she'd defer to Gabby on everything. They ordered broth for entrée, and then a few plates to share: a cucumber salad, a chickpea salad, a kind of beetroot fritter.

'It'll all be very nice,' Gabby said when they were by themselves again. 'Just uninspired, like the rest of the shit we have to do.' Sighing, she draped her elbows over the arms of her chair. 'I tell you, when this cycle fails, I'm going to put my head in a bucket of Kentucky Fried Chicken.'

'Do they have that here?'

'Only at the airport.'

After a moment, Rachel caught herself. 'Well, think positively, right?'

It was the first time she'd heard Gabby laugh, a sound much louder and deeper than her frame suggested. Rachel's back was to the dining room, but she sensed nearby patrons glancing around.

'It's basically failed already. But thank you for the confidence.'

'I'm sorry.'

Gabby shrugged. 'My body stopped responding to the drugs. I think it knows something we don't.'

Rachel was almost afraid to ask: 'What?'

'That it's all a waste of time.'

The waitress brought the soups, which were thin and brown like chicken stock but tasted faintly of lemon. 'I'm sorry you feel like it's a waste of time.'

'This is our eighth attempt. I *know* it's a waste of time.'

Rachel was unnerved by how jovial Gabby seemed, like she could break into that operatic laugh at any moment even though they were talking about something sad. 'It's not very fair,' she said carefully.

'Well, of course not.' Reaching the end of her broth, Gabby lifted the bowl with both hands and tipped the remainder into her mouth, then dried her lip with a thick cotton napkin. 'It's how they do it,' she explained. 'You're allowed.'

'That's okay,' Rachel said. 'I'll just—' She tilted the bowl away, as she'd seen in some etiquette tutorial, and swept her spoon through the last of the liquid.

'Suit yourself.' After a moment, Gabby returned to the topic, though Rachel wished she wouldn't. 'No, it's not fair. But maybe I'll do that thing where you give up and eat a pile of junk food and have unprotected sex once and get a bun in the oven.' Her nose wrinkled. 'All the failure stories end with success, don't you find?'

'I guess. The ones you read online.'

'Everyone I know has a neighbour or a boss or a bloody school-friend who gave up after twenty years of trying, then had one boozy night on holiday and ended up with triplets.'

'I haven't really talked to anyone about it.'

'Your prerogative, I suppose.' The waitress took their bowls and Gabby sat back in her armchair with two fingers held to her lips. She was a smoker, Rachel realised; no wonder she was irritable, if she'd had to quit for the treatment and it hadn't even worked. 'Warwick told the boys, so for us it was open slather.'

'He told his sons you were trying for a daughter?'

'He didn't say the daughter part. Just that we want to have a baby, and we need IVF to do it.' Gabby clucked her tongue. 'He needed the boys to go easy on me, in case I was hormonal. Of course, we both expected it to work right away.' She clicked her fingers. 'What idiots.'

'Were your stepsons nice?'

'They're a delight.' Gabby touched her lip again, then curled her hands into her lap. 'Why don't you talk to people about your infertility?'

Rachel balked at the descriptor. She wasn't infertile, just single and past her peak. But she couldn't say this to Gabby; at least, not the first part. 'It's very personal,' she said, looking around to see if their mains were coming out.

Gabby waited until Rachel was facing her again. 'You don't talk much in the group sessions.'

'I'm not very expressive.' She wondered if she should add *Unlike Meg and Harper* but didn't want to sound like a bitch.

'No,' Gabby agreed. 'And Ian's bloody useless.'

The two women grinned, bonded through shared dislike. Rachel leaned forward and confided, 'And Olga. What's up her arse?'

Gabby shook her head.

'What is it with her?' Rachel continued. 'She runs the place, right?'

'The manager.'

'Doesn't she have better things to do than meet with patients all the time?'

'What do you mean?'

Before she could answer, the waitress arrived, placing their dishes slowly and carefully in the centre of the table. Rachel reached for her water, almost knocked it over, then gulped down the whole thing. As soon as she was done, the waitress made a production out of refilling the glass from a bottle set in the ice bucket. The fertility patients' sad substitute for wine.

Rachel began spooning food onto her plate, keeping her face

down. Gabby took the hint. She filled her own plate, had a deep swallow of lemon water, and asked, 'What inspired you to do this?'

'Come to the clinic? It's cheaper here than where I live.'

'That's not really what I meant.' Gabby dug her fork into the various little piles, as if they were talking about nothing more consequential than the upcoming expo. 'What made you want a child?'

Rachel's throat dried. 'We covered that in one of the sessions.'

'Yes.' Gabby was unbothered. 'I just wondered if you'd thought more about your answer.'

'I don't think I *can* answer.'

Gabby chewed a forkful of cucumber salad and let her gaze slide around the room. She wasn't putting pressure on Rachel, but she wasn't changing the subject, either.

'Why do you want to know?' ventured Rachel, trying not to be defensive.

'Before I was married,' she said, 'when I didn't have children, people didn't mind asking me why that was. I find it interesting that nobody asked Warwick and his ex why they'd decided to have the boys.'

'They'd probably consider it rude. Since the boys exist.'

'I want a baby,' Gabby began, cutting into the magenta-coloured fritter, 'because the idea of a little person in the house who's a mix of Warwick and me, who I can watch grow and learn and interact with her big brothers, it makes my heart swell in my chest. Like something's opening up. Possibility. A whole other world.'

Rachel thought that was a cliché. It was the kind of thing Meg and Harper would say, except Gabby's tone was milder and her eyes were dry.

Gabby chewed her fritter, then swallowed. When she spoke, her teeth hadn't been stained pink at all. 'What about you?'

Rachel had also felt the opening in her chest, but she knew it was from fear, not hope, the way Gabby described it. Rachel had come to terms with the end of her marriage, had no desire to be close to another man, but was filled with hot terror at the prospect of there being nothing more to life than this.

Not that she wanted a baby to plug a void, like Meg had said; not that. Something different. Something less terrible than that.

Rachel just wanted a baby. She hadn't been sure of it for a long time, and now she was. She had to at least try, or she'd regret it until she died.

'I can't describe it,' she said. She didn't expect Gabby to be satisfied, but her cool look of disappointment was a surprise. Rachel lined up four chickpeas and punctured them with the tines of her fork. In the group, Gabby had appeared to admire Rachel's steely demeanour. Well, it wasn't some act for her benefit.

They said little for the rest of the meal. As soon as Rachel had cleared enough of her plate, she put her cutlery down and rested her palms on the edge of the table. 'I'm sorry to rush off, but I'm meeting someone at two.'

'That's fine.' Gabby flapped a hand when Rachel fumbled for her purse. 'It's my treat. I invited you.'

'Really?' Rachel was relieved; there'd been no prices on the menu, and the carpets and chandeliers indicated the food wouldn't be cheap. 'Thanks.'

'Yes, well, I wanted to pin you down. It's very boring here without company.' She touched her lip again. 'I went for a walk with the others last week. Meg and Harper.'

'How was that?'

'They're easy to talk to. Well, listen to. It's difficult to get a word in.'

'They seem like good friends.'

'Friends? They're married.'

'To who? Each other?'

Gabby laughed even louder than before. 'It's legal in America.'

Things unfolded in Rachel's brain. 'Harper's son—?'

'Meg's as well. But Harper carries the babies. At least, I imagine so,' she said. 'It's not like they confessed. Too risky. Who knows if I can be trusted, or if I'd rat them out to Olga for a discount.'

Rachel leaned closer. 'Is gay marriage illegal here?'

'I don't know, but fertility treatment for gay couples is.'

Rachel's mind whirled. She'd assumed Meg wasn't being hassled by Olga to produce her husband because he was real, but it turned out her marriage was just as fake as Rachel's. How were they getting away with it? It was impossible to ask; like Gabby said, Meg and Harper would never reveal the truth.

What had Gabby guessed about Rachel's situation? She resisted the urge to put her right hand on her left and rub the store-bought ring. 'Well. I had no idea.'

'You would if you'd been here seven times before,' Gabby said grimly. She nodded. 'Thanks for joining me, truly. And good luck.'

Emerging from the restaurant, Rachel found the steps to the Promenade blocked by the guard who'd checked them in. Following his nod, she walked along the western side of the building and found a small gravel parking area filled with black cars. Another guard waited in a hut by the entry gate, but when she tried to go around, he shouted and gestured back at the Palace.

'I'm just leaving,' she said. 'Leaving. Go. I'm trying to leave.'

'Not this,' he said. 'Go round. Go round!'

Rachel continued her circle of the building, but at the rear service door she was stopped and sent back the way she came. Retracing her steps, she told the first guard she couldn't get out and asked if there was an exit through the hotel.

'You have booking?' he asked gruffly. His hands were in the pockets of a heavy coat, and Rachel wondered if he had a gun in one. Or both.

'I just had lunch. I saw you before.'

'Booking?'

'I was with my friend. Gabrielle ...' Rachel realised she didn't know Gabby's surname. 'We ate in the restaurant. I came in about an hour ago and tried to leave this way.'

'Promenade is closed.'

'Can I go through the restaurant and out a different way?'

He gazed at her as if she'd posed a timeless philosophical inquiry. 'Only with a booking.'

'She had a booking.'

He shook his head. Rachel breathed through her urge to cry. She hated the stifling humiliation of being trapped, of not understanding. 'If I don't have a booking, how do I get out?'

Taking a hand from his pocket—no gun, as far as Rachel could see—the guard pointed to the main doors. 'Lobby, maybe,' he grunted, then turned back to the Promenade.

Just a few steps over, there was none of the heavy security of the restaurant, car park or back entrance. Two guards manned the base of the stairs, but they were there to stop people from entering the Promenade; a steady flow moved in the other direction, from the boardwalk into the hotel. Rachel entered the Palace lobby, which was as grand as the restaurant with its whorled blue wallpaper, chandeliers like glittering stalactites, and cream-and-gold brocade sofas arranged around low, cherry wood tables. There were queues at the check-in desk and concierge, so Rachel moved through the crowds until she overheard a couple speaking English.

'Sorry to interrupt,' she said, 'but is there a back exit to this place?'

'Exit?' the woman asked. She wore a chartreuse blouse and matching earrings, and her lips were tacky with gloss.

'I was having lunch in the restaurant, and now they won't let anyone enter the Promenade.' Rachel checked her watch; it was five to two. 'I'm late to meet someone in New Town.'

'New Town,' the woman repeated. She ran her tongue around the inner seam of her lips. 'I don't know how you'd get back there. They closed the bridges.'

'And the Esplanade,' her male companion said. 'Protesters.'

The woman rolled her eyes.

'How do I get to the New Town Hotel?' Rachel asked, starting to feel desperate. She didn't particularly care about meeting the bartender anymore, she just wanted to get the fuck out of this building.

The woman licked the inside of her mouth again, her lips swelling and shrinking in the wake of her tongue. It was nauseating. 'I suppose you'd have to get a taxi, go around.'

The man shook his head. 'You won't find a taxi. Maybe a tram?'

'I thought they cancelled the trams.'

Rachel gripped the back of the woman's chair. 'I just need to get out of the hotel.'

'Oh,' the man said. 'I guess if you can't go through the front ...' He nodded at the far side of the lobby. 'There's an emergency exit there, but it might make a racket.'

'The alarm won't be connected,' the woman commented. Glancing at Rachel, she seemed to register the panic on her face. 'Hey, it's okay. Look.'

Her instructions were detailed, a relief after the previous vagueness. Rachel took the back stairs to the mezzanine and turned down a long corridor of function spaces that ended at the tennis courts. Passing them, Rachel found the pool area, where a lifeguard showed her through the public gates. She was surprised to see a handful of bodies stroking purposefully along the outside lanes; it couldn't be more than three degrees Celsius.

Finally free of the hotel, Rachel took a few bracing breaths and followed the road east, planning to cross the river on the far side of the Old Town. After a couple of blocks, she was stopped and told to go south, so she zigzagged until she found the main train station. It was fairly empty, which made sense; everyone within a thousand-kilometre radius was already here.

There was a path that ran parallel to the rail line, and Rachel followed it north over the river and past the Esplanade until there was a street she could turn onto. From there, the New Town Hotel finally came into view. She was an hour late to meet Jess.

She slowed, shivering from the thick layer of sweat trapped between her skin and clothes, tears pinching her eyes. Long power walks weren't recommended at this point in her cycle. She should be resting and planning her rebuttal to Olga.

Tucking her face into her scarf, she hurried through the lobby. She didn't think the bartender would wait this long but didn't want to risk it.

When the lift doors closed without anyone coming in, Rachel let out a choked sob. Bracing her forearms just above the button panel, she tilted her pelvis and looked at the ground as she tried to control her breathing. It wasn't until the doors chimed open and she lifted her head to face the mirrored wall that she realised she looked like a woman in labour.

Jess
Saturday

Something had happened over the past couple of days. After Yara's dire predictions on Wednesday afternoon and the emptiness of the streets like a zombie film set, on Friday the city filled with people. They must have flown in late Thursday, but to Jess it was like they'd popped out of another dimension, lanyards swinging with momentum.

The hotel guest, Rachel, had done the opposite: disappeared. On Friday, Jess waited in the lobby for almost an hour, then headed for the Esplanade in case she'd been caught up in the protests. The bridges had reopened after a sudden lunchtime closure, so Jess continued over the canal, knowing all the time how unlikely it was that she'd spot Rachel's ashen face in the teeming crowds.

Later, working the bar, she'd kept alert to the darkest corners, but Rachel still hadn't shown. If Jess was able, she would've looked for her in the system, but the hotel and bar were separate businesses, and she couldn't access guest records without risking her job. Besides, she only knew a first name. There was the option of door knocking once her shift ended, but someone told her all eighty-three rooms were booked.

She'd finished up later than usual, but the streets were still thrumming as Jess walked back to the flat, the air as dry as a coarse towel against her skin. Tipsy expo attendees played hopscotch on the cobblestones and demonstrated their solar-charged scooters. Bamboo napkins and plant-based utensils littered the ground. Overhead, a line of lights flashed as planes waited to land.

Without Rachel, the article on the fertility clinic was just a big advertorial. Yara might pay her and print it out of desperation, but she'd probably never commission anything from Jess again. Even the thin profile on Cassandra Caspie might've made a better product. It was more relevant, despite the billionaire's trip being cancelled.

Viktor was gone when she woke up, though the rumpled sheets and lingering scent suggested he'd spent a few hours there. She hadn't seen him for days, and they'd only spoken in snatches on the phone as he headed into or out of another meeting.

Jess twanged with anger. He'd been at Elpis's beck and call for over a week and there was going to be nothing to show for it. Her article was the same. For once she'd tried to stretch and do something different, and here it was turning into a big, useless flop. She wished she'd never bothered pitching anything to Yara. It would've been better to take Vera's advice and rent out the flat for the weekend. They could have had four peaceful days in the mountains and returned to a small pile of foreign cash.

With nothing else to do, Jess dressed and power-walked through the busy streets to the New Town Hotel. A queue of coaches idled on the forecourt, ready to take guests to the conference centre. The vehicles were glossy-new, big and silent; hydrogen-powered, according to signage on the flanks. Past them, on one side of the main entrance, a greying man in a three-piece suit was being interviewed by Reuters. On the other, a white-haired presenter in a double-breasted jacket spoke into a Deutsche Welle mic.

Jess peeked into the breakfast room to check Rachel wasn't there, then stationed herself near the elevators with one earbud in and her phone held out like she'd stopped to take a call. She wore an old trapper hat of Viktor's with the flaps pulled low, trying not to be recognised by her workmates.

At last, she spotted Rachel, plainly dressed in a windcheater and jeans. Jess stepped in front of her. 'Hey. What happened yesterday?'

Rachel winced and rubbed her eyes. 'Sorry.'

'Where were you? Are you okay?'

'I got stuck. The roads were closed.'

A woman who'd exited the lift ahead of Rachel walked back to them. 'Is everything fine, Mrs Mather?'

Her accent was tinged North American, but Jess could tell she was local; a rep from the clinic, judging by the soft purple of her blouse.

'We met earlier.' Rachel's limp shrug annoyed Jess. 'We were going to catch up yesterday, but I forgot.'

The woman offered a sparkly smile. She was quite young and stunningly beautiful, as usual. 'And you are?'

'Jess.' To Rachel, Jess said, 'Can we meet after breakfast? I'd love to talk.'

'I've got appointments,' Rachel said. 'But later ...'

'You can do whatever you want, Mrs Mather,' the clinic rep reminded her, the perkiness of her tone jarring against the seriousness of her expression. 'Remember, you don't want to wear yourself out. Anyway.' She eyed Jess. 'It will rain, maybe.'

The idea made Jess want to laugh.

'I run a walking tour of the Old Town,' she explained, feeling a warm beam of pride when both women showed surprise at her fluency. 'You can imagine how bookings have dried up. Your friend expressed interest, and I might have been overly keen to win a client.'

'You weren't asked to stop for the week?' the clinic woman asked. She had the country accent, too. It made Jess like her.

'I'm kind of working off the books. My boyfriend's part of the expo, and we had to hang around anyway.' Jess delivered what she knew would be the winning hand: 'There's always a few officials' spouses who want a private tour. Or at least, I thought so.'

The woman's smile turned genuine. 'It's a spouse-free zone, as far as I can tell.'

'They probably decided to stay home. If only we had a Gucci store, or Louis Vuitton.'

Guests continued to flow out of the lifts, their groups splitting and reforming around the three women. Some threw irritated looks.

The woman from the clinic touched Rachel's arm, convinced by Jess's cover story. 'Well, I think that if you'd like someone to show you around this afternoon, Mrs Mather, that would be okay. So long as you take it easy.'

***

To fill the time, Jess walked down to the conference centre. There was no way for her to get in without credentials, so she loitered for a while, wondering if the IVF clinic had hired a booth. Were they trying to go clean and futuristic, like the rest of the city? Maybe their freezers would switch to hydro power, or the medical equipment could be made with sustainable materials. What was a test-tube baby's carbon footprint?

A plastic stand like an old-fashioned newspaper dispenser held down leaflets for passers-by. Jess took one from the top and examined the list of keynote events. The inventor of a technology that turns used plastic into road bitumen was presenting in the morning. Later, there'd be a panel discussion about developments in global infrastructure so that ammonia could be shipped as a power source.

A penned area had been set up for protesters after the overflow the day before. At the head of the pack was Boris, speaking with a microphone held to his lips, though the power was shut off so that only the converted could hear him. As Jess continued around the side of the hall, the Polish Minister for Digital Affairs passed with a trail of reporters clicking in his wake.

There were no other reasons to stop: no carts, no cafés. Jess took the long way back to the hotel, enjoying the novelty of so much of the Old Town lying pristine. She snapped pictures of the streetscapes, taking fresh joy in the blend of architecture: a baroque general post office beside a prefab office block, the thousand-year-old main square and fountain backgrounded by a commercial strip in blond brick, its eaves dense like a worried brow.

Jess knew she shouldn't be so thrilled at having something to write about. On Thursday, Rachel had seemed devastated, and even now she was flat and suggestible. But that wasn't Jess's fault, she told herself. It was the clinic's. Who knew? If Jess wrote a strong enough article about what they'd done, Rachel might even get justice.

Eventually she was back at the flat, where the yeasty smell of pretzels enveloped her as soon as she stepped in the door. Viktor had left two on a plate in the kitchen nook, still warm, a line of x's for kisses marked on the serviette. So, someone in the vicinity of the conference was open for business. Jess ate the first quickly but took her time with the second, unwinding the plaits to release the steam and watching the layers of pastry separate into translucent flakes that she caught, full of joy, on her tongue.

***

Just after one o'clock, Rachel and the clinic woman came back to the hotel. From a distance, Jess could see the pale moon of Rachel's face, the weight in her shoulders. The chaperone led her through the lobby like she was guiding someone very old or sick, then gestured at the breakfast room. Rachel shook her head. Touching her elbow for a final time, the woman left.

Jess darted across. 'Is everything okay?'

Rachel's arms were crossed so tightly into her solar plexus it was like she was trying to give herself the Heimlich manoeuvre. 'Not really.'

'What happened?'

'They pretty much said that if my husband isn't here in two days, they won't transfer the embryo.'

Jess felt a pull of exhilaration: the story lived! She assembled a concerned expression. 'Why not? Who cares if your husband isn't there?'

'You're the one who lives here,' Rachel muttered. 'You should know why the fuck they do the things they do.'

It was an anger Jess understood. She'd felt it on the tram, swiping her travel card when she didn't need to, then skipping it the next time and getting a fine as soon as she stepped back on the platform. When she couldn't find the cut of beef she liked in the supermarket; when the Greek yoghurt was labelled 'cream' and she poured it on her apple pie. When it was impossible to find a flat with central heating, though the average daytime temperature in winter was below zero. When there were four levels of policing, all equally ceremonial and pointless, just in different-coloured uniforms. When a junior lecturer job came up at the university, but Viktor's application was returned unprocessed. When the parents of the students Jess tutored cancelled without paying because it was the honour day of a saint she'd never heard of. When the cost of a dentist was waived if you completed a series of intricate forms, but the receptionist processed her at full price and wouldn't give a refund. When they closed the airport for six months to redo the runway and had all the planes land at a nearby airfield and passengers bussed thirty minutes to a different airport to be processed instead of having the flights go to that airport to begin with. When drinking water while eating pork was said to be bad luck, when orange juice was served warm, when hairdressers had no basins and refused to cut your hair if hadn't washed it yourself.

There was no answer she could give Rachel. Instead, Jess took her arm and led her outside, where the sky was a heavy grey. She doubted it would rain like the woman from the clinic suggested, but still; maybe. Without speaking, she walked Rachel down the avenue to the Esplanade, then pointed west. 'Have you been up to the castle?'

Rachel nodded, so Jess led her to Penthouse. As a distraction, she explained the story behind the building: the sudden demolition, years of limbo, the final decision, the slow white-anting of public confidence. 'And this is what we got. Fifty apartments, and fewer than five have anyone living in them.'

Rachel gazed up at the cylindrical structure. Jess had meant it to be an example, but Penthouse looked too lovely in the quiet afternoon, tendrils of vines from the green panels dancing in the breeze. She decided not to point out the scorch mark on the Esplanade caused by a sunray hitting one of the windows just right.

'The view from the top floors must be good,' Rachel commented. 'You could see everything.'

'I'd love to see the mountains from so high up. It's the most beautiful part of the country, if you ask me.'

'Do you like living here?'

Instead of giving her usual gushing answer, Jess sucked her lower lip and thought about the question. 'It has its moments.' She inhaled deeply. 'I can't really imagine being anywhere else, to be honest. Even if, in a lot of ways, it feels like it's about to fall apart.'

'I think this place is perfectly fine,' Rachel said. 'It's nice. I just wish they'd change their stupid rules about married couples and IVF.'

'Okay,' Jess said, her excitement growing. 'Let's talk about that.'

She walked Rachel to the edge of the Esplanade and they sat with their feet dangling over the canal. The water level was low, a thin brown track through mud and weeds. They desperately needed rain.

Rachel slouched, pulling at her hands. Jess realised she'd have to prompt her to speak. 'You said the clinic was going to cancel your appointment?'

'If my husband doesn't show up.'

'But they knew he couldn't come?'

Rachel nodded. 'That was always the deal. But now we're a couple of days away and they've changed their minds.'

'Sorry.' Jess cleared her throat. 'But don't they need him there to …?' She trailed off, unsure sure what part of the act Rachel's appointment involved.

'I'm using a sperm donor.' Rachel looked sidelong at her for a moment before her nose crinkled. 'They've already made the embryo. It's five days old, five days post-fertilisation. The sperm part is done.'

'But it's not his sperm anyway?'

'Not my egg, either.'

Could Lena be the original owner of the egg?

'Then the baby won't be related to either of you,' Jess said.

'So?'

She could feel Rachel chilling, but she had to clarify. 'It's like adoption, then.'

'It *is* adoption. Embryo adoption.'

'But they created it for you?'

'Not for me specifically. They created it to be used.'

Jess tapped at the pocket of her jacket. Her phone was in there, and her notebook, both of which she needed to do a proper interview.

'You've got a problem with it,' Rachel stated.

Her demeanour had changed. There was power in her now; her gaze was sharp.

'I just don't understand, I guess,' Jess said. She allowed herself to sound earnest, thinking it would help, the way it had with Olga at the clinic. 'You're going to so much effort.'

Rachel watched her.

'I mean, the world's kind of fucked, right?' Jess laughed, hoping to break the tension. 'We're in the middle of this expo that's offering last-ditch efforts to try and claw a few tenths of a degree back from climate collapse. People are already being affected by it, all over the world. Don't you think we're pretty much doomed?'

'I think there's been a lot of times in history when people said the world was ending.'

But the world really *was* ending, slowly but surely. Couldn't Rachel see that?

'It's not like I expect people will just stop having kids like *that*.' Jess tried to click her fingers, but they slid soundlessly in the cold. 'They'll still have babies naturally, that can't be helped.'

'Lucky them,' Rachel muttered.

'I don't mean myself.'

'You don't want kids, I take it.'

'No.' Jess shook her head firmly, as if being offered a child was the same as being presented with an unappetising plate of canapés. 'I don't.'

'You're what.' Rachel appraised her. 'Twenty-eight?'

'Twenty-six.'

Her eyebrows fluttered. 'When I was twenty-six, my boyfriend didn't want kids, so I thought I didn't either.'

'You think I'll change my mind, too, right?' It was Jess's turn to act cool and knowledgeable. 'My mother used to say the same thing when she saw me playing with my sister's kids. Like I'm not adult enough to decide.'

'I have no idea.' Rachel rubbed her lips together in thought. 'But if you did, it'd be fine, because you've got so much time.'

'I won't.'

Rachel lifted her legs so that her feet rested on the edge of the boardwalk. For a moment Jess thought she was going to climb up and leave, but instead she wound her arms around her bent knees and locked her fingers together. 'Did you decide not to have kids because of the climate? Or do you just not want them?'

'Both,' Jess said, though in reality she didn't know. 'If I ever did think about having a baby, I couldn't live with the fact that I'd be bringing it into a world that's going down the toilet.'

'If you wanted kids, you'd get over that idea pretty quickly.'

Jess was dumbfounded.

Rachel sighed and squeezed her thighs closer to her chest. 'You're assuming it's a rational decision. It isn't.'

'But we can stop ourselves from doing things that are irrational.'

'Can we?' Rachel asked. 'It's easy to pretend you're just being rational when you don't really want the thing anyway.'

Jess looked towards the mountains, wishing for the gentle sight of the cloudfall to bring down the tension. 'Can I ask you something?'

'Okay.'

'I don't want to be offensive.'

Rachel snorted but let her continue.

'Did you and your husband ever think that—you know. That if his sperm doesn't work and neither do your eggs, maybe nature's telling you something?'

'No,' Rachel said coldly. 'I did not.'

Jess shrugged uneasily. 'Sorry. Look, I'll stop asking. I just find it hard to get my head around, you know? You don't seem very happy to be doing this.'

'Talking to you?'

'No.' Jess laughed, and Rachel's expression eased. 'This IVF thing.'

'It's not meant to be fun.' Rachel tightened her elbows into her waist. 'It *is* meant to be straightforward.'

'And now they're threatening not to let you do it,' Jess summarised, getting the conversation back to where it started. 'What does your husband think?'

Rachel tipped her forehead onto her laced hands and let out an odd sound. She was weeping. Given the tension that had bubbled up between them, Jess felt the kindest thing to do was wait.

When Rachel spoke, the edge of her words was ragged. 'It's not like I can do anything. They hold all the power. If they want to cancel my treatment, they can.'

'Can't you complain?'

'To who?'

Who indeed? The municipal police? 'They can't just take your money and send you home. That's a scam, right?'

'Is that what it is?' Rachel's voice strained. 'Is that what they do?'

Now was the time to tell Rachel about the article. Reaching into her pocket, Jess gripped her notebook.

'I have a friend who's an egg donor,' she said, without withdrawing it. 'According to her, it's all legitimate.'

'Nadya?'

Jess frowned. 'Who?'

'Your friend.'

'Her name's Lena.'

Rachel released her legs and exhaled. 'Okay. That's good to know.'

'She did it once before, and the family had twins.'

'Twins,' Rachel repeated, looking distant.

'Are you going to go home? What are you going to do?'

'I don't know. I've still got a couple of days.'

Jess let go of the notebook. 'Let me look into it, okay?'

Rachel nodded, but she didn't seem convinced.

Jess stood and reached out, but Rachel got up by herself. They walked in silence back along the canal until they reached a barrier. The New Town Hotel was in one direction, and Jess's apartment was across the bridge.

'I'm really sorry if I offended you,' Jess said. 'I should've been more sensitive. I know it's personal.'

Rachel was gazing past her, in the direction of Castle Hill. 'You won't know it until you know it.'

Jess thought that was kind of meaningless, but she finally knew better than to say so.

***

It was past midnight when Jess got back from the bar. Viktor was still out, so she lit candles and settled with her laptop in the kitchen. A few streetlights shone weakly, but most buildings she could see from the window were dark. She longed for the next Saturday night, when things would—hopefully—return to normal. Viktor would be back at work, and she'd have thirty crowns in her pocket at least.

The wi-fi was working again. Setting a cup of fragrant tea on the sill, she searched online for information about the fertility clinic, first in English and then the local language. The foreign patients were upsold, for sure—the program included a chaperone, regular spa treatments, chef-prepared meals, psychology appointments and acupuncture; experiences way out of reach for most citizens—but it didn't seem like they were duped. Jess found reviews by women whose treatments had been successful, writing of the babies asleep in their laps as they typed. A few said they hadn't got pregnant, but the clinic seemed attentive and it was just bad luck. None reported having their IVF cancelled because their husbands weren't there.

The local comments were from donors and surrogates rather than clients, but they seemed fine too. A handful posted on a job-seeking forum complaining that they hadn't made as many crowns as the nurses originally predicted, but they didn't say they weren't paid.

Jess was about to close the laptop when Viktor came back. His boots clattered against the wall as he shook them off, then socked feet creaked along the floorboards. The candles were almost out, and Jess blinked when he switched on a lamp.

'You are awake,' he said. 'I am so pleased.'

'How's everything going?'

'Exhausting. Fascinating. Dull.' He draped his arms around her hunched shoulders and kissed her neck. The skin he touched to hers was cold, and his clothes smelled of smoke and whisky, but his breath carried only olives and garlic. 'Still, I see potential. So much potential.'

'Did Cassandra Caspie show up?' she asked, not serious.

He was distracted, looking at her screen. 'What is this?'

'I'm researching the clinic Lena goes to.'

'You are thinking of donating babies?' he teased. She hadn't had the chance to tell him the topic of her article for Yara had changed.

Jess turned in her chair to look at him. 'You'd let me?'

'It isn't a matter of letting, darling. Your body is yours.'

'We could make a lot of money.' She waited for his reaction, but of course this wasn't news to Viktor. 'But it'd mean another woman giving birth to my kid.'

'It depends on what you believe.'

Jess didn't have the energy for another debate. 'I wasn't looking up egg donation anyway. I was trying to work out if the place is legitimate.'

'Of course. What makes you think not?'

Jess outlined Rachel's story, watching as Viktor's expression shifted from concern to resignation. When she finished, he inspected her mug with its cold dregs of tea, then tipped the contents down his throat. 'So. She is not married?'

'She *is* married,' Jess repeated. 'But her husband can't be here. They told her it would be okay, but now it's not.'

Viktor exhaled. 'It will be fine. It is annoying, yes, but they will do the procedure. It is not a scam.'

'How do you know?'

He put a hand over hers. 'Because I know, darling.'

'Then why are they pretending they won't?'

'For show. Can't you see?'

Frustrated, Jess pulled her hand away. 'What show?'

'They must follow the law.' He wiped tiredness from his eyes. 'Fertility treatment is for husbands and wives, even if the patient is from another country, like your friend. The clients sign forms to this effect. They say yes, they are married. Yes, it is a man. No, he can't come, too bad, transfer the baby without him. This is how they do things.'

'That's what they said at the start. But now they want proof.'

'They are going a bit far, I admit.' He took her hand again. 'But I am telling you, when she arrives on Monday, she must only say he tried but still could not come. They know your friend will complain if they cancel. Even if she lied about a husband, they do not want a reputation where people spend money and get nothing. It looks bad for them.'

'Why are they being so weird about it if they don't really care?'

'The expo brings scrutiny. A public servant could lurk around any corner. They must follow the rules to the letter.' Viktor yawned. 'This week, anyway.'

'You're sure.'

'I promise, darling.'

Disappointed, Jess closed the laptop. 'It was going to be my story for Yara.'

'Yara would tell you the same. It is just quirks.'

'I've only got two days left,' Jess fretted.

'Why don't you write about the cloudfall?'

'Like what?'

'That you find it beautiful. Why it happens.'

'Is that news, though?'

'As I have said, Yara's paper does not cover the news.' He

shrugged. 'It is a story about the environment. It will fit with the theme, surely.'

It sounded weak to Jess, but she was running out of options. She thought she might go back to the Palace Hotel and ask Natalya to expand on the lizard-people thing.

Viktor blew out the last candle and Jess put her empty mug in the sink. In their bedroom they stripped to their underwear and cuddled together under the thick quilt, whispering against each other's collarbones in the dark.

'I went past the conference centre today,' Jess said. 'It looked crazy.'

'You should see inside.'

'Boris was protesting.'

'That is his right.'

'Will it ruin the Elpis deal, if they see public opposition?'

'Maybe Elpis will feel jealous,' Viktor mused. 'They see how desirable the land is, and it makes them want it more. Like a jealous boyfriend. No, no,' he continued, aware that Jess could believe him, 'in fact, what Boris does is good. Elpis sees the appeal of an innovation hub and are talking of supporting it. It is a good thing to brand with their name.'

'Boris will be pleased, right?'

'This is the outcome he has been hoping for.'

She was having trouble keeping up. 'So he *wants* the factory?'

'This is the reason Boris makes his fuss.' After a moment, he said gently, 'Did you hear anything about an innovation hub before now, with Elpis wanting the site? No. And this is not a coincidence.'

'So, Boris is arguing the land should be used for an innovation hub to guilt Elpis into paying for it? Couldn't the government have just made them building it part of the deal?'

'But my darling, then they would have the power. They would say no, this is too much, we take our business elsewhere. Instead, they see a grassroots movement demanding an innovation centre instead of the factory, and Elpis thinks they need to make concessions to get their plan over the line.'

Jess thought she understood, but maybe she didn't. 'It sounds unnecessarily complicated if you ask me.'

'We must always play hard to get. Especially when we are desperate.'

She stretched. 'Do you think you'll end up getting work from Elpis?'

'I believe so. It could be very lucrative.' He chuckled at her sigh of relief. 'I know money has been tight. But I promise-promise, it will all pay off very soon.'

'Are you sure?' Jess asked, then worried she sounded too needy. 'No, it's okay. Yara's going to pay me for the article, and if worst comes to worst, I'll go to the IVF place and do some tests for twenty crowns.'

'I have Monday morning free while Elpis meets internally, but the buffet stays closed until Tuesday. Radu is running the scooter out flat with courier work.' Viktor's massive yawn was like a hippo's gulp. 'I will see if any students stayed in town. Some may want last-minute tutoring.'

'It's too bad you and the others don't have a car, or you could drive the casts of thousands back to the airport.'

'Ah, we must not worry.' He snuggled his nose against Jess's neck. 'I promise to come up with something, darling. Here, there is always a job to be done.'

Rachel
4DPO

Rachel dreamed of climbing Castle Hill. Every time she thought she was near the top she'd look up to see the steps stretching endlessly away. Then, when she was about to give up, Ana and her mother blocked the way, faces twisted with grotesque concern. *I want to get down*, Rachel tried to tell them, but her mouth filled with berries, her teeth sticking together, tongue swollen with the tartness of the fruit.

The chime of the housekeeping bell dragged her from the heavy dream. She checked her phone: six o'clock in the morning. The sweat chilled on her skin at the prospect of a message from Olga, or worse, Olga herself, come to search the hotel room for Rachel's missing husband.

Gabby stood in the dusky hallway, an emerald trench coat buckled around her small frame, light makeup charming her face despite the still-dark hour. A black rolling case stood at her feet, and she rested her palms on its extended handle. 'Sorry to wake you,' she said. 'I just wanted you to know that we're leaving.'

'Leaving?' Rachel asked, bewildered. She looked both ways down the hallway. 'For what?'

'Back home. We decided last night.' Gabby's grip tightened. 'This cycle isn't going anywhere.'

'I'm sorry.'

'Not your fault,' she responded throatily, rocking back on her heels. 'Everything happens for a reason. I'm meant to say that, aren't I?'

'I don't know what you're meant to say.'

'Nor do I,' Gabby said. 'Your transfer's tomorrow?'

Rachel felt a squelch of unease. 'Fingers crossed.'

'Best of luck.'

'Thank you.'

The two of them hesitated, deciding whether they knew one another well enough to embrace. Apparently not: Gabby took one hand from her suitcase and held it out. 'Don't tell me if you do fall pregnant,' she instructed. 'I'll die of envy.'

'My expectations are low, if that helps.'

'Not really,' Gabby said. 'But thanks.'

Rachel watched as Gabby wheeled her case towards the lifts and pressed the button, then stood with her legs slightly apart while she watched the floor numbers change. The slightness of her build and her stance like a determined child filled Rachel with melancholy, and she closed the door.

In the en suite, Rachel inserted a progesterone pessary, then returned to the bed to let it absorb. She shut her eyes, wondering if she'd be like Gabby and Warwick tomorrow, leaving without the thing she'd hoped for most. If the embryo transfer was refused, would Ana and her mother be allowed to drive Rachel to the airport? Would they give her time to change her flight, or just dump her three days early?

Anxiety rose in her like a chilling tide, and as soon as the half-hour was up, she got straight into the shower. Her hair was still dripping when she burst out of the hotel, desperate for a cooling slap of fresh air.

By the time she got to the Esplanade she could breathe but barely see, so strong were the tears streaming out of her. The light was weak and the air near the river reeked of brine. A couple of early-morning fishers sat with legs dangling, flinching at the noise she brought to the stillness of the water. The only sound aside from her sobs was the peal of bells from the Old Town as the cathedral clock marked seven a.m.

Wiping her eyes on her coat sleeve, Rachel crossed the Twin Bridges and followed the avenue towards Cathedral Square. The Gothic building loomed, blackened and forbidding. The early Sunday morning service was underway, the large doors cracked open for latecomers. When Rachel peeked through the gap she was hit with the strong smell of incense and the emptiness of most of the pews, the dozen or so attendees clustered at the front. In the pulpit, the priest's robes were a drape of rich colours, ruby and gold and sapphire, heavy sleeves dancing as he gestured. Rachel couldn't understand a word he said.

She and her brothers had never been taken to church; she knew the main stories of Christianity, the general morals she was meant to adhere to, but the specifics escaped her. The religion here was probably different, anyway. Maybe the priest was describing the end of the world as he'd seen it in a vision. The listeners were stilled with awe.

Six stained-glass panels lined each of the two main walls, with a larger one, the thirteenth, serving as a backdrop to the priest. Through them a story was being told, though like the sermon it was indecipherable to her.

Shaking her head, Rachel stepped back from the door and took in the façade of the cathedral again. There was signage off to the right-hand side, an arrow at the bottom pointing around the corner. Rachel followed it and found another door, this one propped open with a round, white stopper, revealing stone steps leading into a candlelit cellar. A sign on the inside of the door said *Ossuary*.

Rachel descended, holding the thin, peeling handrail. The space smelled cold and damp, but somehow cleaner and more welcoming than the thick air inside the cathedral.

The steps ended at a bricked floor. The front part of the cellar was about four metres wide with candles in holders on each of the side walls. The space was bisected by a glass panel, and on the other side piles of bones filled a dome shape that had been carved out of the earth. At the top was a row of skulls with smaller ones at each end.

A plaque in English was fixed on one side of the glass. Bending to read it in the low light, Rachel learned that these were the bones of plague victims from the fourteenth century, uncovered when part of the cathedral was renovated a couple of decades ago. A third of the population had died in the epidemic, including half of all children. Little infants, like the bones on display.

Rachel stayed for a few minutes, thinking of nothing. When she turned to go, she saw a plastic school chair pressed against the back wall, a wooden box on top with a slit in the lid for donations. She took a note from her pocket and pushed it through.

The grounds were empty when Rachel came out. As she passed the cathedral entrance she heard the priest, still droning on. She crossed into the centre of the square and gazed up at the imposing building again, cradling her feelings from the ossuary like a child.

Rachel thought of that word, 'child'. In this process, it wasn't a term she used, instead saying 'transferring an embryo' or 'falling pregnant' when speaking to the nurses. There was something emotional about the concept of *a child*.

As soon as she acknowledged this, Rachel imagined her child: a girl with dark hair pushed behind her ears, cheeks rose-gold from sunshine, knees grey and scabby. She stood beside Rachel in the square, polite but uninterested, looking around at the other buildings. The child was all life, giving off the background hum of woodland insects and smelling of bark and sweet berries. Her child was a native: Nadya and Georgi were from here, she'd been conceived here. Rachel, her mother, would effectively be a virgin, and a vessel. Was the religion being practised behind the doors of the cathedral inherent in the child? Was that why she'd appeared at last, faced with the bones of her ancestors?

Rachel put a hand to her face, letting her cold fingers calm the burning skin. When she took it away again the figure was gone, but not in a sad way. Now the child was the embryo frozen in its dish: perfect, static potential. From this moment anything and everything could happen. No wonder the child thrummed with resonance.

The transfer was twenty-four hours away, but the decision had to be made today. Once the blastocyst was allowed to thaw, it would have to be transferred into Rachel, or else discarded. It was safest to call it off now, leave the embryo in storage until she could return with a better plan. It could last for years fixed in time. The child would wait.

But Rachel couldn't. She couldn't abandon the child now that she'd seen her. It wasn't that she expected Monday's procedure to work, but even if it failed, she'd still have the child with her when she left this place.

She couldn't bear not to do it; she could not go back alone.

***

Gabby and Warwick weren't the only ones who'd finished the program. Harper and Meg were done, too, but in the way they were meant to: The embryo transfer had taken place on Saturday, apparently without Meg having to show Olga a husband. Now Harper was on modified bed rest for two days before going back to the States.

Ian offered Rachel one of his gormless smiles. 'Just you and me today!'

Rachel tried to smile back. At least she wasn't spending her final counselling session with Olga, though she expected the woman to appear at some point, demanding video footage of Ben entering the country.

'Today's session is meant to focus on growth, but we can be pretty loose if it's just the two of us.' Ian shook out his arms so that they flopped against his chair. 'I must say, you've been pretty quiet so far. Maybe you'll find it more comfortable talking one-on-one.'

She shrugged. There was no chance in hell she'd mention visiting the ossuary and seeing the child.

'Is there anything you want to talk about, that you'd like to ask?'

'Not really.'

Ian's forehead folded. 'Nothing at all?'

'No.'

'I can give you a chance to think about it.'

'That's okay.' Rachel felt the strength of Gabby flowing through her. She felt the certainty of the child. There was nothing she needed to say or to prove.

'Well.' Ian seemed stumped. 'We can do the growth session, then, but you usually need a partner for—'

She stood. 'Is it alright if I go?'

'Go?' He peered up at her, blinking. 'Well. Of course.'

'Yes? I don't have to do this?'

Ian got to his feet as well. 'This is your treatment. You dictate what you want. Aside from the medication and those things, it's all optional.'

'All the therapy? The acupuncture and massage?'

'Most patients enjoy it, but nothing's mandatory.' Ian put his large hands to his equally large stomach and held it. 'We want to provide a relaxing and open environment, but different people relax in different ways.'

Having won too easily, Rachel now wanted to fight. 'You're not saying that all we need to get pregnant is to relax, are you?'

'No,' Ian said. 'But it's far more pleasant than being upset, isn't it?'

Rachel went into the waiting room—finding it through the first door she tried—and beckoned for Ana, who was leaning on the reception desk and chatting, to follow her. Escaping the clinic without encountering Olga was the key to Rachel relaxing fully, and in the back seat of the town car she closed her eyes as Ana and her mother's soft murmuring flowed over her. They'd given her all the advice she'd need to handle Ben's non-existence at the appointment the next day: she'd say his flight was turned back for some reason—smoke in the cabin, dodgy landing lights, whatever. Extraordinary circumstances, something totally out of their control. Her husband tried his hardest, but he couldn't make it. How could they deny her a service she'd paid for when it was nobody's fault?

Back at the hotel, Rachel went to bed and caught up on the sleep she'd missed after being woken by Gabby. She didn't dream of climbing the hill, or of the child.

The doorbell ringing gave her déjà vu. Opening her eyes, she wondered if it was the morning itself that had been the dream. If the ossuary didn't exist and Gabby would be at the group session, the two of them gritting their teeth at one another as Ian droned on.

This time Jess, the bartender, stood there. 'Hi. I wasn't sure you'd be here.'

What was it with this woman? Rachel was beginning to wish she'd never spoken to her.

'I don't remember giving you my room number.'

'I heard your surname yesterday, with the clinic lady,' Jess explained. 'I need to talk to you about your appointment.'

Rachel shivered at the reminder of their conversation the day before. She hadn't gone so far as to confess she was single, but she'd come close. Surely Jess had guessed.

Holding the door half-open, Rachel said, 'It's fine. I have a plan.'

'I have a better one.'

Rachel hesitated, wringing the doorknob in her hands. In the silence Jess lifted her eyebrows, and Rachel felt a spike of anger: she was sick of people questioning if she wanted this. Huffing out her bad energy, she stepped back to let Jess in.

**

It was embryo transfer day.

The forecast was zero degrees, so Rachel dressed warmly. Before they'd gone their separate ways the day before, Jess told Rachel some of the news channels were predicting sleet. There was none when Rachel stepped out of the hotel into the grey air, and the ground below was dry.

Again, she walked to the Esplanade and crossed the canal to the Old Town, then continued down the main avenue. The footpaths were a steady kind of busy, pedestrians yawning with hands wedged in their coat pockets. This morning, Monday, the cathedral was quiet, the big wooden door closed and bolted.

A lone figure sat on a bench in the square, bent forward with hands laced between spread thighs. Hearing the scrape of her footsteps, he looked up.

She stopped beside him. 'Viktor?'

'Good morning,' he said. His voice was warm like Dimitri's had been, but Viktor seemed closer to her age. His curly hair was threaded with grey at the front, and deep lines caught the skin at the corners of his eyes. 'You are Rachel?'

'Thanks so much for doing this.' She turned, expecting him to stand and follow, but he remained seated. 'Is everything okay?'

'Would you like to sit for a minute? Get to know one another?' His grin was cheeky. 'We are meant to be married, after all.'

She didn't think he was flirting, but she left a space between them when she sat. The cold bled through her coat and slapped her ears. 'You're sure this will work?'

'Undoubtedly so.'

His confidence was reassuring, but this was the point of no return. 'I don't want to be rude,' she said, 'but if they hear your accent—'

'I have a different one,' he said, his words coming out like Jess's. 'This is how they expect a foreigner to speak.'

Rachel smiled, though she still felt uneasy.

'I will say very little. Believe me, they do not care. They are just thrilled to see a male body accompany you.'

'It's ridiculous, isn't it?'

'Ridiculous, yes. Is nothing ridiculous where you are from?'

He stood and smoothed the thighs of his trousers, and together they walked towards New Town. More people were in the streets now, and she felt aware of having a man beside her for the first time in years. She glanced down and saw that Viktor was wearing a ring, like Jess had promised.

'How long have you two been together?' she asked as they reached the History Bridge, aware that questions like this would have to stop when they reached the hotel.

'Six years.'

'Have you ever lived in England?'

'For six months, which is enough,' he said cheerily. 'I am lucky that Jess agrees to be with me here.'

'She seems to like it.'

'I am lucky,' he said again.

'You guys don't want kids.' Rachel sucked her teeth, surprised at herself. 'Sorry, that's personal, I know.'

'I am about to attend your conception. Nothing is too personal.'

She smiled tightly. 'Still. It's none of my business.'

'Jess and I live in a precarious way.' Rachel was amazed at his grasp of the language: would she, a native English speaker, use a word as precise as that? 'This is a difficult place to have a family. The natural environment is changing in a way that makes me unhappy. And,' he shrugged, 'I do not have much feeling for children.'

'I think that's good.' She was making a different argument than she had with Jess. Would they compare notes? 'To have that certainty.'

She was relieved he didn't comment on the certainty she must have. Even with the reassurance that came with having finally glimpsed the child, Rachel no longer wanted to try to justify her own convictions. She just wanted this to be done.

The town car pulled up just as they reached the hotel and Ana got out. 'Good morning, Mrs Mather. You have been for a walk?'

'This is my husband,' Rachel said.

Ana looked at Viktor. He touched his hand lightly to Rachel's shoulder. 'Hello, I'm Rachel's husband.' He used the English accent, almost too plummy to be real.

'Well.' Ana folded one hand over the other at her waist. She was trying to keep her expression neutral, but Rachel detected relief. 'I have spoken with the laboratory, and the embryo has thawed with success. The transfer will take place in one hour.'

Anxiety turned Rachel to stone. A flash in her peripheral vision was the child, dancing in and out of sight.

'Good,' she said at last. 'Let's do this.'

＊＊

In a room at the back of the clinic, Rachel and Viktor waited to be called through for the procedure. Under her paper gown Rachel was naked below the waist; plastic nets encased her hair and feet. Viktor wore a similar gown over his clothes and sat reading something on his phone.

The space was separated into three cubicles. Each had a recliner for the patient and a smaller armchair for a partner, a locker for their belongings and side table with a plate of dried berries and pot of mint tea. Rachel's nerves made her talk, though the quiet and her unfamiliarity with Viktor suggested she shouldn't.

'At least if I'm the only one here, they shouldn't mix up the embryo.'

Viktor looked up and gave a small smile.

'I'm busting for the toilet,' she said. 'Sorry. T-M-I.'

The door whooshed open and Olga entered, dressed in eggplant-coloured scrubs, hair wound under a matching cap.

'Mrs Mather,' she said coolly. Rachel stilled her jogging feet.

'Preparations are almost complete. You will go through in five minutes.'

She was studiously ignoring Viktor, who sat with impeccable posture and followed every word. When they arrived, the receptionists had called him 'Mr Mather', but the nurse who came to get them only nodded at his presence.

'You have been taking your progesterone?' Olga asked, eyes fixed on Rachel.

'Three times a day.'

'Not this morning?'

Rachel shook her head.

'You recall the next steps. On leaving, we recommend forty-eight hours of rest, keeping to your hotel suite and minimising activity without being completely sedentary. Every two hours, walk around the room. Shower and toilet as normal, but do not take a bath or put anything warm on your abdomen. After Wednesday, you are free to fly home. Seven days after this, attend your local clinic for a pregnancy test.' Olga gave a tight smile. 'We wish you every luck.'

'Okay, thank you.' Rachel couldn't resist nodding at Viktor. 'This is my husband, by the way.'

Olga nodded without looking.

'He managed to take holidays after all.'

'Yes.'

She seemed tired. Of Rachel? Of having to deceive her patients? Of being alert to a government crackdown? Feeling sudden sympathy, Rachel said, 'Thanks so much for all your help with everything. The treatment here has been great.'

'I appreciate that. It is our aim.' Olga nodded again. Turning her head in Viktor's direction, her eyes closed for a moment before she glanced back at Rachel. 'As I said. We wish you every luck.'

***

'Thank you,' Rachel murmured to Viktor in the back of the town car. Her thighs shivered and she was sore from the speculum, but her stomach felt light and flittery.

'You are welcome,' he said. The fake accent, barely needed, had been dropped. There was no need for pretence now, with the embryo nestled where it couldn't be taken away.

'I hope you didn't have to miss anything important.'

'I was free. But I have one meeting this afternoon, at the Palace Hotel.'

Ana caught what he said and turned in her seat. 'We can take you there, if this is convenient.'

Viktor's eyes were merry. 'If my wife doesn't mind.'

The four smiled conspiratorially.

Ana's mother took an exit heavy with traffic. As they rolled slowly forward, Viktor said to Rachel, 'I do not wish to be rude, but I think this is the last time we see each other.'

Realising what he meant, Rachel reached for her purse and counted notes until she reached the amount she and Jess had negotiated. She knew how much of her own currency this could be exchanged for, and roughly how many bowls of Honey Morning Milk it would buy, but she had no idea what it meant to Viktor.

He slipped the money into his pocket. 'There is not much permanent employment here,' he explained. 'Not in my field. We take odd jobs where we can.'

The driver made it through the orange light and turned onto the avenue. Viktor unclipped his seatbelt, ready to jump out.

'Thank you so much,' Rachel said. The car slowed. 'And thank Jess for me as well.'

'Please let her know when you have news,' he said. 'We are on your side in this.'

As Viktor disappeared into the crowd, Rachel committed him to memory: the kind smile, the heavy fringe, the slender bearing. This was who she'd describe if she returned home pregnant and needed an imaginary partner to populate her story. After all, he'd been there when it happened.

Jess
Monday

Though the expo wasn't quite finished, things were already returning to normal. Locals in their white jackets were back on the streets, and businesses were either open again or preparing to. Flags advertising the expo had loosened from a few poles and now hung upside down, like old washing needing to be brought in.

As Jess alighted from the tram, she saw a few hopefuls carrying umbrellas or wearing plastic ponchos over their clothes. It was the first day of spring and grey clouds sat on the city, their edges swollen purple like bruises, refusing to break open and deliver the downpour. There were still ten days to go, but it was looking like yet another March without rain.

Yara called her in when she knocked, and Jess opened the office door to see the editor at her desk, squinting at a screen, paper cup of black coffee held aloft. The downstairs bakery was back in business.

'Jessie.' Yara didn't look up. 'What exposé do you have?'

Jess held her own laptop tight against her waist, the casing damp with nervous sweat. 'It's nothing like that.'

Finally, Yara closed her computer and raised the pink pencil marks of her eyebrows. 'I know.' She crossed her arms. 'I tell you, we are not spies who must meet in secret. Have you heard of email?'

'I didn't want to send it straight to you,' Jess said. She rested the laptop on the edge of Yara's desk but didn't open it. 'I need to give a bit of a preamble first.'

Yara looked pointedly at the chair opposite until Jess sat down. 'Preambles can also be emailed.'

'There wasn't much to say about the fertility clinic in the end. It was all pretty straightforward.'

Yara nodded. 'I thought the idea would be boring.'

'Yeah, well.' Jess tried not to feel hurt. 'Some weird stuff went on during the expo, but Viktor explained it all to me.'

'Wise, wise Vika. So, two stories that went nowhere. Perhaps a record.'

'In the end,' Jess said, raising her voice a notch in the hope of shutting Yara up, 'I thought it was best to write something I'm passionate about, right? And what do I love most about this country?'

'The warmth of the people?'

'The smooth efficiency of its democracy.'

The pink eyebrows jerked up again.

'I'm joking.' Jess opened the laptop and spun it in Yara's direction. 'I'm sure you'll think it's over-the-top earnest and dumb, but it's content.'

Yara narrated under her breath as she read. Tense with nerves, Jess turned side-on and read some of the front covers papered onto the ceiling.

'Ecotourism opportunities in the east,' Yara summed up when she reached the end. 'A way for a declining region to preserve a precious landscape and make money at the same time. Well! It seems the proposed innovation of the past week rubbed off on someone.'

'I was kind of inspired by Cassandra Caspie. You know, doing our best to address issues that aren't going away.'

'You spoke to her after all?'

Jess shook her head before realising Yara was pulling her leg.

'You want the entire population of the east to reorient their economy around the cloudfall because you think it's nice?'

'No,' Jess said defensively. 'I think it's an untapped resource that—'

'Yes, I know.' Yara nodded at the laptop. 'You say so here.' She began to type.

'What are you doing?'

'Fixing. The deadline is soon, and there are many problems.' The delete key clattered. 'But there are some useful opinions here. You spoke to the head of the tourism body?'

'She didn't have much else to do. She wasn't invited to the expo.'

Yara snorted. 'And here is a current tour operator.' She smirked. 'A wordy man.'

Jess had managed to get all of two lines out of the coach driver, both of which she'd crammed into the article. 'Visitors like to see the east' was one; 'this job has been in my family for many years' was the other.

'And at the end, you comment on potential artistic links. Good.'

Even if they hadn't been at a loose end, the manager of the outdoor theatre company would have spoken to Jess anyway when she said she was with Yara's paper. It was another of the owner's big, mysterious investments.

Yara hammered more keys. 'This is fine. It will fill the page, at least.' She lifted the laptop on the flat of her palm like a waiter offering a dish. 'I also like the cloudfall.'

Jess took her computer back. 'You do?'

'And the under-use is worth comment.' Yara sat back. 'Especially as it soon slips through our fingers.'

'Because of the changing climate.'

'I was thinking of the more immediate threat.' Yara's eyes searched Jess's face. 'You know, of course. Elpis's expansion.'

'What do you mean?'

'Solar panels and batteries require components that come from the earth. Like lithium.'

Jess's heart dropped. 'Is the factory going to cause pollution?'

Yara pursed her lips. 'What does Viktor say?'

'I've barely seen him all week,' Jess admitted.

'I'm sure you will have many robust discussions once the deal is signed.'

'He's hoping to turn this into ongoing work.'

'Why not? Opportunities must be taken where they can.' Yara frowned. 'We would sell the cloudfall itself if it meant a bit of cash and international recognition.'

Before Jess could respond, Yara pressed her palms together and rapped the sides of her hands against the desk. 'Well done, Jessica. You have saved me from the horror of the blank page.'

'Thanks.' Jess cleared her throat. 'So. I think we agreed on thirty crowns.'

'Was it not twenty-five?' The editor broke into a grin. 'That was a joke. Yes, you have earned it. Come back on Wednesday when the money is here. And who knows.' She wrinkled her nose. 'I may even have another assignment for you.'

***

Jess took a tram to the Old Town depot and walked south. Passing City Park, she saw that Sandy's cart had reopened and went over. 'You're back.'

'It wasn't exactly a holiday,' Sandy grumbled, as if Jess had accused her of taking one. 'Had to see all the family one at a time. God forbid they make arrangements that suit us when we're the ones coming all this way.'

Jess asked for two pretzels. Sandy made them fresh, taking a noodle of pre-made dough from a cooler at her feet and winding the ends around one another, then sliding it into her portable oven. 'I hear things were a nightmare here,' she remarked.

'It was pretty weird. So many people around, and yet so many places closed.'

'Stupid decision, suspending the permits.' Sandy started looping another shoestring of dough. 'Money left on the table everywhere.'

'I guess they wanted to ease congestion.'

In the oven, the first braid of pretzel was beginning to brown. Sandy whipped it out, sprinkled salt and poppy seeds over the top while it was still warm, then wrapped the horseshoe end in greaseproof paper. Jess reached for it, but Sandy stayed still. 'I think you still have a debt.'

Trying not to sigh, Jess added the money for last Monday's pretzels to the basket.

Nodding, Sandy passed the fresh pretzel over. 'Ask yourself, who was allowed to stay open? The Palace, the New Town Hotel, the bigger restaurants. Fine. But why a two-room coffee shop on the Promenade, and not the Castle Hill buffet?'

'What coffee shop?'

Sandy slid the second knot of dough into the oven. 'You must know.'

'Dimitri's, on the waterfront?'

'Exactly. And who is Dimitri?'

Jess didn't know.

'The son-in-law of the Minister for Business Development.'

'Seriously?'

'I understand Subway staying open. The Pizza Hut by the event plaza. They want to keep those businesses happy. But Dimitri doesn't even serve traditional cuisine.' She removed the second pretzel at the perfect moment, doused it in salted seeds and handed it over. 'Not like the ancient art of breadknotting, hmm?'

Threads of intrigue tickled Jess's brain. 'Did the news report on this?'

'Sweetheart,' Sandy drawled, emptying the contents of the coin basket into the bag around her middle. 'What makes you think they care?'

Walking away, Jess held the pretzels in one hand so she could type a message to Yara with the other. *Did you hear rumour of minister's café owner son-in-law getting pref. treatment during expo?*

Dimitri? Yara responded. *Everyone knows that.*

Arriving at the Palace Hotel's service entrance, Jess took a seat in the smokers' courtyard, nodding at two off-duty parking attendants drinking from cans of low-alcohol beer. She meant to wait, but the smell of the pretzels was so good that she couldn't resist biting into one. The bread was still warm and slightly chewy: heaven.

Lena emerged, puffer coat zipped over her cleaning uniform, and Jess held out the uneaten pretzel. Lena took it as she sat down. At the sight of her, one parking attendant checked his watch, swore and nudged the other. They went through the rear door, sipping from their cans.

'What is this for?' Lena asked. She pressed her nose to the bread's pinched tip and inhaled. 'Mmm, so fresh.'

'I wanted to thank you for taking me to the clinic.'

'Are you going to take Olga's offer?' Lena asked, unwinding the pretzel. It was common to try to recreate the original noodle of dough without tearing the cooked bread. Sometimes there were YouTube challenges on it.

'To be honest with you, I was going to write a story on it for Yara's paper, but it didn't really go anywhere.'

Lena frowned. 'You were going to write about me?'

'No, no,' Jess said hurriedly.

'I am not ashamed, Jessie, but it is private.'

'I know. I was just getting background info.'

After a moment, Lena's face relaxed and she went back to her pretzel. It had torn, so she gave up and began to eat.

'I spoke to a patient, and for a while I thought it was all a big scam. It turned out to be a misunderstanding, but if it wasn't, the clinic could've been shut down. You wouldn't have got all that money for your eggs.'

Lena waved her free hand. 'The clinic would not be closed, even so. But thank you for worrying about me.'

'I was worried, but I wanted a story as well. I needed the money.'

'You want to make money; I want to make money. I understand.' Lena took another bite and spoke with her mouth full. 'They will pay you to do their tests, remember. Obligation free.'

'I don't know. Olga didn't seem to like me.'

'Who cares if she likes you? She needs only to like your ovaries.'

'Did your results come back okay?'

She smiled. 'Everything is good. I start medicines when my period arrives.'

'Well, good luck.'

'Thank you.' Lena chewed the last bit of her pretzel with her eyes closed and an ecstatic expression. When she was finished, she said, 'Are you meeting Vika now?'

Jess was surprised. 'Is he here?'

'He went into a breakaway suite a little while ago.' Lena checked her watch. 'The closing drinks start in the lobby now, so they must be almost finished.'

With the cloudfall story filed, Jess had nothing else to do. If she caught Viktor, she might be able to join him for some free food.

Lena hugged Jess goodbye, then let her in through the staff door. The lobby was crowded with guests in coats and scarves making toasts with recyclable wineglasses, rolling suitcases and carry-on luggage beside them. They were ready to leave as soon as they could.

Jess didn't see Viktor, so she went up to the mezzanine floor and along the eastern wing of the hotel. Three middle-aged men headed towards her from the pool area wearing damp business shirts with swimming shorts and slides, each of them talking into a mobile phone. Most of the meeting rooms she passed had their doors open, stragglers chatting with their arms full of folders while cleaners pushed vacuums across the patterned carpets, but Viktor wasn't among them.

A door labelled *Private* opened across the corridor from Jess. She turned quickly, ready to hurry away from a suspicious hotel manager, but the man that emerged was familiar.

'Jessie?' Viktor asked, his mouth falling open.

'Lena said you were here!'

A couple of others filed past, glancing at Jess with curiosity before continuing towards the lobby. Viktor gave them a curt nod.

'Sorry,' Jess apologised, 'if you're still—'

'Vika, could you come back for a second?' a woman's voice called from the meeting room. She had an Australian accent: *Vee-kah.*

'Oh, whoops,' Jess said. 'It's okay. I can wait.'

Viktor shook his head, flustered. 'Let us talk about this later.'

'It's fine. I'm not here. You go back.'

A woman poked her head through the doorway. Jess assumed it was the Australian, but when she spoke, it was pure United States. 'Viktor? Sorry, Cassandra has *one* more question.'

'Of course. Excuse me, this is my girlfriend,' Viktor said. 'Jessie,' he continued, voice firm enough to stifle Jess's shock at the revelation that Cassandra Caspie was a few feet away, 'this is Marnie. She works for Elpis.' He stepped back inside.

'Okay,' Jess said dumbly. 'Hi.'

'Hi, how are you.' Marnie didn't wait for an answer before sweeping the door closed.

Unsure what else to do, Jess returned to the lobby. In the short time she was gone, the space had grown so packed that guests could barely move, fenced in by their garment bags and suitcases. Servers squeezed through the smallest gaps, holding canapé trays over their heads, and attendees passed fresh cups of wine along in a chain from the tiny bar.

Feeling claustrophobic, Jess left through the main entrance and took a deep breath at the top of the steps. The sun was setting, giving Castle Hill a soft orange glow. Taxis and town cars packed the avenue, but the Promenade was oddly quiet.

Jess's phone chimed in her pocket and she fumbled with it, hoping for Viktor. Instead it was a video from Feodor's wife: she'd gone shopping in the town at the foot of the mountain and captured a spectacular cloudfall. Jess watched it again and again, the cloud sliding like grey steam along the emerald incline and vanishing before it touched the ground.

The battery icon went red and she pocketed her phone. A steady stream of guests had begun to pour past, and Jess watched for Cassandra Caspie even though she knew the billionaire would leave secretly, disappearing like she'd never come at all.

By the time Viktor emerged, it was dark. He took her arm in his reassuring grip. 'Darling. Let us talk.'

Jess felt shaky. She wasn't sure what they needed to talk about, and that was part of the problem.

They crossed the avenue past the backed-up cars and climbed the rocky steps up Castle Hill. Viktor took the rear, prepared to catch her if she slipped, murmuring his encouragement: *darling, darling, darling.* At the summit, it was warmer than Jess expected, though maybe that was the exertion. The sky above had cleared and was full of stars.

They sat on a bench facing east, the mountains faint in the distance. Viktor reached into his shoulder bag and took out a container of peanut butter whirled with chocolate spread and a sleeve of malt biscuits. 'For sustenance,' he said.

The peanut-and-chocolate paste was a staple of his diet; he'd packed half-a-dozen jars in his luggage for the semester he spent at Jess's university. His willingness to share the thick nectar with her had been the first sign they weren't just a fling.

Viktor dug a biscuit through the spread and handed it to her. A peace offering.

She took it but didn't bite down. 'You met with Cassandra Caspie after all.'

'Yes.'

'I can't believe you're the first person to see her in public for a year.'

'Oh, Jessie.' He smiled. 'That is just a story, of course. Miss Caspie meets with staff. She does business.'

'I thought she kept her camera switched off during calls?'

'Not always.'

Jess was disappointed. 'So it's not remarkable?'

He shook his head. 'And no-one needs to know about it, even so.'

'Well, what was she like?'

Viktor licked the tip of a biscuit. 'Like anyone.'

'Is she having triplets? Was her face burned off?'

'No and no. She is normal.' His forehead crumpled in thought. 'What else to say? She is very short.'

'When did you find out you were going to see her?'

He sighed. 'It was a delicate situation, darling.'

'I wouldn't have tried to make you get an interview,' Jess said, not knowing if this was true or not. 'I knew you didn't think it was ethical. You didn't have to lie.'

'This is not why it was kept private.'

'Then why?'

He ate a biscuit packed with spread before responding. 'The factory deal was getting too much attention. Miss Caspie preferred it to cool down.'

'But people want the factory to be built, don't they?'

'It was not the factory she cared about this much. It was the land acquisition.' Sensing her confusion, Viktor reached out and squeezed her hand. 'The farmland, darling. My grandfather's.'

'What for? To put down panels?'

'For the mineral reserves below the surface. Lithium is needed for the battery and panels.'

He tightened his grip as Jess reared back in shock. 'They're going to dig up the farm?'

'There is agreement, as of this afternoon.' Though he was trying to sound sombre, his excitement bled through.

Viktor's grandfather would be spinning in his grave. 'They're going to *dig up* the farm?' she repeated.

'The farm is unworkable, darling. It has been so for many years. Grandfather knew this better than anyone, and he had other plans for the land.'

Jess couldn't believe it; the old man was so proud. Maybe she'd just misunderstood why.

'He knew of the metals beneath and expanded by buying surrounding plots when they came for sale. One day, he believed, the deposits would be valuable.'

Jess was ashamed that she immediately thought of money; what Caspie and Elpis believed his grandfather's land was worth. It was nothing to do with her, anyway. She and Viktor weren't married. Maybe he'd at least agree to pay a larger share of their rent.

Viktor ate another biscuit. 'Ask any question you want.'

'Will it destroy the cloudfall?'

'Oh.' He looked at the mountains. 'There is to be an environmental study. And the clouds are just weather, anyway.'

Irritated, she ate three spread-heavy biscuits without asking anything else. Viktor leaned over to take one for himself, and their fingers touched.

'Miss Caspie likes the cloudfall,' he said. 'She would not want there to be an impact.'

'Did she see it up close?' Jess mumbled.

'There was a brief tour.'

It was hard to swallow her mushy biscuit. 'Did you take her out there?'

'She had to see the area. Others came with us, of course.' His tone lightened. 'You know her grandfather was born on a farm down the road? He emigrated when the crop began to fail. He knew of the minerals also but made a different decision.' Viktor paused. 'In fact, my grandfather bought the boat ticket for him and was given the plot in return.'

Grandfather conspiracy, Jess thought. 'And what did Cassandra Caspie think of that?'

'Miss Caspie is a practical person.' Viktor adjusted his buttocks against the bench. 'As we drove, she explained the grandfather story as one that brings her full circle. When he could not make the most of the land, he gave his granddaughter the best life in another country so she may return and complete what he started.'

'Your grandfather did the same, though. Except he didn't leave.'

Viktor shrugged. 'It is just a story.'

'It's not,' Jess insisted. 'It's real life. How many people are going to get kicked off the land so Elpis can dig it up?'

'I thought you were in favour of green technology. You talk as if she plans to dig up coal.' When Jess looked away, Viktor brushed her arm in apology. 'Few will be forced off, but we expect many to leave even so. This is why Elpis has set up a fund for them. We agreed this point today.'

Jess nibbled on a malt biscuit and listened as Viktor told her how he'd got Caspie to allocate money for people like Boris's grandfather, who would need support to leave the land. They'd get priority employment in the factory, the mine or the tourism ventures that Elpis planned to underwrite. Caspie liked the idea of Cloudfall Tours too, and there was room for Jess if she wanted.

'Is she serious?' Jess asked, overwhelmed.

'I suppose we only have her word.'

Viktor went quiet, allowing her to absorb the information. The mountains would be dug up, but the cloudfall preserved. They could move to the east and have money, but a mine might blight the view. She and Viktor could both work with Elpis while it tossed neighbours off their farms. But it was all for the greater good: the greater good, and the bottom dollar.

'You're happy with this, right?' Jess asked, anxiety climbing in her throat. 'You think it's the best way to save the planet?'

'My darling.' Her naivety made Viktor sorrowful. 'Such things are no longer possible. We just move the deckchairs around.'

Strangely, Jess felt steadied by his statement. The ship was going down. Might as well do what you can: enjoy the cloudfall, eat chocolate spread. Good thing they didn't have kids.

She lifted the biscuit and took another bite.

Rachel
8DPO

On her last morning, Rachel considered going back to the ossuary, but in the end, there wasn't time, what with lying down to absorb the progesterone pessary, breakfast and packing. And anyway, she felt no real pull to say goodbye to anything. The city was just a place where she tried to change her life. Really, with the amount of time she'd spent in her hotel room and the clinic, she could have been anywhere.

Ana was waiting in the lobby, accompanied by a man who held Rachel's bags. With things back to what was meant to be normal, Ana's mother was no longer filling in. The driver who shook Rachel's hand had a lined, grey face and distracted eyes, and spoke no English.

As they slowed with the traffic Rachel looked for evidence that the expo had taken over the city for almost a week, but there was nothing. The banners were gone, the marquee on the Esplanade dismantled, the roads reopened. If they'd managed to fix the world's problems, then Rachel could see no sign of it.

Ana was quiet, leaning her head against the glass. Rachel wondered what her life was like. Did she live with her mother? Was she married? Did she have children of her own? She felt guilty at having treated Ana like their relationship was only professional, when really, they'd shared such intimacy.

'What are you doing after this?' Rachel asked. 'Back to the clinic?'

'I must go home and study.'

'What are you studying?'

'Nursing.' At first Rachel thought Ana was being short, resenting her last-minute attempt at friendship, but then she added, 'The clinic work is good because I get experience.'

'Do you want to be a fertility nurse?'

Ana's cheeks went slightly pink. 'I would like to be a midwife. Deliver babies,' she clarified, as if uncertain she'd used the right term. 'The vocation runs in my family. My great-grandmother helped to deliver my mother on the floor of a laundry. Formal education is required these days, so that is what I do.'

'Was your mother a midwife, too?'

'She was a doctor. A gynaecologist.'

Rachel wanted to comment on the shift from being a medical professional to a chauffeur but knew it wouldn't come out the way she meant. 'It must've been nice to spend time with her.'

'She was busy when we were children. Too busy, I think. This is why I do not want to be a doctor. Nurses work hard, of course, but they are also given family time.'

'You work hard, too. You were always there for me when I needed you.' Tears rose in Rachel's eyes, and she turned to the window again.

'I am glad.' The younger woman touched Rachel's wrist, her fingers cool and soft. 'That has been my aim.'

At the airport, when Rachel's bags had been unloaded, Ana initiated a brief, firm hug. 'We wish you the best of luck with your journey.'

'Do they tell you if the patients you chaperoned get pregnant?'

'Not officially.' Ana smiled. 'But there is always talk.'

'What about the others? Gabby and Warwick, Meg?'

Ana wrinkled her nose in a pretty way and didn't reply.

'Well, thanks for everything.' Rachel wanted to hug Ana again, but the younger woman was back by the idling car, one hand resting on its roof. 'I really appreciate it.'

'It was my pleasure,' Ana said. 'Goodbye.'

***

The queue to check in was short but slow. Rachel remembered the ease of her arrival, travelling through private hallways with Ana, but the clinic no longer needed to impress her now that the treatment was over. Maybe their contact would get sparer and sparer, until they sent her pregnancy test result by way of a thumbs-up or thumbs-down emoji.

This part of the terminal had just the Kentucky Fried Chicken Gabby had longed for and no shops, so after Rachel's bags were sent to the plane, there was little to do but go through security. Beyond passport control there were more options: duty-free concessions, a burger place, an Asian food stand, a bar, a souvenir stall, a newsagent-bookseller, and a shop called 'Essentials' with a whole wall of coloured neck pillows.

Rachel's flight wasn't boarding yet, and after two days in her hotel room she wanted to walk. She browsed the duty-free, bought a fridge magnet with a picture of the cathedral, and flipped through the few English-language books and magazines in the bookshop. In the Essentials shop, she selected a tube of hand sanitiser, a sleeve of tissues and bag of chewie lollies, not bothering to calculate the exchange rate. She'd spent so little over the last two weeks, even less than she would have at home.

Around the next corner was a toiletries display: condoms and lube, sanitary products, and there, in a place that sold barely anything, several boxes featuring a stick with two pink lines. In the bottom corner was the number six surrounded by exclamation points. Rachel knew the meaning of the text without being able to read it: accurate results up to six days before the tester's missed period.

Six days before a missed period was the same as eight days after ovulation. For Rachel, that was today.

She took a box and carried it with her other purchases to the counter, where a young man with a scattering of small pink pimples scanned them and pointed to the credit card machine. The entire transaction was completed in silence, and Rachel walked out of the shop and straight to the nearest toilet with her heart fluttering in her throat.

Her official blood test was scheduled for the following Wednesday, the day her period was technically due. Whether the transfer was successful or not, the progesterone she was on would prevent her bleeding, making a test the only way of learning the result. The clinic recommended waiting until then to take any at-home tests 'to avoid confusion or disappointment', but how was she supposed to last another six days? She'd followed the rules so strictly: she had a permanent headache from refined sugar withdrawal, hadn't drunk anything with more caffeine than tea for three months, and reduced her exercise regime to walking and light yoga. She'd lived the life of restraint they wanted.

All the stalls were occupied. Rachel waited with the parcel stuffed into her shoulder bag, shifting her weight. Nerves had brought on the real need to pee. At last, there was a flush in one of the cubicles and a bright-eyed teenager in jeans that were more rips than fabric shimmied over to the sink. Rachel went in, locked the door carefully—how terrible if it swung open while she had the stick between her legs to catch the stream—and hung her bag over the hook.

When she opened the carton, the paper-wrapped test jumped out and bounced on the tiles. Rachel grabbed it, then pulled down her leggings and underpants one-handed. Some urine was already dribbling out by the time she popped the plastic wand from the paper, and she pushed it deep into the bowl so the results window was splattered with yellow. Once the tip was drenched, she snapped the cap back on and lay the stick flat on the tiles.

Results in two minutes was the other phrase she could guess without knowing. Rachel wiped, and fixed her clothes, her entire body trembling. A sharp emotion had collected in her throat, and she didn't know if it would come out as a laugh or a cry. Swallowing it down, she put her head in her hands and counted the seconds under her breath.

Acknowledgements

Most of this novel was written on Whadjuk Noongar Boodja, around Boorloo and Walyalup, and I pay my respects to the traditional owners of these lands. Thank you for telling your stories for thousands of years.

My most sincere thanks go to my editors, Georgia Richter and Rachel Hanson, for helping me to work through this novel's inevitable tangles and snarls. Our talks about character and motivation left me energised, and your understanding of and commitment to the novel as a whole was as reassuring as ever.

I am exceedingly grateful to the Fogarty Foundation, whose cash prize for the 2021 Fogarty Literary Award enabled me to travel to Central Europe for a whistlestop tour of cities that inspired the unnamed capital in this book. Their support, along with that of Fremantle Press, has been life-changing, and I would not be anywhere near publishing a second novel without them.

Parts of *Last Best Chance* were drafted during a Katharine Susannah Prichard Writers Centre Flash Fellowship, and I thank KSP for awarding me this opportunity. Unfortunately my stay was cut short by mild Covid, but before going home I managed to sneak in a couple of illuminating and encouraging conversations with my co-Fellows, writers Trish

Versteegen and Karen Herbert. Thanks so much to both of you, and I'm glad I didn't spread my germs.

In the final days of writing the first draft, I was lucky enough to attend the City of Geraldton's Big Sky Festival, where fellow author David Price gave me sage advice on a scene that was missing from the novel. Now I can't imagine the book without it, and I'm very grateful for your wisdom.

I worked on various drafts at Mattie Furphy House with a great, and evolving, group of writers. Thank you Barry (the original BD!), Maria, Sharron, Sasha, Polly, Holly, Natasha and Emma for your company and excellent chats, and sorry for distracting you from your own projects!

Jess's difficulty with the more technical and jargony parts of a second language were inspired by a conversation with the beautifully bilingual Annie Morgan. While all the characters in this novel are fictional, and so is the physical setting, language and customs, the country's assisted reproductive technology industry was inspired by reading about IVF treatment in the Czech Republic (now known as Czechia). Writing by Julia Leigh, Sheila Heti, Meg Mason, Mieko Kawakami and other women, both published and unpublished, helped me to think of fertility, motherhood and childlessness/childfree-ness in new ways. The decision to continue to try for a baby without intervention, undergo IVF or end fertility treatment are all courageous ones, and the strength of these hopeful parents can't be underestimated.

Thank you to fellow writers, friends and family for your reassurances, companionship and willingness to listen and share. My parents Lesley and Peter have been incredibly supportive not only of my writing, but also of larger things—I'm very lucky.

Finally, to my husband Andrew: it's impossible to encapsulate all the things you've done for me and the ways you've picked me up over these last thirteen years. You're the best thing in my life and I love you so much.

Also by Brooke Dunnell

Julia Lambett heads across the country to her hometown where she's been given the job of moving her father out of his home and into care. But when Julia arrives at the 1970s suburban palace of her childhood, she finds her father has adopted a mysterious dog and refuses to leave. Frustrated and alone, when a childhood friend crosses her path, Julia turns to Davina for comfort and support. But soon Julia begins to doubt Davina's motivations. Why is Davina taking a determined interest in those things Julia hoped she had left behind? Soon Julia starts having troubling dreams, and with four decades of possessions to be managed and dispersed, she uncovers long-forgotten, deeply unsettling memories.

Brooke Dunnell's novel teases literary domestic drama into a slow-burn psychological mystery; its insights into, and intimate perspective on, family relationships are vivid and unsettlingly drawn. Sydney Morning Herald

... a slow-burning domestic noir, evoking the intensity of childhood and adolescent friendships and the inexorability of old patterns of behaviour when such bonds are revisited in adulthood. The West Australian

from fremantlepress.com.au